FOREIGN PLANET

This Foreign Universe – Book 2

A Novel by

J.S. SHERWOOD

FOREIGN PLANET
This Foreign Universe - Book 2

FIRST EDITION SOFTCOVER
ISBN: 1622537459
ISBN-13: 978-1-62253-745-7

Editor: Becky Stephens
Cover Artist: Sam Keiser
Interior Designer: Lane Diamond

EVOLVED PUBLISHING™

www.EvolvedPub.com
Evolved Publishing LLC
Butler, Wisconsin, USA

Printed in Book Antiqua font.

BOOKS BY J.S. SHERWOOD

ARC ONE: THE BATTLES THEY FOUGHT
Book 1: *Foreign Land*
Book 2: *Foreign Planet*
Book 3: *Foreign Home*

ARC TWO: THE EARTH THEY LEFT BEHIND
Book 4: *Almost Pathless*
Book 5: *Almost Homeless*
Book 6: *Almost Earthless*

ARC THREE: THE SEEDS THEY PLANTED
Book 7: *The Engineer*
Book 8: *The Explorer*
Book 9: *The Sage*

DEDICATION

For Meaghan,
Forever my person.

PART ONE

Chapter 1

It didn't take long for all three hundred seventeen survivors to hear about Tashon's ability or, to some, "alleged" ability, to see the fourth dimension around them. To see, as if from his own personal mind-drone, a view of what was going on around him from the Fourth, while also seeing the world the traditional way: with his eyes. Tashon wasn't sure how the news spread so quickly. It seemed the human tendency to share news that was not one's own hadn't ended.

It had been one week since they sent Aleron and his monster back to the Fourth, but Tashon was still being pulled aside by those who had lost someone in the terror. Asking him if he could talk to their late husbands or brothers or girlfriends.

He was standing in the shade of a flowering tree. When they had first arrived, the trees had been adorned with large, yellow leaves. Those leaves now layered the ground and had been replaced by dark red flowers that roughly resembled the shape of a human heart. The veins that ran up and down just under the bark had turned into more of a pinkish-red. Thin clouds hovered in the sky, scattering the red rays of the rising sun into beams that shot off to the horizon.

Since Aleron's eviction, the forest had come alive with small creatures. White worms wriggled in the soil near the base of the trees, some with two rear legs that allowed them stand and lift their bodies vertically into the air. Little six-legged, furry animals whose shape resembled that of a lizard. Dozens of insects, each similar, yet different than those found on Earth. And Tashon's favorite: the moths.

Using his Fourth sight, he saw someone walking through the trees toward him. He watched the middle-aged woman step lightly, her hand brushing against each tree she passed. He also saw himself, from the side. The tree behind him casting his face in shadow. He now always saw himself in third person, while simultaneously seeing everything through his natural eyes. The first few days it had been dizzying, but he was getting used to it. And, as always, Laos, the man Tashon had killed, floated just above him in his fourth-dimensional form. A glowing gray that more often shone closer to a pure white than not, with a human form that was to Tashon what Tashon was to a two-dimensional rendering of a human. Laos did not haunt Tashon. He had grown to be more of a comforting presence.

The woman came into the peripheral of his human sight. He turned, smiling, and then nodded to her.

"Chief Tashon." She smiled as she stopped at his side.

Tashon turned to face her. He quietly inhaled. "Just Tashon, ma'am. How're you doing, Mandolin?"

She shrugged. "I'm here."

Tashon smiled, knowing why she came to talk to him. She'd lost her entire family in the fight against the terrorists. She wanted to ask him if he'd seen anyone from her family in the Fourth. To perhaps receive a message of love or encouragement from the other side. Tashon wasn't looking forward to disappointing her.

"Have you seen...." she said, her eyes wet. "Can you really see the dead?"

Tashon shook his head. "No, not like that. I mean, I can see the Fourth all around us, but I can't call on the souls of the dead or anything like that. I've seen beings that look like people who've died, but only a few."

"So when they died—when we die—it's not over?"

"No, it's not. A part of us is in the Fourth, but—"

"So, you've seen my family?"

Tashon glanced away, catching a glimpse of Smith walking through the trees in the distance, a smokie at his side. He looked at the ground. "I wish I had, ma'am, but no."

Tears filled the woman's eyes. Her face tightened, and her eyes narrowed. "How do you know they're still alive then?" Her voice got louder. "If you haven't seen them?"

Tashon closed his eyes. Let his Fourth sight take center stage in his mind. Laos was there, as always. Tashon narrowed his sight in closer to him. Laos was the only constant companion Tashon had from the Fourth. He saw his sister, his parents and Evalee regularly. A handful of others, some he didn't even recognize, would periodically pass by. But he had never been successful in searching out specific people. Tashon looked intently at Laos, and asked him if he'd seen Mandolin's family. He hadn't. Tashon opened his eyes.

Tashon turned back to her. He looked her in the eyes. "I've seen enough... souls to know that this life isn't it."

She nodded and stepped back. She opened her mouth to speak but all that came out was a choked sob.

Tashon's eyes filled with tears. He hated seeing others in so much pain and looking to him for some semblance of peace or closure, only to disappoint them. He moved to her and placed a hand on her shoulder.

She fell into him, wrapped her arms around him and freely wailed, snot and tears streaming down her face.

Tashon hugged her back, thought for a moment to say he was sorry, or that he understood. But would those words make her feel any more at peace?

He held her until she loosened her grip and pulled away, thanking him quietly as she walked away, leaving him to wonder why he'd been given this new vision. Was it a blessing? A curse? Or something that just happened, a one in a million chance? He sighed and leaned his shoulder against the nearest tree. Felt its rhythmic pulsing against his skin. The same beat that moved through each tree in the forest. Closing his eyes, he slowed his breathing to match the rhythm. If only he could turn off his view from the Fourth. Even when he slept, Laos and that higher plane were there, a presence he could never shake. He could tune it out, but never completely turn it off.

With a slow exhale, he stood straight and opened his eyes.

"Rosa," he said with a smile. "Always good to see you."

"How are you?" she asked as she leaned against a tree.

"I'm good, ma'am. You?"

"Great, though I'm sure you haven't seen Cosima?"

Cosima. Rosa had broken the girl's wrist after she attacked Tashon with a knife. But Cosima had ended up sacrificing herself to save others from Aleron's shadow. Rosa had been hoping to talk to the girl through Tashon, but Cosima's fourth-dimensional essence had not been found.

Tashon shook his head. "I'm sure she's out there, though. Like the others."

"Yeah. Is Laos still following you around?"

"I think he always will be."

"Must make pissing difficult."

Tashon snickered. "He closes his eyes and turns around."

"How nice of him."

"You'd think he'd do more to haunt me. Or at least annoy me. I did kill him."

From the Fourth, Laos reached out and told Tashon yet again that he had forgiven him. Again, a slight shiver ran down Tashon's spine as his eyes grew wet. He didn't understand the kindness of Laos, even though Laos had explained that Tashon had been doing what he needed to save those on the Ship of Nations. Tashon knew it was true, and he had mostly forgiven himself. But the fact that he'd taken a human life sill weighed on him, keeping him awake some nights.

"Did you see Smith come this way?" Rosa's question brought him back to the present. "We're having another discussion about moving forward."

"I'm sure he's meditating with the trees again. I'll go get him."

Rosa nodded and walked back to the shelter of the grounded Ship of Nations. Another discussion about "moving forward." Tashon walked slowly, in no hurry to interrupt Smith's meditation, or to join in yet another meeting to argue about all the things that could go wrong, and all the safeguards that should be put in place. They wanted all the details ironed out and written in stone as soon as possible, as if they couldn't change and adapt them as humanity grew and expanded on Aethera.

Tashon stopped walking. Ahead, Smith sat cross-legged, his back against a tree, eyes closed. A smokie sat a few feet away, at the base of a tree. It stared down at a broken branch that lay amid the drying leaves. The head broke apart from the body, stretched into a line of black, wrapped around the branch and lifted it gently into the air. Tashon watched as the branch floated off the ground and stopped at its broken counterpart that stuck out of the tree. The line of smoke twisted and spun gracefully around the branch. When it pulled away, the branch was whole. The smoke returned to the shape of a head, and floated back to join its motionless body. In the last week, Tashon had seen a smokie fix branches and trees half a dozen times, but it still filled him with wonder. A part of him even hoped the engineers would never figure out how the smokies worked. He liked seeing them as fantastic creatures that could not exist anywhere else.

He turned his attention to Smith and moved to wake him from his meditation.

Chapter 2

The trees had become Smith's therapists. A few times a day, when the losses he'd suffered threatened to drag him into the earth, he walked away from the ship and the survivors and the incessant discussing. Find a tree—any tree—as long as he couldn't see the ship. He'd sit in the dirt or the crumbling leaves and lean his head against the bark.

The bark, unlike the first time he did this, remained hard. He thought it was because, somehow, the trees could tell that he was okay, that there were no intruders in his mind. Then, eyes closed, he let his thoughts go back to his favorite memories of those he'd lost. His first date with Evalee. Singing with Fritz. Jonstin telling Smith his horrid childhood, telling Smith how much he respected him. Sylvia, bringing strength and hope to the survivors after the crash. Evalee, the night before she died. Wide-eyed with excitement for the adventure to come.

Then he would remind himself that those people were gone from this dimension. But that Tashon had seen their souls in the fourth dimension. Gone, but not gone. But damn, he wished Evalee were with him. At times he wished the tree would suck the back of his head into its bark again, let him drift away into the fake memories of Evalee.

But no.

He would open his eyes, see the trees towering above him. Feel the soft earth beneath. Breathe in the fresh air, stare into the sky. Remind himself of the beauty of Aethera. Stand, stretch and give his son a hug.

Footsteps approached.

He stood, turned and then smiled. "Tashon," he said. "Good morning."

"It is." Tashon smiled and pointed his thumb toward the ship. "Rosa's looking for you. Everyone's supposed to be talking about what we're doing next."

Smith nodded and the two walked side by side through the trees, the leaves crunching under their feet. A white worm lifted its body off the ground and then skittered away.

"You talked to Abe?" Smith asked.

"About what?"

"The role he wants to play in everything."

Tashon shook his head.

"He wants to explore. Document everything he finds. Useful. Interesting. Beautiful." Smith paused. "And dangerous."

"You don't want him to?"

Smith laughed. "No, I do. I'm excited for him. When he told me, he was so happy. Just happy. Like I haven't seen since Ev died."

"And?"

Smith was silent for a moment. Imagined Evalee's soul in the Fourth following Abe through the adventures he would soon have.

"And nothing," Smith said. "Just good to see is all. Surprised he hasn't said anything to you."

"I'm sure he will."

The ship came into view and Smith sighed. A lot had been done to clean it out and make comfortable living quarters for all the survivors. To turn it into a home. But, to Smith, it all felt like a temporary façade. The illusion of a home. But perhaps it was just the absence of Evalee that made him think that way.

"How's Evalee?" he asked Tashon.

The boy smiled. "Good. Keeping an eye on Abe, I think."

"You see her?"

"No."

"Then how do you know?"

"She's not watching you. Where else would she be?"

Smith nodded and smiled. They walked into the clearing just outside the ship, a soft breeze scattering leaves here and there. Most of the adult survivors sat in a half circle of crates and logs, chatting or simply enjoying the real air and sunshine. With all that had gone wrong, everyone still agreed that it felt good to breath fresh, natural air after so many years of recycled oxygen. At the front of the half circle were three chairs. Johann sat in one of them. In the second, a woman named Theresa. She had helped Tashon after Cosima attacked him. In the past week, she had protested nearly every policy Johann tried to put in place.

The third chair was for Smith. He slapped Tashon's shoulder, walked through the crowd and took his seat. He nodded to Theresa and Johann, the latter slowly running a wooden comb through his beard. With a cough and a nod, Johann pocketed the comb and stood up.

"Before we get to questions from everyone, we've finalized the group of explorers. Of those who will see what resources they can find, as well as what dangers they can protect us from."

And with that, five people emerged from the airlock to join Johann. Winona, a young bald girl with dark skin and piercing blue eyes. Abe stood next to her. Then stood Galvin, the man who would be their leader. He stood a head taller than even Smith and had large biceps and protruding pectorals. He held hands with his wife, Astrid. They had lost all three of their children when the Ship of Nations went down. Last was the oldest of the group. Ballas. He was bald on top but let his white hair grow long on the sides. Despite his age, he was extremely limber and agile. Plus, he had spent most of his life researching and writing about alien life in all its potential forms, from bacteria to intelligent species. Out of any human still alive on Aethera, he was the most qualified to explore and record what they found. On the Ship of Nations, he had been in charge of analyzing videos sent to them by the colonies.

"These five," Johann said as he spread an arm out wide, "will leave within the next few weeks, once we've all decided where they'll go first. Wish them all good luck before then."

The crowd clapped briefly, and silence returned.

"Now, that is all I have for today. I believe Theresa had some things to bring up."

Theresa stood up and thanked Johann. She cleared her throat. "So, at this time, Smith, Johann and I have been acting as your interim leaders. Unless there are any objections, I move that we vote to make our positions permanent."

She waited. Smith briefly considered objecting, only to withdraw himself from leadership. But he knew he could do good in the position, so he said nothing.

"Great," Theresa said. "Anyone opposed to doing it right now by raising hands?"

"I am," Smith said.

Theresa turned to him, an obvious look of annoyance on her face.

"I agree with Smith," Johann said. "The anonymity of ballot voting is crucial. It prevents unnecessary divides from splitting up friends, families."

"But shouldn't friends and families be able to share their opinions and ideas and votes without fear of rejection or hatred?" Theresa asked.

"Of course," Smith said. "But we don't live in a perfect world. Remember when everyone's votes were released to the public back on Earth? In California, I think."

Theresa huffed but had no response. No doubt she knew that the state had fallen into chaos the week following the release of votes. Friend fighting friend, son torching father's car. Each violently blaming the other for the terrible state of the nation.

"Okay," she said. "We'll organize the vote for later this week."

Smith stood up. "And if you want to put a name in of someone else you think should be among the leaders, you are welcome to."

"Right." Theresa sat down, giving Smith a look that seemed to scream, *Why would you say something like that?*

"Okay," Smith said. "I know we're all concerned about food and water. Food won't be a problem. Plenty of biotech seeds survived the crash, and we have enough room for a sizeable farm."

"What about water?" someone asked from the crowd.

"Engineer Dousten has more on that," Smith said.

A young woman slowly made her way to the front. Her engineer's uniform was torn on one shoulder and covered in dried blood. She wore it proudly.

"We need to start rationing water," she said with a high-pitched voice that seemed a bit too cheery for the words coming out of her mouth. "Less than half the ship's water tanks survived the crash, and with the farm, we need to make this water last as long as possible."

"What's the ration?" a man asked.

"Each person will vary, depending on age and daily tasks that they are required to complete," she said and smiled, as if talking about the beautiful sky. "Those tasked with more physical labor will require more, and so on. But approximately sixty ounces a day, give or take ten."

Smith heard the grumblings of the crowd, but knew no one would protest. It was what had to be done, and Smith trusted them to be civil about it. But what if the water ran dry before a solution was found? He pushed the thought aside.

"You mentioned a possible solution," Smith said.

"Right. Wells. We believe there are underground rivers. First, we need to find them, and then start digging. We need volunteers. Come find me, or any other engineer, and we'll get you to work."

She smiled, and then walked back to her seat.

"That's all we have for today," Johann said without standing. "Does anyone have anything they want to bring forward?"

Rosa rose from her seat on a log, walked to the center of the clearing, and stood at an angle to meet eyes with the tribunal and the crowd simultaneously.

"I—no, we—need a spiritual guide. A teacher. We need some purpose higher than ourselves."

No one spoke.

Theresa shifted uncomfortably in her seat.

Smith smiled, a gut feeling telling him what Rosa was going to say.

"I move that Chief Tashon be appointed our spiritual guide," she said.

Chapter 3

Tashon stood, eyes on the ground to avoid the stares from the crowd. Why would Rosa suggest that he be the spiritual leader? That he be the one to give humanity a "higher purpose?" He could see beyond the veil of reality, of course. Knew, in a way no one else did, that death did not end life indefinitely.

But what about that knowledge gave him the ability to lead a church? It gave him no knowledge of a higher purpose for himself, let alone anyone else. The most it could do was bring some sense of comfort to those still living. It did not give him the knowledge to guide others on a spiritual journey.

Voices erupted from the crowd. Some cheered the idea. Others denounced it, saying it went against what Humans for Humanity had stood for.

"Quiet," Johann called. "Okay. This, uh, motion from Rosa was not brought to us beforehand. Tashon? Do you want to add to this?"

Tashon took a deep breath and locked eyes with Smith.

With a fake smile, Smith shrugged back.

Tashon shook his head.

Smith stood up. "Rosa, have you discussed this with Tashon?"

"No," she said, "But had I, he would have refused."

Tashon silently agreed with her. But why, of all people, was Rosa the one to try to make him some sort of prophet?

"Then we can't vote on it if he doesn't want the job."

"I know. I just... he... we've never... I'll talk to him."

Usually, Tashon would love spending time with the old ninja woman, but he was not looking forward to his next talk with Rosa.

"Okay." Smith sat down.

Johann dismissed everyone.

Rosa walked straight to Tashon.

He considered making a break for it, but knew she'd corner him eventually. He gave her a half-hearted wave as she neared.

"Chief Tashon," she said, a hint of regret in her voice. "I should have talked to you first."

"Yeah." He patted the log next to him and Rosa sat down.

"But this... what you've seen, what you can see has never happened before. We can't let it fade away or disappear."

Sometimes I wish it would, he thought.

"Why?" he asked.

She laughed softly. "This changes the way we see," she said and spread an arm out wide. "Everything. Life. Death. After death."

"But how does that give us any higher purpose?"

She clicked her tongue and looked to the sky. "It gives us hope. Is having hope, real hope, not something higher, something better?"

Tashon moved his head, something between a shake and a nod. He had felt more hope, more peace, than he had in his entire life. But he could actually see those who had died, their souls. How could others feel that hope if they didn't see what he saw? It suddenly occurred to him that Rosa never questioned what he said he saw in the Fourth. Smith even seemed doubtful at times. But Rosa? She had taken everything he said as fact.

Tashon lifted his gaze to hers. "Why do you believe me, Rosa?"

"We all saw the beast that took Aleron and the others. It came from the Fourth. If something that purely evil and dark lives there, it only makes sense that the opposite would live there too. And everything in between."

An idea crept into Tashon's mind. "Do you think the beast used to be a human?"

Rosa inhaled. "Who knows? Maybe the Fourth contains the souls of all species, intelligent or not. Even ones we don't know about."

"Or the ones that are buried in the red mountain caves."

"Exactly," Rosa said. "But, if so, the beast must have been awful in its life in the Third, too."

"You think?"

"I don't think our souls would change their nature. It doesn't make sense."

Tashon nodded, silently acknowledging her logic. It made sense and explained why most of the souls he had seen in the Fourth were varying shades of gray. Most weren't completely good or evil, but somewhere in between.

The wind picked up. A small twister of leaves twirled around a few feet away.

"Look, Rosa, I like talking like this, about this. But that doesn't mean I'd make a good spiritual guide."

"Maybe," she said. "Just see what more you can learn about the Fourth. And then tell people about it. I think most people believe you, at least a part of them does."

"Right."

"I'll talk to you later."

Rosa stood and strode off, leaving Tashon alone. Or, almost alone.

Laos reached out to Tashon from the Fourth. The man floated outside Tashon's physical sphere. But words floated as waves from Laos to Tashon's mind.

"She's not wrong, Chief."

Tashon stood and walked into the trees, toward the Red Mountains, while Laos's words continued to swim in his thoughts.

"Hope can save lives. Save souls. Aleron had lost his hope. Hope in himself. In humanity. He saw that absence of hope in me and the others. Filled the absence with purpose. Direction. Anger."

As Tashon walked, the trees became denser around him. From the left, a smokie appeared and walked by his side. When he had been on top of the ship, thinking of how he could throw himself off, was it hope that had stopped him?

No. It was seeing the beast speeding through the trees. He didn't jump because he needed to warn the other survivors.

"I was there that night. Laos's words came again. *When you almost jumped."*

Tashon paused for a moment, then kept walking. Had Laos somehow stopped him from ending his own life?

"No, I don't have that kind of power. Don't think anyone here does."

Tashon let out a breath. He was glad he hadn't jumped, and glad to know it had been his decision. He didn't like the idea of unseen beings controlling his actions. Fate, destiny, whatever one might call it, did not seem to exist. And Tashon found that to be one of the most comforting discoveries he could have made. Tashon stopped and leaned against a tree, smiling as a handful of moths danced through the leaves above him.

They were about the size of his hand, and the tips of their pointed wings ranged from white to green to orange. The rest of their bodies were a soft gray.

The moths had shown up minutes after the beast was sent away.

Tashon loved the moths.

He sat down and watched as they fluttered in and out of the leaves. After a few moments enjoying watching them in the Third, he closed his eyes and put a small piece of cloth in each ear, dulling his awareness of the third dimension. After a few deep breaths, all he could see was the fourth dimension. Laos was next to him, glowing more brightly than the last time Tashon had looked at him with his Fourth sight alone. Behind Laos, in the distance, was a city of buildings that may have been the same one in which Tashon first saw the souls of his dad, mom and sister. But he didn't know for sure.

The moths that had been in the forest fluttered around him, aglow with all the mesmerizing colors of the Fourth. They existed simultaneously in the third and fourth dimensions, the only such creatures Tashon had discovered. He could sit in the Fourth for hours, watching them dive and dance through the colorful wind of that higher plane.

Eventually, the moths flew off and Tashon pulled his attention back to the Third just as Abe and Ballas, the old navigator, walked up to him.

"Abe, Ballas," Tashon said. "What are you doing out here?"

"We wanted to go to the caves. Found something I want the old man to look at."

Ballas smiled, not bothered that Abe had called him old.

"What did you find?" Tashon asked.

Abe smiled. "Why don't you come with us?"

Tashon thought for a moment, remembered what he and Rosa had talked about. Perhaps if he went to the catacombs, he could see Aethera's past inhabitants in the Fourth. "Let's go," he said.

Chapter 4

Abe had been hoping Tashon would go with them to the caves. Though he had been in there by himself, he always felt safer with Tashon around, because he would be able to see if any danger from the Fourth.

Some nights, Abe imagined that Aleron's beast hovered above them, watching. Waiting to find a way back to the Third and finish off humanity. And if it wasn't that, he had nightmares about the biotech beetles boring holes all over his body.

He rubbed the stump where his arm had been amputated and took a deep breath. It'd become a nervous habit for him to rub it anytime his anxieties threatened to get the best of him. His stump grounded him, reminded him that he was still alive, that though a part of him was gone, the rest of him remained.

"Have you seen Aleron, or any of his, uh, appendages?" Abe asked Tashon.

Tashon laughed. "Ha. Appendages, I like that. But no, I haven't."

"Good," Ballas said, as he walked with a skip in his step.

The man never walked normally, Abe had noticed.

Abe found little comfort knowing Tashon hadn't seen Aleron. Yet. Just because something couldn't be seen didn't mean it wasn't there, watching him. A bird flew overhead, and its shadow passing across the forest floor made Abe jump.

"Shit," he mumbled.

Ballas laughed, but Tashon stopped and placed a hand on Abe.

"Abe, I don't think it's coming back. I think we're safe. From Aleron and his appendages, at least."

"Yeah," Abe said, trying to sound confident.

But he had thought that their colony was going to land safely, that he would be building a home on a new planet with his dad and mom. But he had thought wrong. He had thought his arm would be healed, that they would all survive the chaos and destruction. But they had lost Sylvia, Jonstin and so many others. Again, he had thought wrong. He wasn't sure there was any reason to think the good endings would be the real endings.

At the door that led into the tunnels of the red mountains, Tashon pulled it open and let Abe go in first, then Ballas. As soon as the door closed, they were greeted by the floating white orbs that lit the hallways. The hovering lights seemed to dance randomly, though they never bumped into Abe. And when he tried to touch one, it evaded him.

"Abe," Tashon said, "I'm... I'm sorry about—"

"Thanks. Me too."

Tashon nodded, and they continued in silence. Abe hated all the apologies about his mom, his aunt, his arm. It wasn't their fault, and their apologies wouldn't fix his arm or bring his mom and aunt back.

"So where is this mystery you want to show me, Mr. Abe?" Ballas's voice always seemed to change pitch, and Abe had to pay attention to the man's words to know when he was asking or telling.

"At the coffins," he said.

They walked the rest of the way in silence. Down the hall, to the right, through a door and down the stairs until they were standing inside the square room, surrounded by metallic coffins encased in the walls, placed in distinct rows.

Abe walked to one and pushed a button on it. A holographic picture shot out, showing the face of a native. Yellowish green skin, lips curled slightly upward exposing rounded teeth. Elongated lines that never disconnected, but somehow looked like writing, floated next to him. Abe wished he could read the language, wanted to understand what had happened to this species. Ached to be able to find even just one of them alive.

"This place is amazing." Tashon's voice broke into Abe's thoughts. "Like an advanced, technological catacomb."

"But weren't those more like underground mazes?" Abe asked.

"On Earth, yes," Ballas said. "But why would they have to be the same as Earth to be catacombs? What did you want to look at?"

"Right," Abe said. "Crisp."

He moved to the center of the wall opposite the stairs. Just below his head, where another coffin should have been, was a circle of nine buttons. Each button had its own shape, some round, some triangular, others ovals or diamonds. And each was engraved with a symbol, some of which were smooth and delicate while other were thicker and jagged.

Abe randomly pressed a few of them, but nothing happened. "I think it's some kind of keypad that needs a passcode. I want to figure out what it's hiding. But it's a completely different language."

Abe scratched his head, pushed six more random buttons. This time, a short melody chimed out of the keypad, but that was it.

Tashon leaned toward the buttons and examined them. "I mean, it looks like letters, maybe. But from two completely different alphabets, maybe even languages. Or maybe just pictures. Art."

Ballas put his hands on his hips and leaned in closely to the keypad. "If they even have or understand alphabets and languages and art the way we do," he said.

"Huh?" Abe said.

Ballas sighed. "Didn't you take courses on logic back on the ship?"

"Guess not."

"Okay, it's fairly simple. Follow me, please."

Abe raised his eyebrows. "To where?"

"No," Ballas said. "Follow my thought process."

"Oh," Abe said.

"Okay," Tashon said.

"Now. Two people from different countries on Earth understand the world differently, because their cultures and their experiences differ."

Abe nodded. "Okay."

"And the farther apart they are, the bigger those differences become. At least, differences in the way each person logically understands the world. One is not inferior to the other, just different.

"So, for example, a man in seventeenth-century England sees the stars and logically understands them to simply be the heavens that God created, untouchable by man."

"But we logically understand the stars in a completely different way," Abe said quickly, excited he was catching on. "Pure O_2."

"Right, and neither us nor him could completely understand the other's understanding without having the same experiences."

"Okay, so this species that left all of this," Abe said. "We have no idea what their experiences are, so we wouldn't even be able to guess at what the code to the keypad is. Or if that even is a keypad."

"Exactly," Ballas said and smiled. "We could spend years trying to figure it out and not get anywhere. What do you think, Mr. Tashon?"

Abe and Ballas turned around. Tashon stood there, eyes closed, arms hanging loosely at his sides.

"Tashon?" Ballas said.

He didn't move, didn't respond.

"Tashon, you okay?" Abe asked.

Abe took a step toward him, reached his hand out to touch him. Before he did, Tashon's eyes opened.

"Sorry. I was thinking. Hold on, let me try something."

Tashon walked to the keypad, quickly pressed each of the nine buttons in what looked like a random order. The sound of air releasing came from inside the wall. The floor trembled, then started slowly sinking downward.

Tashon smiled. "It's like an elevator."

Chapter 5

Inside the ship, Smith, Rosa and Johann sat around a small table inside one of the living quarters. A blanket hung over the couch that Johann often slept on. The blanket, he had said, was one of the few items he had brought from Earth, along with the beard comb he always kept with him. His dad had sown the blanket using his mom's old shirts.

"We can't have a government-sanctioned religion, Rosa," Johann said.

"It's not religion." Rosa shook her head. "It's hope. I want to give people hope. Don't you think Earth would have been better if more people had held onto hope?"

Smith shrugged and nodded. He knew hope was needed, especially after all that had been lost.

"Rosa, I get that." Smith paused, searching for the words. "Tashon has brought me more hope than I thought possible. But the leaders of the people cannot appoint a spiritual leader."

"Why?" Rosa asked.

Smith looked to Johann.

The old man pulled his comb out and ran it through his beard several times before speaking. "Rosa, you know this. Think back to the crusades. Or, more recently, reawakening agents that ran rampant through North and South America burning down entire neighborhoods. We will not make people feel we are telling them what they have to believe."

"But this isn't about just belief. We have new information about a higher dimension that is, in fact, an afterlife."

"Rosa, there is no actual proof of that," Johann said as he placed his comb on the table.

"Tashon has seen it!" she shouted. "And that monster that took hold of Aleron—what was that?"

"Tashon has seen it." Johann exhaled. "He claims." He put up a hand to stop her protests and continued. "With any religious or spiritual event, or the belief of an event, different people have different reactions. In the case of Tashon, as with any other prophet—"

"Prophet?"

"I believe that's how history will view him. But, there will be those like you, Rosa, who take Tashon's story as fact. It is what happened. Then there will be those like Smith, who believe strongly in Tashon's story and message, but cannot cite it as fact for there is no way to prove it. Then there will be those who disbelieve it, but ignore it. But...." Johann stopped and looked to Smith.

"Rosa, I know you're doing what you think is right." Smith sighed and stood to stretch. "But if the leaders of the people say Tashon is the spiritual leader of the people, the people who don't believe and ignore will eventually oppose it. We can't draw that line between the people."

Rosa nodded. "Okay, I get that, but I need to do something."

"Rosa, hold meetings whenever you want. Talk with everyone why there is reason to hope. If he will, get Tashon to go."

"And you'll be there, Smith."

Smith smiled. "I'll try."

Rosa nodded, then stood and left.

Smith scratched his face, wondering briefly how the future historians of Aethera would record this moment. Had they just made a wise decision, or a foolish one? Or, perhaps, it was simply the decision that had been made, and nothing more. But it was never just a decision, was it? Every choice changes the outcome of the future. Had Smith chosen to stay on Earth, he never would have met Evalee.

Never would have lost her, either.

If he could, would he go back and do it differently?

No chance in hell.

"What are your thoughts on Tashon's visions, his fourth-dimension connection?" Johann asked.

"I believe him," Smith said. "I've known him since he was kid, saw him every week after his parents died. Then every day once he became my apprentice. He's not one to lie, Johann. His mind is sharp, clear too. And I saw that monster latch onto his mind. It had to have some sort of effect."

"But if that effect is, in reality, insanity?"

Smith thought that over before responding, imagined discovering that Tashon was indeed insane. "If he is, what harm will his insanity cause?"

"Right now? None. But what if those spirits he sees in the Fourth start convincing him to hurt or kill?"

A burst of laughter escaped Smith. "That," he said, catching his breath. "Is the most insane thing I've heard."

Johann raised his eyebrows.

"But I'll keep an eye on him," Smith said.

"A keen eye, Smith. I love that boy, and I hope what he says is true, but there's no knowing what actually happened to his mind when that shadow latched onto it."

Smith nodded, knowing that, though it was unlikely, Johann could be right about Tashon.

Footsteps echoed from the corridor and Smith turned to see who was passing. Theresa walked into the room and took a seat before anyone had the chance to offer it to her.

"I heard Rosa talking," she said. "You two signed off on her starting a religion?"

"You could say it that way." Johann smiled.

"That's how I'm saying it, and that's what happened. I'm glad you didn't decide to let her spirituality be supported by the government, but next time I need to be included in those discussions."

"Copy that, ma'am." Johann saluted her with a smile. "Is that all?"

"No, it's not." She turned to Smith. "You suggested that, when the vote comes, people could write in other names if they chose to."

"I did," Smith said.

"Why?"

Caught off guard by the question, Smith took a minute to answer. "Theresa, I'm surprised that bothered you this much." Smith inhaled, not ready to speak his next thought. "But I think it's arrogant to just think everyone is okay with us three being leaders. We just sort of... assumed the roles with no vote or anything."

"I agree with Smith," Johann put in.

"Of course you do," Theresa said, seeming to roll her eyes without actually rolling them. "You already told the people that they could put other names down, so we can't go back on it now."

Something clicked in Smith's mind and before he knew it, he was speaking. "We shouldn't be calling everyone else 'the people.' It separates them from us. We are 'the people,' too. We are no different, no better than them. And putting the leaders and government up like that will only separate us more. We—"

Smith's thoughts ran faster than he could speak, but he felt he was onto something. An idea that he knew he'd heard or read about somewhere but hadn't occurred to him until that moment.

He took a moment to calm down and collect his thoughts. "I don't want any leader, or leaders, to end up with too much power. We should let everyone, including ourselves, simply live their lives. And when an argument or something comes up, it can be brought to the leaders. For now, us three—or whoever are chosen. As we grow and expand, that job can be spread among others."

"Okay, I like it," Johann said.

"I'm not against it," Theresa said. "But what about laws? Consequences for breaking those laws? If someone steals, or maims, or any of a hundred other crimes?"

Johann stood up, pacing back and forth. "I remember reading of a small group or tribe that relied more heavily on mercy than on justice."

Theresa scoffed.

Smith smiled. The idea seemed unique, like a great way to start humanity's history on Aethera.

"People, of course, still had to be accountable for their actions," Johann said. "But the consequence, or judgment, was handed out by the offended party. If someone stole from me, I would appear before a leader or judge with the one that stole, and tell what sentence I was giving the thief. One week free labor on my farm, for example."

"What's to stop the offended from handing out a sentence that's too severe?" Theresa asked.

"That's what the judge is there for, but what we want to do is set out the procedures and laws in the right way, a way that teaches us all to show mercy and kindness."

"You say you read this in a book?" Theresa asked.

"Back on Earth, yeah. During my military days."

"Was it fiction?"

"Does it matter?"

Smith laughed and told Theresa he agreed with Johann. If they could create a culture that valued and understood kindness and mercy, they had to try.

Theresa agreed to discuss it with everyone and put it to a vote, then left.

Johann went into the small kitchen and pulled two bottles off the shelf, opened both and gave one to Smith. He took a sip. Warm cola. Cola had been Evalee's favorite drink, her guilty pleasure, as she called it. He smiled at the thought then turned to Johann.

"Did you really read about that?"

"Yeah, but it was definitely fiction," Johann said and laughed. "A tribe on an alt Earth planet in some old comic book."

Smith chuckled and raised his eyebrows in surprise. "You read those back on Earth?"

"Yeah. They got passed around the ranks when I was enlisted. Mostly just to distract us from everything going on, but some had decent ideas."

"So the beginning of human government on Aethera is based on a fictional tribe from a comic book?"

"You got it, Smith."

They both laughed and sipped their colas in contented silence.

"You know what I really want, Smith?"

Smith shook his head and shrugged.

"To raise up a people who don't need a large, overarching organization to govern them. To have us, humanity, be able to govern ourselves with kindness. And mercy."

Smith set his cola down and popped his lips. "Is that possible, though? We, humanity, tend to be selfish. We get angry, violent. We hurt each other."

"But we aren't all like that, Smith. I like to think the majority of humanity has, at the very least, something inside them that tells them right from wrong."

"A conscience."

"Yeah, but what if," Johann said, a smile spreading across his face as he spoke, "we could create and cultivate a culture that taught the importance of that conscience? That raised children in a way that doing the right thing is an integral part of life?"

"An idealist idea."

"Maybe. But wouldn't it be wonderful?"

Smith nodded his agreement. "It would be. But I have no idea how we would even begin. For now, let's stick with mimicking that tribe from your comic book."

Johann laughed and lifted his bottle to his lips, but Smith could tell he wasn't done with the idea.

Chapter 6

While Ballas and Abe had been talking about the relativity of logic and understanding, something in the Fourth had approached Tashon. The soul of one of the dead natives of Aethera. She had appeared next to Laos, just a few shades darker than pure white. Tashon had felt that she was happy to see him, happy he was at the burial site of her species. She wanted him to do something for her, for her species. She didn't put words into his mind the way Laos did.

His mind was pulled somewhere far away, and he was in a cave. At first, the cave was empty, then a bright light flashed above the ground and a body fell out, then stood up. It was a woman, a native of Aethera. Pale green skin, flowing yellow hair. Tashon watched as she walked through tunnels for hours, days, weeks.

She was utterly alone.

Weeks, then months. Tunnel after dark tunnel with no end in sight. At some point, she collapsed, distraught and overcome by loneliness.

She lay on the floor, virtually motionless, for days.

When the ground trembled, she rose to her knees and dug her hands into the ground. Threw rocks and dirt behind her for hours, the pile towering above her. Her knuckles bled, but still she dug, relentlessly, hour after hour. The hole reached farther into the earth, and she stepped into it, her face barely visible above the top of the hole.

She paused, breathing deeply and heavily. Her hand, now full of clay, rose into the air and dropped the wet soil onto the ground. Handful after handful of clay plopped on top of each other until there was a pile the same height of the woman. She lifted herself out, knelt by the mound and began sculpting.

First feet, then legs, hips, torso. A head, hair, a face. She was making company. No, a man. When she was done, she stood directly in front of it, placed her lips on the lips of the sculpture, and breathed life into it. The brown clay slowly changed colors until its skin matched her own, its head tilted back, inhaled, and the entire form was alive.

These were the first two natives of Aethera, the beginning of their species. The first critical moment of their history. An image flashed in Tashon's mind. A symbol.

To Tashon's physical eyes, the symbol made no sense, a jumble of straight and curved lines, with no discernible image. But with the part of his mind that hung in the Fourth, he knew the symbol represented the species' birth, their first mother, and the symbol also appeared on the keypad Abe had found. Once Tashon understood this, more scenes flashed into his mind, each a critical moment in the species' history, each with its own corresponding symbol that appeared on the keypad.

The invention of melody as the highest form of communication.

The first venture outside of the caves.

The first war. Tashon saw the death, the hatred, the bloodshed. Saw the symbol in his mind as he wiped tears from his eyes.

The discovery and harnessing of their power source, a raw energy that ran through parts of the planet's crust like streams and contributed to the beating that echoed through the yellow trees.

When their first ship went out to sea and discovered another intelligent species on a distant island. Tashon felt the excitement at the discovery, the trepidation at finding something so foreign, for the other species had pale skin, with four long legs connected in the middle by some sort of neck, from which protruded an elongated, oval head. Tashon wondered if the species still lived, but his new fourth-dimension companion didn't know.

The next symbol commemorated the treaty signed between the two species that laid out everything from trade to border lines to disagreements and acts of aggression.

Then Tashon saw the leader of the four-legged species murdered by a rogue member of the other species' military. War broke out, and the west side of the mountains was hit by some sort of chemical bomb, leaving the gray desert that was now there.

And the last symbol represented the species going into hiding underground, beneath the coffins. They were still alive, then. Still on Aethera.

Tashon's attention returned to the third-dimension and he walked to the keypad, knowing he had to press the symbols in chronological order. As he did so, the floor started moving down, and he knew they were about to meet living members of one of Aethera's native species.

"What...?" Abe questioned.

"How the hell did you do that?" Ballas asked.

Tashon smiled and shook his head, too excited about what they were going to find to explain everything. The floor continued down, exposing more coffins, what Tashon now suspected were actually stasis chambers.

The floor stopped. The three turned around and found a small opening that led into a brightly lit, white-walled hallway. Tashon took the lead and they walked through single file, Ballas at the back muttering about how beautiful and confusing all of it was. The hallway ended at a door. Tashon pushed it open, and the three stepped through.

Five natives were sitting on the floor surrounding a small fire. They jumped to their feet and all at once began... singing. More likely, they were attempting to communicate, but to Tashon it sounded like a jumble of melodies, each trying to overpower the others. But the most important fact, to Tashon, was that they did not react violently, nor did they seem fearful.

Each had skin of varying shades of green, and each vastly different from the shoulders up. One had bright yellow hair, cropped short, exposing small holes that seemed to be ears. Another had a stripe of red hair, like a Mohawk, but off-center. The third was bald and had a wide, dark red scar across the forehead. The next had white hair with a tinge of yellow that was braided into five ponytails of differing sizes. And the last one, shorter than all the rest, had a handful of strands of long, white hair.

Eventually, they stopped singing, glanced at each other, then back at Tashon and his companions.

Tashon opened his mouth to speak, then closed it, knowing they wouldn't understand him. He considered reaching a hand out to them, but for all he knew they would perceive that as an insult or a challenge to fight.

Ballas stepped toward them, looked to where they had been sitting on the floor, and sat down.

One by one, each of the natives sat down, followed by Tashon and Abe.

The native with cropped yellow hair let out a short melody. It was calm and deep but ended with one high pitched note.

Tashon had no idea what it meant. He let his mind focus in on the Fourth, hoping that the ethereal native could translate for him, but when she tried, all he heard was a melody in his mind, though this time he got a very distinct feeling: happiness, overwhelming joy.

The natives were happy to see them. Or maybe, Tashon realized, they had known the humans had been there for a long time. Perhaps the smokies somehow recorded everything that was happening outside the caves, and they were just waiting to see what kind of species the humans were. Thankfully, the natives had decided the humans were a race they were happy to meet.

Tashon smiled at the five new faces. Each of them attempted to imitate the action, but their mouths curved up only slightly, making them look more mischievous than happy.

Abe laughed, then stopped himself by covering his mouth.

The natives covered their mouths and stared at the three with their hands on their faces.

Tashon, and evidently Ballas, felt bad for this so they covered their mouths as well.

So, the eight sat in a circle, hands over their mouths, eyes bouncing between the others in the room. Did they think this was some sort of greeting or ritual?

Tashon dropped his hand and the rest followed.

The native with the red scar waved his hands in front of him and turned his palms upward. Two thin, stiff wires folded up out of the skin of each palm. A wall of light between each wire formed, creating a box. He stretched his hand outs, expanding the box, and shook his hands twice. The cube of light surrounded them. The room filled with images of a sprawling metropolis that covered the west side of the red mountains, which was now only barren desert.

We watched your boat fall from the dark void, alight in flame,
A beacon foretold by Mother, awaited by many,
Doubted by few.
A star-sent blessing or curse, we do not know, cannot know for certain.
Yet still we fought to stop the fall of all your Frames.
Fought to stop the stopping of all your Frames,
As Mother said we should, all that time ago.
Did not, could not, keep all your Frames moving.
Many, too many now, are still filling us with a pain,
A pain as if it were our own to stop moving.
These new Frames, like us, unlike us
Were said by Mother to come for a purpose.
Come to wake us, to wake the rest of us from their endless,

Living sleep that Mother, too, foretold.
Yet still, we were not ready.
And while our loves, our others, sleep rotations through,
We five find no such blessing.
We five, awake, waiting for the saviors Mother said would come.
Though they do not act like we thought saviors would.

Chapter 7

Abe stared in awe at the images filling the room. The gray desert they had crashed on, that his mom was buried in, had once been a glowing, vibrant city. A bridge made of white stone extended out of a tunnel in the red mountains, supported by black pillars that sunk deep into dark green earth. Vines snaked around the black pillars, reaching over the top of the bridge, lining the walkway with the blooming blue flowers that grew from them.

Hundreds, maybe thousands, of the natives walked across the bridge, each adorned in various brightly colored robes, pants and coveralls. Some walked into the red mountain tunnels while others walked toward the city. The entire metropolis was lifted above the ground, supported by the same pillars that kept the bridge from falling. Rounded, cylindrical buildings stretched high above the white walkway, some connected by tubes through which walked even more pedestrians. Sections of green gardens were spread throughout the city, between and on top of buildings. Green, yellow and brown trees cast shadows on outdoor markets.

Abe shook his head. These natives, these *people*, had once been an advanced, abundant species. What had once been a beautiful, living, breathing city was now empty, save for the biotech beetles and the rotting corpses of Sylvia and the others who died in the hailstorm.

He turned his attention back to the images of the city. The people walking through the city exuded a joy that Abe had never seen shared among so many at the same time. One of the natives, this one with long white-gray hair, began to communicate. To sing.

As the notes left her lips, they swam at Abe with a physical presence. He could not understand the words, but he felt the meaning behind the notes, the words. He felt unequivocally happy, completely safe. Not a care in the world, just as he knew the people in the images felt.

Like nothing bad could happen.

Abe softly laughed with the joy that feeling brought him and noticed Tashon and Ballas doing the same. Then the image shook.

The soil underneath the city rippled, came alive. Biotech beetles burst from underground, charging up the posts that held the city aloft. A wave of the mechanical insects flooded over the city's edge and swarmed over everyone, dragging each to the ground. Some were dragged over the edge and dropped to their deaths while others ran away, only to trip and be torn apart bit by bit, the insects spiraling into their flesh the same way the one had in Abe's arm.

Smokies ran out of the tunnels and dragged as many people as possible back into the caves, but the rest were left to be thrown to their deaths or slowly ripped apart by the grinding of state-of-the-art bioengineered insects.

It went on for minutes until, at last, every native who hadn't gotten away lay still. Each beetle sped away, hundreds stopping on each support beam under the city. Then, simultaneously, each beetle exploded, and the city crumpled to the earth in a cloud of dust and fire.

Back in the cave, a native with an off-center mohawk and a tattoo on the left side of his face let out one long, deep note.

It sunk into Abe's chest, reverberated through his ribs, shook every bone in his body. Tears poured from his eyes as he tried to catch his breath. He felt empty, alone, angry. Why would someone do that to such a beautiful city? Such a peaceful people?

Abe turned to Tashon and Ballas, who were both overcome with the same raging emotions.

Then, the deep tone stopped, and Abe's body calmed. He wiped his tears, slowed his breaths. What a language to be able to communicate such powerful and personal emotions to those of another species, of a completely different world.

They sat in silence. Abe, Tashon and Ballas looked to the ground. The natives had hands placed on each other's shoulders, eyes closed. The overpowering despair and anger had left Abe, but he still felt a rage for what had happened. Why? Who? No matter what logic he tried to put on it, he could find no sensible reason for such an act.

"Why," he choked out. "Why?"

"I think I know," Tashon whispered.

And he told them of what he had seen in the Fourth, or, what had been shown to him. The rogue native killing the leader of the other native species on Aethera.

Abe shook his head and lifted his eyes to the five in front of him, whom he now considered friends. "I'm sorry this happened to you, and your people," he whispered.

He knew they wouldn't understand the words. But if they could transmit emotion with their melodies so effectively, maybe they could receive them as well, for Abe truly felt a deep pain for detestation of their people.

He never once questioned whether that pain was valid, or even real.

The scarred one shook his hands again, and a new image filled the room. It was Abe, Smith and Jonstin, walking alone through the gray desert, on their way to find the fallen Ship of Nations.

A weight fell in Abe's stomach when he saw Jonstin alive and well. Jonstin, who had died saving Abe. Jonstin, the man Abe had thought was an arrogant bastard until the last few days of his life. And damn, he missed that bastard. Jonstin had wanted to spread out through Aethera, see what possibilities existed on the rest of the planet. Jonstin was the reason Abe had decided to be among the group setting out to explore their new home.

In the image at the center of the room, lines of biotech beetles stormed Abe, Smith and Jonstin. Abe turned away, knowing what was about to happen. He had been there, after all. A soft, piercing melody came from one of the natives, though Abe couldn't identify which one.

He looked back at the image as the smokies surrounded the three. The melody grew louder, and Abe realized the smokies hadn't been there by chance. The five sitting in the caves with him had sent them. The five sitting in front of him had saved him that day. He smiled and nodded, opened his mouth to thank them, but stopped short, anger replacing gratitude.

"Why the hell did you only save us?" he screamed. "You left Sylvia and the others to be pounded to death by chunks of ice falling from the damn sky, for shit's sake! You let Cosima and Jonstin and damn near all of us die by that beast! And then send your shit-face dogs to save the rest of us at the last minute, after we did damn near everything!" He stood up, his blood boiling. "You let my mom die. And then try to tell me I should be thankful you saved me, but let nearly every other damn person die? Bullshit." Abe turned and left the room. He made his way to the keypad, and realized he had no idea which buttons to push. "Bullshit," he whispered as tears fell down his face.

The stopping of a Frame, the ending of its Melody
Does stop for a time the Melody of all Frames
That have woven with the stopped Frame, the silent Frame

We see no Melody within these new Frames
Their Frames, designed like ours
Yet their Windows-opaque, imperceptible, almost
Full of
Blind
Dark
Rage
Not as Mother said they would be
Not Angels sent from above
But not Monsters, no
Something in between, a swirling that cannot be deciphered
In just one look, or five,
If ever they can be.

Chapter 8

Smith stood in the bottom of a large, round hole with a shovel in his hands. Winona dug next to him. The deeper they got, the softer the ground became. But still no signs of water.

Smith paused to stretch his back. "Thanks for helping, Winona," he said.

She nodded and kept digging. "You got it. Hard work is good for the soul," she said, wiping sweat off her forehead.

Smith smiled at the memories the saying brought. On Earth, Winona's parents had fought out of deep poverty to earn just enough to gain the education and training that eventually landed them on the Ship of Nations. Once on the ship, anytime a difficulty was encountered, they were always among the first to step up to the plate. Smith was glad to see their work ethic had bled into their daughter, even in their absence.

"Your parents were some of the best people I've known," Smith said.

Winona kept shoveling dirt. "They were, weren't they?"

"I miss them."

Winona nodded. Smith went back to shoveling, the act bringing back the all too fresh memory of burying his wife. But this time, he reminded himself, they were digging for water. For life. Not the same, he reminded himself.

Winona paused and looked at Smith. "Where's Abe? Haven't seen him all afternoon."

"He's off with Ballas," Smith said. "He found some engravings that looked like a language in the caves. Thought Ballas would have some insight."

Winona nodded and went back to her task. She had been spending more and more time with Abe, for which Smith was grateful. The young girl brought a light to Abe's eyes that Smith had never seen. It gave him hope for the future.

He looked to the ground and pushed his shovel in as far as possible. The dirt made a soft, gurgling sound that could only mean one thing.

"Mud," Winona said.

They dug faster, throwing increasingly wet dirt to the side. Soon, a drop of water appeared. Then a trickle.

"Water," Winona said. "Water!"

Smith laughed as three engineers appeared above them. They reached down hands to help Smith and Winona out, then quickly got to work putting together a pump and siphon system using various salvaged parts from the ship. Winona stayed to help. Smith left to see how the farm was doing.

The sun had passed its highest point in the sky, the shadow cast by the ship stretching into the forest. The forest floor that had been cleared when the other half of the ship was sent back into the Fourth was now being converted into a farm.

Rosa and a handful of other volunteers were putting the biotech seeds in the small trenches that had been dug earlier. Smith watched as a young girl ripped open a sealed box full of biotech seeds that would grow into blooming pink peach trees within the next few weeks. They had been Evalee's favorite trees in the farming sector, and her favorite fruit to eat after a long day. Smith figured if his wife wasn't alive on Aethera, at least something she loved would be.

Smith shook his head and smiled at how sentimental he'd become. The girl dumped a small pile of the seeds into one end of a trench. The seeds moved out in a straight line, one stopping every few feet, until the trench was filled with fifteen evenly spaced seeds. Smith stood, walked along the trench, and pushed each seed into the soil with his finger. Smith stretched with a contented sigh and picked the seed packet off the ground. 'Pink Peach Trees,' it read. 'Now with temperature-regulating nanites!'

Smith smiled, glad it was those seeds that had survived. No matter how cold Aethera got, the trees would still produce food. A breakthrough creation, masterminded by the woman who taught Smith nearly everything he knew of biotech farming.

The sky darkened as the sun continued to sink into the horizon. Abe still hadn't returned, Smith realized. He felt his son was okay but being away from him was hard. Especially when 'away' meant much more than just being on another floor of the ship.

He sighed. Sometimes, when he was falling asleep or waking up, Smith found himself wishing that what had happened to Tashon had happened to him instead. He wanted to be able to sense those things of a higher dimension, to know with utter certainty that there was something more, that his late wife was truly watching out for his son.

Somehow, Smith had accepted that his wife was dead. He wasn't free of the hurt from it, and probably never would be, but he had accepted it. True, Tashon's vision in the Fourth had helped, but it was more than that. Smith knew that life was moving on, that he would be okay. Maybe it was because he survived all the horrors that followed her death, or maybe it was the beauty of Aethera he had decided to open his eyes to, or perhaps Ev's soul was close to him, and brought him comfort. He didn't know for sure why he was okay as he was, but he was glad for it. And, at times, guilt-ridden as well.

He could tell Abe hadn't accepted his mother's death. It was as if the boy hadn't completely realized she was gone until after their lives had calmed down and some type of normalcy had begun on Aethera. There was nothing more to fill him with purpose or fear or anger other than the absence of his loving mother.

And Smith had no idea how to help him. A part of him wanted to always keep Abe in sight, to never let him be alone. But he knew he couldn't do that. Knew Abe would only grow to hate him if he didn't let him leave to explore Aethera. Smith only hoped the journey would bring Abe some type of peace.

Rosa walked to Smith's side. "You okay?"

"Yeah," Smith said. "Yeah, I'm good. We found water."

"Hot damn," Rosa said. "That's good news."

Sweat trickled down both sides of Smith's face. "Thirsty?"

Rosa nodded and the two walked back to the ship. The engineers had fashioned a manual pump by connecting intact but now useless oxygen pipes to the water tanks, bringing the water out of the ship to the corner of the farm. The handle and nozzle were made using various parts from faucets in the housing district. Soon, those pipes would be connected to the new well.

Smith held his bottle under the faucet as Rosa worked the handle back and forth, the water splashing out in rhythmic surges.

"How's Abe doing, Smith?"

Smith took a sip from his bottle, then held Rosa's under the faucet as she resumed pumping.

"Better than I would have thought," he said. "He's excited to get out there and explore Aethera."

"I'm still surprised you're letting him leave."

"I wasn't going to, but"—Smith shrugged—"I don't think him staying around here is going to help that any."

"And Tashon said Evalee's watching over him, so you don't need to worry."

"Right," Smith said.

He did believe Tashon, but there was still no way for him to know for sure if Evalee's spirit was truly watching Abe, or if Tashon's mind had simply been compromised when the tentacle pierced his brainstem. And even if Tashon was right, what could Evalee's spirit do for Abe if he got stuck in a sinkhole, or mauled by some undiscovered Aetheran beast?

Smith looked at the setting sun and turned to face the red mountains.

"Abe and Ballas should have been back by now. They went to look through the red caves hours ago."

"Let's go find 'em then, farmer."

Chapter 9

Abe took a deep breath as the tears dried on his face. He turned around as Tashon stood and walked toward him, Ballas and the five natives close behind. The five natives spread out in a circle. Each opened their hands, palms up. The wires flipped out of each hand, and the larger room was filled with the image of Aethera's sky.

Colony Six's ship burst through the atmosphere, already being ripped into two pieces. Flames poured out of one side of the hull as gravity pulled it toward Aethera's surface. The image panned out. A dozen smokies sped through the gray dirt toward the falling ship. One bent and lifted off the ground to catch a man spinning to his death. But just as its last leg was about to leave the ground, hundreds of biotech beetles exploded from the dirt and attacked the smokies. One by one, each nanotech dog was overtaken, and their interior rods dragged away, out of sight.

Another melody floated from the five, this one deep, heavy and filled with regret.

An apology.

The weight of their sorrow poured into Abe, the might of their wish that they could have saved everyone shrouding him in a cloud that did not dissipate until their melody was complete.

The five silently looked at the three, their hands over their mouths.

Abe felt he needed to tell them he accepted their apology, that all was forgiven. But how could he do that? They wouldn't understand him. Or would they?

"Why did they show us that they tried to save us?" he asked.

"A show of good faith, maybe," Ballas suggested.

"But why specifically that? They already showed that they saved me and my dad and Jonstin. They wouldn't show that unless—"

"They understood what you were screaming at them," Tashon said. "They wanted to show you that they tried to save Evalee. To save everyone."

"How the hell...?" Ballas asked.

The three looked at each other, then back at their new acquaintances.

No one spoke, or sang. Footsteps echoed from above them. They all looked up to find Smith and Rosa staring down into the sunken floor.

"Oh, shit." Rosa whistled.

The mohawked one ran to the keypad, pressed each button, and the floor began to rise. As it did, Abe's heart pounded as the reality of first contact began to sink in. Every science teacher he ever had talked about the possibility of another intelligent species, of what that would mean for humanity. Would it be their salvation or their destruction? Would it lead to peaceful, fruitful treaties or to war and bloodshed?

First contact, and he had just yelled at the new species. And they had responded by apologizing to him. To Abe, the future between humans and the Aetheran natives was going to be one of peace. But they needed to have a real name. Simply calling them "natives" didn't feel right to Abe now that he knew they were alive.

The floor stopped. Smith and Rosa looked, wide-eyed, at the group standing in front of them. The five looked back and placed their hands over their mouths.

Abe stepped forward. "Dad, Rosa, these are the—" Abe said, then paused. "The Singers."

The Singers dropped their hands and turned their lips upward in a forced smile. They opened their mouths, a separate tune from each blending together in a melody that made Abe feel loved and important. He looked around and saw smiles on every human face—the melody had affected them each in the same way.

"Singers," Smith said. "Did they tell you that's what they're called?"

Abe shook his head.

"I picked the name because every time they communicate, it sounds like they're singing."

"That's how they... communicate?" Rosa asked.

Abe, Tashon and Ballas nodded, then took turns telling Smith and Rosa everything they knew about the Singers.

The five Singers stood quietly, their eyes not focusing on any one human in particular.

"Smith, we need to let everyone else know," Rosa said.

"I know, but do we take them with us now, or...?"

"This could be a crucial moment, Chief Smith," Ballas said. "If we leave them, that could negatively impact our relationship from the start."

Smith nodded. "So they can communicate with us, in a way, by giving us emotional reactions using specific notes."

"It seems that way," Ballas agreed. "A very emotional species, I think."

"But how can we communicate with them? How could we ask them to come with us, or find out if they even want to?"

"But they did understand Abe when he screamed at them," Ballas said.

"Maybe they can understand our language, but not speak it." Tashon said.

"Perhaps," Ballas said. "But if they can, why haven't they tried to tell us anything?"

The humans looked at the Singers, who stood silently, seemingly patient, as if they could stand there forever.

Abe moved in front of the Singers, looked each one of them in the eye, and each one avoided his gaze.

"We would love it if you came with us," he said.

The Singers looked at him, then at each other. Their heads moved back and forth as their mouths silently opened and closed. Abe and the others waited, thinking they must somehow be communicating with each other. But when their mouths stopped moving, no images rose from their hands, no notes escaped their mouths.

"That worked well, son," Smith said.

"At least I tried, old man."

"I think we should just start walking," Ballas said firmly. "If they want to follow, they will."

"That actually makes sense," Rosa said as she turned and slowly walked down the hall.

The rest hesitated briefly, then followed suit, Abe the last to move, not wanting to leave the Singers. But they, too, followed Rosa away from the catacombs and down the hall, the one with the scar walking next to Abe.

"Dad," he called. "Don't you think—I don't know—maybe someone should run ahead and tell everyone?"

"Your son's a smart one, Smith," Ballas replied. "That's a smart idea. Maybe even corral everyone into the ship, wait outside for us with Johann and Theresa."

"Yeah, good call," Smith nodded. "I'll run ahead."

This young Frame shows a Melody,
One full of
Rage

Hurt
And hope
Hope unseen, unknown by young Frame,
Hope to disparage fear, chase off doubt
Burns invisibly to him, within him
A burning sung of by Mother, remember?
Could young Frame
Be the one to wake us to save us
Yes, only if, as Mother said,
Young Frame so chooses
For we all choose if we will save
Or if we will destroy
If we will wake
Or force endless sleep.
But a contradiction, hear?
For if one can choose to wake or sleep
Why can't we five sleep,
Or our others, any of them, wake?

Chapter 10

Smith jogged away from the group, thankful for the few minutes alone to figure out what had happened. They had made first contact. No, his son had made first contact, and then yelled at them, blamed them for Evalee's death. Smith chuckled out loud as he opened the door out into the forest.

The sun had gone down, a thick mass of clouds hiding the stars and the moon. He slowed as he moved through the cool air and trees, trying to decide what he was going to say to everyone. Given the darkness and the cold, though, most people would be huddled inside the ship in their living quarters.

A smokie sat just outside the clearing around the ship as Smith slowed to a walk. Two figures sat outside the airlock, quietly talking. Johann and Winona, the young girl on the exploration team with Abe.

"Smith!" Johann called. "Everything okay? Where you been?"

Smith laughed. "Everything is hard to explain. Winona, head inside please. And find Theresa, tell her she needs to be out here now."

"Yes, sir." She smiled. "And come back with her?"

"I don't think that—"

"Oh, let her come, Smith. She was just telling me how she wants to learn about government and leadership."

"Okay, okay. But hurry back, Winona."

"You got it, Chief Smith."

She ran into the ship and Smith sat next to Johann with a heavy sigh and a chuckle.

"What the hell's going on, Smith?"

Smith shook his head, sighing deeply.

"Something that Ev should've been here for."

"Okay." Johann looked to the trees Smith had walked from. "That doesn't tell me anything."

"Right. Let's wait for Theresa and Winona."

"Okay."

Smith inhaled deeply, held the air in his chest as long as he could, then blew it out. What they faced was unprecedented, impossible. Yet there he was. There they were, a small, lost branch of humanity at the cusp of something immeasurable. He looked to the sky, still shrouded in clouds. Out of all the universe, he had ended up on Aethera, with a species that mesmerized. A species that, he hoped, would be a part of human civilization and culture from that day forward.

Theresa and Winona burst out of the airlock, breathing heavily.

"Smith?" She looked at the farmer expectantly.

As quickly and clearly as possible, he told them everything that had happened with the Singers. When he finished, Winona and Theresa stared at him, eyes wide.

Johann smiled and stood. "Let's meet our new neighbors with open arms, then," he said.

"Wait, no," Theresa said. "We need something better than that planned. We're not ready for this."

"Ready or not, they're coming," Johann said, then laughed.

"This isn't funny, Johann. We need to make sure we're not too kind. Give off an attitude that shows we respect them but won't be pushed around."

Johann scoffed. "Were you not listening to Smith? They don't see human attitudes the way we do. Abe screamed at them, and they offered up some sort of apology."

"But then we don't understand their actions any better than they understand ours. So how do we know it was an apology?"

Johann looked to Smith and both shrugged.

"Exactly," Theresa said. "So we need a—wait, what the hell is that?"

A bluish white light glowed deep in the forest. It slowly moved toward them, gently bouncing up and down. It grew closer and Smith started to make out faces in the glow of the light. Tashon and Abe walked in the front of the group, the mohawked Singer walking between them. Mohawk's hands were facing forward, the wires popped out of the skin, a ball of light glowing, hovering off each palm.

Smith, Johann, Theresa and Winona waited in silence as the group came into the clearing and formed a half circle in front of the ship.

"Greetings, Singers." Theresa stepped forward and stuck out her hand. "We are plea—"

"Cut the bullshit, Theresa." Johann pushed her hand down. "They can't understand you."

"But I thought they understood Abe?"

"Yes," Ballas said. "I've been thinking about that. And my theory is that they understood him because of his intense emotional state when he yelled at them."

"So, if I want them to understand me, I need to be more... sincere?"

Ballas laughed. "No. You can't fake emotion. So your cheap political bullshittery won't work on them."

Smith smiled. "Phenomenal."

"Brilliant," Johann said as he stroked his beard.

"Political bullshit? I was being sincere."

Abe shook his head. "This shouldn't be about politics. Let's learn how we can get to know them. How we can communicate with them."

"But we need to start off on the right footing," Theresa argued. "We can't seem too weak, or too strong. We're going to be political partners, neighboring countries."

"Woah, wait," Winona joined in. "What do you mean? We're on the same land, a couple miles apart, at most. Why can't they be a part of the same country? Fall under the same government?"

Johann smiled. "See, Smith? I told you she should join us."

Theresa rolled her eyes and huffed.

"And I don't get the feeling they think the way we do about power and control, anyway," Abe said. "They seem more... honest than that. More evolved."

"So how are we going to communicate with them?" Johann asked.

"They used their... notes and melodies to convey emotion to us," Tashon said. "But they used images to convey facts."

"Not necessarily objective facts," Theresa interjected.

"We should treat them as honest and friendly until proven otherwise," Johann stated firmly. "Go on, Tashon."

"Right. So, we should use images to convey humanity's history to them, the same way they did for us. Does anyone have a working cube with them?"

Winona pulled one out of her pocket and tossed it to Tashon, who caught it and sat on the ground in front of the Singers, placing the cube in front of him.

"Ballas, where should we start?"

Ballas joined Tashon on the ground. "I think when the Ship of Nations left Earth?"

Tashon told the cube to produce the available footage of the day they left Earth. The image burst into the air in front of the Singers, and they flipped their palms down, the lighted wires disappearing into their hands.

As the video played, Smith kept his eyes on the Singers. Their eyes and faces betrayed no emotion the way a human's would. They stood, eyes glued to the images of the Ship of Nations leaving Earth, of life on the massive generation ship, of the first five planets to be colonized. They watched silently, seemingly emotionless, for over an hour. By the time Tashon gave the cube back to Winona, the clouds had dissipated, and the moon cast a dim light over the entire group.

The Singers looked at each other, then back at the humans. The one with the scar sang a short melody of four slightly different notes, and Smith distinctly felt that they understood what they saw. At least, as much as they could from their own perspective.

"Wonderful," Ballas said. "Don't know if I'll ever get used to feeling the emotions of another species."

"It's wonderful." Johann smiled as he sat on one of the many logs that surrounded them. "Historic."

Two of the Singers awkwardly sat on their own logs.

Smith was about to join them when Theresa grabbed his wrist and pulled him to the side.

"Hell, Smith," she whispered with a hiss in her voice. "This is not a time to kick back and relax with these things that we know nothing about. What are we going to tell the people? They'll be waking up soon."

"The who?"

"Oh, shut up, Smith. Everyone. They need to know they're being protected, that we'll take care of them. That we won't let these aliens—"

"We're the aliens."

"Shit, Smith! The people need to know they're going to be kept safe."

Ballas walked toward them, his eyes narrowed, a slight frown on his face. "Kept safe? From the people who lived here before us, who were decimated by another nation on the other side of the planet?"

"You're all batshit," she said. "Johann! We need to figure this out."

With a sigh, Johann stood and joined the small group.

"We need to take this one step at a time, Theresa," he said calmly. "First, what do we tell everyone?"

"The simpler, the better, I think," Ballas suggested.

"Simple?" Smith asked.

"Straightforward. Simply tell them the facts as we know them," he said, then looked directly at Theresa. "No conjecture."

"But they're going to have questions! How do we answer those?"

"Theresa," Smith said. "We don't need all the answers right now. And I don't think anyone will expect us to."

Smith waved Tashon and Abe over, leaving Winona and Rosa alone with the Singers. As they walked over, he wondered if Singers felt the humans were being rude having conversations away from them. But they were an intelligent species. They should understand the humans were only trying to figure everything out.

Smith looked at the three who had found the Singers. "Anything else that you remember?"

"No."

"Nothing."

"Sorry."

"Okay," Johann said. "That's okay. What questions do we have? Everyone else will most likely have some of the same ones."

"I do," Theresa said. "Are we sure there's only five left? I'm worried that there's more, and that they could take us out."

"Only five?" Tashon asked. "There's way more than that. Those coffins aren't coffins. They're stasis chambers."

"Shit," Theresa said. "Why didn't you tell us? How do you know?"

"I thought I did," Tashon said. "Sorry. One of the Singers who died in the attack told me."

"From the Fourth?" Johann asked.

Tashon nodded.

"How many?" Smith asked.

"Hundreds, I think. More than we have."

"Shit! We need to play this right." Theresa started pacing. "Or they could wipe us out or enslave us or—"

"Theresa, shut up," Johann said. "If we think like that, we're going to start a war. There is no reason to fear the Singers."

"Yet," she said. "But have you considered that maybe these emotions they're inserting into us are only meant to control us? To make us perceive the reality they want us to see?"

No one answered her. Smith looked at Rosa and Winona, smiling as the Singers made butterflies fly across a screen that spread out of their hands. His gut told him Theresa was wrong, that they could trust the Singers. But more often than not, his gut was wrong.

The new Frames have sailed the void
Pierced the dark with their boats
Seen and done more than we can know, or dream
Yet still their Windows are dark, silent
Was Mother right? Will they wake us?
Can they wake us?
Or must we wake them from their darkness,
From their pain, their rage?
Could we do so?
Perhaps Mother only foretold
Part of the story.
Or, this may be heresy,
Was Mother wrong?

Chapter 11

Tashon excused himself from the group, telling them he was going back into the Fourth to see what more he could learn of the Singers. They all readily accepted it, though Tashon could have conversed with someone in the Fourth whether or not he was surrounded by people. No, he just needed to get away and think.

He walked to the nearest well, a hole ten feet deep with a shallow layer of water at the bottom. He sat down, his feet hanging into the new water source.

His memory told him that the Singer from the Fourth had told not only him, but also Abe and Ballas that the coffins were, in reality, stasis chambers. And that Abe had then told Smith, who told everyone else. Logically, Tashon knew that was not reality, but his memory told a different story. And his memory of how it happened was more real to him than the reality of what happened, and that scared him.

He looked around at what he could see with his physical eyes. The trees, their bark pulsing to a rhythmic beat. A large leaf tumbling across the ground in a gentle breeze. A smokie sitting in the shadows, watching the meeting of species. This was his world. The world he had always occupied, the world he hoped to occupy for decades more. But now a part of him was constantly away from that world, no matter how much he tried to pretend it was only the Third that existed.

Yes, he was happy for the knowledge seeing the Fourth had brought him. Relieved to know that Laos forgave him, and that death was not the end. But it seemed to him that he was no longer able to keep the two realities separate, and he worried it would continue to confuse his mind and memory.

Laos, as always, hovered in that higher plane, and Tashon wanted to close his eyes and focus in on his ethereal companion, to see if he could glean any understanding of what the constant connection to the Fourth was doing to his mind.

"Can you see my mind or my soul, Laos?"

"No, Tashon."

"It feels like my mind is being split apart. My physical mind here, and my soul's mind up there."

"I think you've got a handle on it. If that happened to me, I'd be completely insane in an hour."

"Maybe I'm going insane, then. It's just taking its time."

"Trust yourself. What you've seen, what you will see."

"Yeah. Yeah, you're right. I just need to keep track of what I see in the Fourth, and what I see in the Third."

The thin rays of the morning sun poked out over the horizon. He looked back to the group, now all back in one huddle. He jogged back to join them, seeing his movements through first and third person, wondering if he would ever get used to the sensation, worried that the two might bleed together until he could not decipher between the two planes.

Three of the moths fluttered over his head and landed on a tree by the Singers.

"Did you learn anything else?" Theresa asked as Tashon rejoined the group.

"No, sorry."

"All good, Tash," Smith said as he slapped Tashon's shoulder.

"Where're Johann and Winona?"

"Went inside the ship. Getting everyone awake and gathered, bring them all out at once."

Tashon looked at the Singers, smiled and waved, then turned to Ballas.

"You think that's a good idea? Won't it scare them, or overwhelm them?"

"I don't think so. They showed us that they've been watching us. They know how many of us there are."

Tashon agreed. He looked back at the Singers, the five of them standing there, looking around as if nothing strange or amazing was happening. As if first contact was a normal occurrence for them. On the tree, the moths' wings fluttered in unison. In the Fourth, their wings did the same, though there they floated in the air with no tree to rest on.

An idea struck Tashon and he walked to the Singers, placing himself in the middle of the five, facing the moths. The Singers turned to look the same direction he was. He stretched his hand out, placed it on the bark of the tree, and the moths floated away. The pulsing of the tree beat softly into Tashon's palm and he looked at the Singers. They watched him, seemingly emotionless, as he put his other hand on his chest, over his heart. He wanted to know more about the trees. Did they all share one beating heart that pumped life through their roots?

One of the Singers placed a hand on the bark, a bracelet of rectangular stones wrapped around the wrist. It locked eyes with Tashon and lifted its other arm up, placed its hand on the middle of its back, just below the neck.

"That's where your heart is?"

The Singer that had visited him in the Fourth, in the caves, reappeared, hovering by Laos, whose face shone with a bright smile. The two looked down on the scene, a flock of moths gracefully circling above them. The moths also burst out of the leaves of the trees that towered above Tashon, and he was filled with the sense that he was in the middle of something more significant, more historical, more precious than anyone could comprehend.

The Singer made no movement, no sound. Tashon moved his hand off the tree and cautiously moved it toward the Singer's back. It moved its hand away and Tashon gently placed his hand on its back. The Singer's heart beat under his hand, far slower than a human heart. He pressed harder, but the flesh under his hand didn't give at all, as if the Singer were made of rock.

"They're on their way out," Theresa called, interrupting the wonder Tashon was being filled with.

He looked at her, saw the skin around her eyes and lips tightened in defensive fear, and a heaviness fell in his gut as he realized she would not be the only one to react to the Singers' presence with trepidation.

Johann and Winona walked slowly out of the ship, followed by the rest of the survivors. As they filed out, gasps, screams and hushed mutterings filled the clearing. They slowly sat on the rocks, logs and dirt. Some kept their eyes fixed on the strangeness of a new species, while others kept their eyes down.

Above him, Laos and the Singer stood side by side, each intently focused on the events unfolding on Aethera.

The rests of the humans shuffled out of the ship, stood around the edges of the clearing, and quieted down as quickly as they could. Smiles spread across many of the faces, while others shared the same look Tashon had seen on Theresa's face. Uncertainty. Distrust.

Johann walked to the front of the crowd, waited for the last whisperings to die out, and took a moment to scratch his beard before speaking.

He smiled. "Good morning. I think we should all welcome our new... wait, no." He paused and ran his hands through his thinning hair, as if considering something of utmost importance. "We can't really welcome them. They were here long before us. Centuries, at least. And we've crashed two ships into their planet. They've been aware of us the entire time, and done nothing to harm or even threaten us. So, let's just all say hello."

Some of the audience verbally said the word, but most nodded, all with varying degrees of nervousness or excitement displayed on their faces and by their body language.

Johann then went into a quick summary of everything that had happened with the Singers, all that was known about them at that moment. When he was done, he looked at Tashon and the Singers.

"They really are a beautiful species, and I'm hopeful that we will have a positive relationship with them as we grow here on Aethera."

Tashon smiled and looked at each of the Singers around him. A minute of silence, then two, three. All of Aethera's humanity stared at Tashon and the Singers. Another minute of silence and Tashon stepped back, placing only the Singers at the center of everyone's vision. As if that movement was their cue, the Singers opened their mouths.

A different note came from each mouth, some of them pitches that Tashon knew humans would never be able to imitate. The notes continued, blending into a melody at once happy and slow, sending a calming warmth into Tashon's heart, his soul. And as it did, he suddenly, inexplicably, felt more at home on Aethera than he ever had anywhere in his life.

The Singers had officially welcomed the humans onto Aethera.

Chapter 12

Abe was standing to the side of the ship by his dad when the Singers began their melodious communication. The sounds swam through his skin, into his veins, spreading a relaxing chill throughout his entire body that made him feel awake, alive and at home. He smiled and turned to his dad, who had the same look of contentment spread across his face.

One by one, the Singers' voices stopped until all was silent. They stood for a moment, then, without ceremony, turned and walked back toward the caves. Once they were out of sight, the clearing erupted with the sounds of excitement, confusion and concern.

Theresa and Johann stood at the front, waiting patiently for the noise to die down.

"Shouldn't you be up there, Dad?"

"Right." Smith nodded. "Right."

Abe shook his head as he watched his dad walk slowly to the front, a dazed look in his eyes. But how else would he look? Abe felt the same way, as if he were living through his time on Aethera through a haze, an out-of-focus lens. Something inside him wasn't letting him fully appreciate the momentous time he was experiencing. Not something, but the lack of something.

The absence of his mom.

He thought he was doing okay, but then he lost it on the Singers when he saw that they could have saved her but didn't. He was embarrassed with himself, but glad that they seemed to be an understanding species. He hoped it didn't turn out that they were simply passive-aggressive.

Theresa raised her hand and the crowd went quiet.

"It looks like we're all still figuring out how to feel about all this. It's historical. But I want to ensure our safety moving forward. We need to tread cautiously here."

"Obviously, I agree with Theresa," Johann said. "As far as being careful and ensuring our safety. But I don't see any reason to fear them.

We should be hopeful, not fearful, about our future with the Singers. As far as I can tell, they are welcoming us with open arms. But we want everyone's thoughts on the issue."

"If they're so welcoming, why didn't they come out to us? Why did we have to discover them?" a man called from the crowd.

"That's a good question," Smith said. "And, to me, the one fact about them that seems questionable. But everything else they have done shows, to me, that we can trust them."

"But what decision are we really trying to make?" a woman asked as she stood up. "It's not like we're going to kill them. Some of us are nervous about their existence, others are excited. But either way, they're here. We need to accept that."

"Yes, well said." Johann nodded. "Other thoughts?"

"Did you say something about another intelligent species on Aethera?"

"Yes," Smith said. "But I think Abe or Tashon can explain that more. The Singers showed them some images about them."

Abe looked around, but Tashon had disappeared, perhaps to be with the Singers. He took a breath, cleared his throat and walked to his father's side.

"So, from what we could understand from the images, this other species destroyed most of the Singers' population, turning the other side of the mountains to desert. The Singers that survived went into the caves. The biotech beetles were made by the other species. If there's a species we need to be worried about, it's those."

"So, a different race of Singers?"

"No, no. The images we saw showed four-legged creatures. The legs came up and together underneath a head, I guess. A long, kind of egg-shaped head."

It went quiet as everyone considered what that meant. Two completely different intelligent species on the same planet. Abe hadn't thought about it much, but now that he did, it seemed nearly impossible that both species were native to Aethera, and he wondered which of the two had been there first.

"Why did they attack the Singers?" A woman asked.

"A Singer went rogue and killed the leader of the other species."

"At least, that's what the Singers told you?" Theresa asked.

"Right."

"And how do we know that's the truth?" a man from the crowd asked.

"I, uh, we—"

"We don't," Theresa cut him off.

"I-I," Abe faltered. "I think—feel—we can trust them."

"I think we can too," Johann said. "And, again, I think it's better that we move forward with hope, not fear."

Many in the crowd called out their agreement. Others muttered their concern.

"But why do you feel that way?" Theresa asked. "Don't the Singers communicate casting emotions on us? Couldn't they also use emotions to manipulate us to their will? That's my concern."

Some in the crowd agreed, though far less than those who sided with Johann. Abe understood her point, and believed she was truly concerned for everyone's welfare. But he didn't like the fear she was putting into everyone. Her concern could cause everyone to mistrust the Singers before they even understood anything about them.

"It is possible," Johann said. "But we can't let that fear stop us from trying to build something good with the Singers. Smith, what do you think?"

"I agree that we should work toward something good with the Singers, but let's be cautious, just in case. Pay attention to how they make you feel, and when they're not around, consider if what you were feeling seems normal for you."

"Okay, agreed," Theresa said. "Be cautious, everyone, and enjoy this unprecedented time in human history."

She disappeared into the ship.

Abe turned to his father and smiled.

"You did good, son."

Abe laughed. "Don't lie."

Smith chuckled and put an arm around Abe, pulling him toward the outskirts of the clearing. They stopped just before they were covered in shade, the rays of the rising sun warming his shoulders.

"You don't think the Singers are actually dangerous do you, Dad?"

Smith shrugged. "I don't think we can know for sure. I don't think they are. But I get where Theresa's coming from, especially since there are hundreds more Singers in stasis that could wake up anytime and probably take us out if they wanted to."

"Happy thought."

"I've had far worse."

Abe turned away from his dad, turning his eyes to the ground, then torward the ship. "Me too," he whispered.

Smith looked at him. Abe could feel the worry that filled his dad.

"I'm okay, Dad, really. I just...." He shrugged. "I need to get away, do something."

"Yeah, I know. But you still want to, even with the Singers here?"

"I was thinking that we should take a couple of Singers with us. Go to this other species. Be—I don't know—peacemakers between the two."

Smith blew out a long slow breath.

Abe waited in silence, hoping his dad would understand why Abe wanted to do this. Part of it was he was worried that the other species would send another attack if they discovered the Singers were still alive. He didn't want Aethera to be thrown into a war before humanity even had a chance find their place on the planet.

But more than that, he believed, without question, that the Singers were good. That they would do everything they could to help humanity. They had already saved Abe at least once. Even though they failed to save his mom, Abe was convinced they were a morally upright species. Save for the few outliers, like the one who murdered the leader of the other species.

"Damn, Abe. You remind more of your mom every day." Smith wrapped an arm tightly around Abe's shoulders.

Abe closed his eyes, imagined for a moment it was his mom, then opened them again. He looked at his dad and smiled. "I would rather be more like her than you."

Smith laughed. "Who wouldn't?"

Chapter 13

Tashon walked through yellow woods, farther than he ever had, in a direction he'd never gone. The moths had flown past him while Theresa was talking, and he'd decided to follow. They fluttered through the third-dimensional trees, then floated through the waves of air in the Fourth. The forest grew more crowded, the trees closing in on him until he was twisting and squeezing his way through the biggest gaps he could find. But he kept going, his third-person eye following him every step of the way, showing him that soon the yellow trees would fade away and be replaced by thin, black sticks that shot out of the ground, leafless and branchless.

He saw this, from his extra eyes, before he truly saw it, and was denied the wonderment of surprise when he found himself among the new plants. A flat rock, about knee height, came into view at the edge of his Fourth sight. He walked to it and sat down. With a deep breath, he pulled his knees to his chest and closed his eyes.

There was the ever-present Laos, smiling at him. The moths halted, hovering motionlessly by Laos's side. Tashon wondered if Laos had seen any of the species that attacked the Singers in the Fourth.

"No, Tashon."

Tashon turned away from Laos, vision keen to notice every detail of the Fourth. Again, in the distance, some type of city of towering, improbable shapes. He let his gaze move until he noticed something in the distance flicker. A light, a mesmerizing shade of green that he'd never seen, blinked. On, off. On, off. Each time it flashed on, it was bigger and brighter. Was it growing bigger, or moving closer?

He waited, and watched. On, off. On, off. Brighter and bigger, until he was sure the light was not moving toward him. He asked Laos what it was.

"I don't know, but it's beautiful, isn't it? Inviting."

Tashon agreed. He wanted to go to it. Touch it, bask in it, sleep in it. But how? The only piece of him in the Fourth was that part of the essence pulled there by the beast. He closed his eyes tighter, willed that essence to move laterally toward the light, but it would not. If he walked his body through the Third, he might be able to reach it, but that could take days.

He clenched his teeth in frustration. Held his breath, tensed his body. Blew it all out. He realized he'd never assessed his connection to the Fourth. Was it possible for him to pull his physical body to the higher plane with Laos? With all the others? Act as his own tesseract engine?

As this thought came to him, his essence in the Fourth rose, above Laos. It began to pull on his physical body, an invisible tether connecting the two. His physical eyes closed and his body rose off the rock. All he wanted in that moment was to be with Laos, to travel with him to the green light.

Pain pulsed in his brain. Everything went white. Something hit his body, pushed through it, and burst out the back of him. The oxygen exploded from his lungs. He lay, or sat, or floated in nothing but bright white, trying to suck oxygen back into his body.

The light faded. His breathing slowed. He opened his eyes. The side of his face was on a semi-translucent surface. Through it he could see the rock he had just been sitting on, far below him, but it was empty. In the distance, below Tashon and to the left, was the ship and the clearing. He rolled to his side, sat up, and looked at Laos, at the moths, at the wind swirling everywhere.

He was back in the Fourth.

He slowly rose to his feet, his legs shaking underneath him. His head spun, pounded, slushed. He fell to his knees and vomited, the bile blowing away in the fourth-dimensional wind. Exhaustion washed over him, but he wouldn't succumb to it.

"Laos, can we talk normally now?"

"Yes, Tashon." Laos smiled. "Welcome back to the Fourth."

"Yeah, I... uh...." He paused. "I guess I can move between dimensions."

Laos laughed. "Not effectively. You look miserable, and your vomit just blew through my being. It was wet, and warm."

"Sorry."

"You should be. I swear, that was worse than when you killed me."

Tashon coughed and looked away, a wave of guilt washing over him.

"Too soon?"

"Yeah. I might just have to kill you again."

Laos laughed and Tashon smiled at the sound. To hear the voice of the man he murdered, laughing and happy, was a comforting relief.

"But now what?" Tashon asked. "I'm no good to walk, can't figure out what that light is."

"It's gone anyway."

"Huh?"

Tashon turned all the way around, his gaze passing by the structures, the moths, and landing back on Laos. The green light had disappeared.

"Huh."

"I haven't seen it before, either."

Tashon nodded, but a sense of loss came over him. Getting to that light had seemed so important, as if getting there would change his life. But now it was gone.

Another wave of nausea hit Tashon, and this time he turned around before releasing the bile from his gut. His entire body trembled. He looked at his hand, which visibly vibrated, sending tremors all the way up his arms, to his shoulders and down his torso to his legs and feet.

He lay down, wanting nothing more than to be back in his own dimension. With eyes shut, he pushed that part of him that had been living in the Fourth away. The essence slid out of his head, and hovered near him, a visible tether connecting it to his brainstem. The tremors stopped. Tashon stood and turned to face the way the ship lay. If he remembered right from his time in the Fourth, he would only need to take a few steps to be above where the ship lay in the Third.

"Yes, that will work," Laos said.

With the land of Aethera stretched far below him like a board, Tashon took one step and left the rock behind. Another, and the yellow forest was right below him. He stopped and looked ahead, far past the ship. On the other side of a vast ocean stood another continent, with towering rocks that were flat on top. Caves and tunnels connected the towers to engineered structures, to other towers, forming an ant-like maze. It was the land of that other species.

It hit Tashon that this species was not as far away as they would like to think. And, with the Singers being their new neighbors, they would all need to decide what to do about the evidently violent species before they attacked again.

A form sped toward Tashon, and before he could move, it was in front him. The Singer who had shown him the code in the caves. She lifted her arm and pointed toward the land of the species that nearly destroyed the Singers. Then she spoke, and the melody that left her lips was one of heavy foreboding. The images that filled Tashon's head as she sang showed a mass of the four-legged species scurrying in and out of their tunnels in a hurried effort to build—something.

The creatures ran on their four legs, but where those legs connected, at the bottom of their elliptical heads, two skinny arms protruded. From what Tashon could tell, each of these arms had at least two joints and ended with hands that had an impressive number of fingers. These hands held various objects that made no sense to Tashon. Some held spheres or squares of metal, perhaps stone or plastic, while others carried what looked like fresh organs and flesh.

They carried these items into a large, spherical building, inside which yet more of them used the items to build large biotech creatures. One looked like a mix between a lion and a praying mantis. Another like and alligator with wings. And countless more.

The Singer's tone grew deeper yet, and lion mantis came to life, the flesh of its joints bending beneath the metal. One of the four-legged species tossed a chuck of meat into the air, and the lion mantis leapt into the air, caught it and ripped it to pieces. The winged alligator dove to snatch a piece that had fallen the ground. But the lion mantis whipped its pincher around and crunched the alligator's head off in one swift movement. A black, blood-like substance oozed out of the headless body, spreading out until it was under the feet of the four-legged species. They walked through as if it wasn't there.

The creature was massive, strong and violent. They seemed like enlarged versions of the beetles that had killed so many of the Singers. Tashon realized then that they would serve the same purpose as the smaller insects.

To kill, to destroy.

Tashon's head spun and he collapsed to his hands and knees. They were building an army. Somehow, they knew the humans were there. That the Singers had not been completely wiped out, and they were preparing an attack. But how could he be sure? Maybe the manufactured beasts were to serve some other purpose.

The Singer touch Tashon's shoulder, and he knew the truth. Knew that he needed to help Singers and humans alike. That he needed to go and, somehow, stop the attack before it reached the ship and the caves.

He coughed and heaved, crawling slowly until the clearing and the ship were directly below him. He sat down, crossed his legs and then closed his eyes. Saw the clearing, in his mind, from a first-person view. Felt the gravity of Aethera beneath him. His head twisted and pulsed, and he fell onto his side.

Again, bright white light engulfed him, and an immense pressure forced the air out of him. He slammed into the Aetheran ground and opened his eyes. Abe, Smith, Johann and dozens of others stared silently at him.

Chapter 14

Smith sat in a circle with Theresa and the five who would be setting out to explore Aethera. A handful of smokies wandered around the clearing as they talked. Ballas and Winona were willing, and already excited, to be a part of Abe's plan to mediate between the Singers and the species across the ocean. But Galvin and Astrid, husband and wife, were unsure of the idea.

"What responsibility do we have to these Singers?" Galvin asked. "Why should we keep them safe from those across the ocean?"

"Right," Theresa said. "And how do we know they're not emotionally manipulating us into doing their bidding?"

"Why don't you trust them?" Abe asked. "The Singers?"

"Why do you? I think it's natural to mistrust a new species."

"No," Abe looked at the ground. "That's human."

"Since when is being human bad?" Astrid asked.

"It's not," Smith said. "But I don't think our tendency to mistrust something just because it's new is good, especially when our future is at stake."

"That's exactly what we're concerned about," Galvin said. "Our future."

"Then don't go with us," Abe said, obviously upset. "Ballas, Winona and I will go. And I bet we could get two others, maybe Tashon and Rosa."

The adults looked at each other, silently assessing the boy's statement. Smith was proud of his son, but worried his stubbornness would get him in trouble. If he had talked to a board member on the ship like that, he would have been harshly reprimanded. Thankfully, Theresa only laughed.

"Just like your mom, Abe. You really think you're doing the right thing?"

"Yes."

Theresa nodded.

"I think the majority will agree with you, too," she said. "But we still need to be careful about how we handle this. We don't have to sacrifice ourselves to save the Singers."

Abe shook his head.

"Jonstin died saving my life," he whispered. "That is what human should mean."

Again, Abe's words silenced the group.

Smith leaned back and smiled at Theresa, who sighed and shook her head. At least she wasn't impossible to work with, Smith decided. And there were bound to be times when they would need someone more cautious and careful. He did, for a moment, wonder if this was one of those times. But the fire inside Abe at being an ambassador between the two Aetheran species was contagious and Smith felt, almost knew, that what Abe was planning had to be done.

A body appeared in the air, six feet off the ground, then slammed into the dirt. Tashon rolled onto his knees, dry heaving uncontrollably. Two smokies flew two his side, followed by Smith and Abe. They helped him sit on the ground and lean against a rock. Rosa appeared next to him, holding a cup of water. Smith handed it to Tashon, who greedily sucked it down. His breathing started to slow, and he opened his eyes.

"We...." He coughed, then spit into the dirt. "We need to stop them."

"Who, Tash?"

Through labored breaths, Tashon told them what he'd been shown in the Fourth. The battalion of mechanically-enhanced, biological creatures that would soon be on their way to finish the job the beetles started.

"You're like a prophet," Rosa whispered.

"Huh? No, I'm not. What I saw, what I was shown, can be explained now that we have proof of our connection to a higher plane."

Rosa smiled. "You have proof. And I believe based on the proof you say you've seen."

Tashon shook his head and looked away. "I'm no prophet. I'm just the one who barely got away from Aleron's beast. My connection is only because the beast didn't finish turning me into one of its puppets."

They went silent. Smith wanted to talk more about Tashon's ability, more about Rosa's faith. But, if Tashon was right, they needed to get group moving as fast as possible.

"Let's get you going with the others, then."

"Right, yeah. I'll go get the Singers. We'll need at least one of them with us."

"And we'll get supplies together."

Tashon stood and jogged off.

Smith watched him disappear behind the trees, then turned to Rosa "Go see if any med bikes are up and running. Abe! Go get supply packs. Looks like you're heading exactly where you wanted to."

Abe and Rosa ran off to prepare. Smith stood and turned, and Theresa grabbed his arm, pulling him away.

"Smith, what the hell is this?"

"You heard same as I did."

"And you just believe it? This is going to cause mass panic."

"And your fear of the Singers won't?"

She scoffed.

"The Singers are a potential, present threat. This, this other species might not even exist."

Smith looked her in the eye. "I. Trust. Tashon. With my life."

"Gah, I know, I know. But what if the spirits, or whatever, are lying to him?"

"I trust Tashon, and his judgement."

"We need to put it to a vote."

Johann walked up to them.

"Vote," he said. "On whether or not we let five people go out into Aethera to stop a potential massacre on us and the Singers?"

"If you put it that way—"

"I'll put it exactly that way when I talk to everyone about what's happening."

"But what if the Singers are manipulating us?"

"We still have the rest of us here," Smith said. "Sending a small group out doesn't weaken us."

"Fine," Theresa said.

"Good."

"One thing we can discuss with everyone," Johann said. "Is what to do while they're gone. We need to be prepared if this other species does launch an attack."

"And ready if the Singers do anything," Theresa added.

"That too," Johann gave her a nod.

Rosa jogged out of the ship.

"Smith, none of the med bikes we have left are holding a charge."

"Dammit." He looked around the crowd. "Winona!"

The young girl walked to him, a gleam in her brown eyes.

"Yes, Chief?"

"You've heard what's happening?"

"Yes."

"And you're still good going, yes? Tashon and Rosa will be joining you, Ballas, and Abe."

She smiled. "Chief, I'm going."

"Good. Abe's getting packs together. Can you go help him?"

She nodded and ran to the ship. Smith rubbed his eyes and turned to Rosa.

"I sure as hell hope Tashon's wrong," he said.

"Me too. But he's not," she said.

Smith nodded, considered yet again the firmness of Rosa's faith in Tashon. But he could feel it, too. Something was coming. Or, rather, they were being pushed toward something inevitable, as if whatever were going to happen was always going to happen, like the certainty of destruction at the hands of an impending hailstorm. He looked at the faces around him, saw them shift to fear or confusion or disbelief as each heard the news. Their bodies tensed, they turned to those closest to them, whispering, shouting.

Abe and Winona emerged from the ship, Abe carrying two packs with his one arm, Winona carrying three. They dropped them at Smith's feet, breathing heavily.

"Tashon's not back yet?"

"No," Smith said. "And we need to figure out how you're getting there. Med bikes aren't an option, and it's on the other side of an ocean."

"Smokies, Dad."

Smith looked around at the black creatures walking around the clearing, in and out of the trees.

"That could work," Smith agreed. "But that's way farther than they carried us across the desert."

"Right, they might not have enough charge."

"I bet the Singers have machines that could get us there, if the smokies won't work."

"I was thinking about that," Abe said, sitting down on a pack. "How are we going to tell the Singers about this? Everything we've communicated to them was about our past, events that we had footage of. How can we tell them this? That the species that nearly destroyed them once is mounting an even greater attack?"

"That's a damn good question."

"I'm sure Tashon will know how," Rosa said.

"I don't think so," Abe said. "He's not a god."

"He's a prophet, Abe."

Ballas rejoined the group, silently listening to the conversation.

"Maybe," Smith said. "But we still need to tell the Singers what's going on. I don't think images will convey that. Tashon saw it all because he was in the Fourth."

"Right," Abe nodded.

"Then why did Tashon go get them?"

"This was their home first. They need to know what's happening."

"Don't you think they already know?" Ballas asked. "They had footage of the colony ship going down, of the Smokies saving Smith, Abe and Jonstin. They've been monitoring us. Don't you think they're monitoring them?"

"Maybe," Smith said. "If their tech can travel that far, and not be noticed. It's not like there are satellites floating around Aethera."

"I'm worried that they won't want to do anything," Ballas said.

"Why?"

"Think about it. Their city was decimated by that species, and the Singers didn't retaliate. They went into hiding, most of them in stasis. They don't seem like an aggressive species."

"You don't think they'll protect themselves?"

"They might, but I don't think they'll actively move on another species."

"A high morality?" Rosa asked

"It could be. Or maybe just cultural. Or maybe even genetic."

"You're saying they could biologically be incapable of violence?"

"An unlikely theory." Ballas shrugged. "A thought, really."

"That'd be something, though," Abe said.

Smith laughed, though he agreed with Abe. After all the hell he'd been through, the violence and corruption on Earth caused by human hands, it would be inspiring to have found a species incapable of such hate and destruction. And if the Singers were like that, and it was culturally bred, could humans reach that point? Smith shook his head and rubbed his eyes. But if humans did reach that point, would they be so non-violent that they wouldn't even fight to keep their families and homes safe? He couldn't imagine that, nor could he imagine the Singers would do nothing to protect themselves. But he'd been proven wrong before.

Chapter 15

Tashon found the Singers in the same place as the day before. The five of them sat in a circle on the floor, a pile of food in front of each. They looked in his direction, then back at their meal. They scooped the food up with their fingers, licked it of with think, dry tongues. Tashon had to look away, and was surprised to see that a species with such advance tech didn't have some form of eating utensils.

They ate quickly and stood, walking slowly to Tashon.

"We need to go." He beckoned them with his hand, but they didn't follow. "Right. Dammit."

He ran a hand through his hair and sighed. How was he supposed to communicate with them? He reached into his pocket and pulled out a cube. He placed it on the ground and pressed a button. An array of words and colored spheres rose out of it. Tashon paused to think. It had been months since he had to search through the menus, and he had to be sure he could find what he was looking for. And he hoped it would help the Singers understand what was happening.

He flipped his finger across the screen until he found it: a holographic globe of Aethera.

"Okay, here." He pointed.

The Singers stepped closer and looked at the screen. Tashon placed his finger on the map where the other species were creating their biotech army. As soon as he touched the glowing continent, a trembling hum left the Singers' mouths and Tashon was nearly overcome with a sense of dread. He bent his pinky into his palm and placed his thumb and three other fingers on the map, hoping the Singers would understand it symbolized the four-legged species.

He walked his fingers slowly along the map, toward their caves. As he did, their humming grew deeper until Tashon no longer heard it, but felt it in his bones, the intensity of it vibrating the stone ground. He stopped with his hand right on top of the Singers' home, and they went silent.

"Understand?"

One of the Singers, a scar on her face, crouched next to Tashon. She lifted her hand up, showing that she had an opposable thumb and three fingers. From what Tashon could tell this was natural, and not the cause of some accident. She made her thumb and fingers match what Tashon was doing with his. Her other hand rose up, palm turned upward. The two stiff wires flipped out, and a screen lit up between the two. Tashon noticed that, somehow, the wires were a part of her and not some type of implanted tech. Or so it seemed to him.

An image appeared on the screen that floated from her hand: a four legged creature. The Singer held the image right next to her upside down hand, as if to confirm that Tashon was referring to the other species.

"Yes." Tashon nodded, knowing they didn't understand any of that.

He gently wrapped his hand around her wrist and guided her hand, along with the image protruding from it, along the map to the land that housed the species and their weaponized biotech. He held it there for a moment, briefly distracted by how cold her skin was, then slowly moved it toward the land of the Singers, and stopped.

She pulled her hand away and stood, arms straight to her side. A guttural note vibrated from her chest as she stared blanked in front of her. The others echoed the sound almost identically, then the red mohawk ran to the keypad and punched the buttons. The floor rose, and as soon as it stopped, the Singers ran down the hall, faster than Tashon thought they could, one of them repeating the same sound over and over, and Tashon figured it was Singer for 'shit.'

He struggled to keep up with them, pumping his legs as his hard as he could, his heart pounding in his chest. At least they understood him, he told himself. But their reaction made him even more terrified of what was coming. They reached the door before he did, four of them running into the forest without waiting for him. The last Singer held the door for him, as Tashon passed, he noticed that this Singer had two different colored eyes. One yellow, one red. Tashon jogged past, the door swung shut behind them, and the Singer sped past him again, disappearing into the trees.

Tashon didn't like that the Singers would get to the clearing before him. He didn't know what had happened at the ship after he left. How everyone reacted to the news. But there was nothing he could do other than catch up with the Singers as fast as he could. Smokies emerged around him, all following the Singers. Ten of them—no, a dozen. Maybe more.

Tashon burst into the clearing. The Singers stood in the middle, a circle of humans around them. But the Singers didn't seem to notice, their attention focused on a smokie that stood in front of them. The shortest of the Singers, with wispy strands of hair, was looking directly at it, waving her hands, and singing a sharp staccato of high notes.

As soon as she went silent, the smokie dropped to the ground. Its legs bent up and to the side so that only its belly and chin rested on the ground. The Singer let out one quick note, and the smokie lifted ten feet off the ground. Two more notes and it flew off in the direction of the other species, and their weapons.

Another Singer, with the braided hair, stepped forward. She lifted her hand up and produced a screen. Already, Tashon realized, he was becoming used to the wires popping out of their hands, the images they produced. This time, it was actual footage. Trees and ground rushed by on the screen. Tashon turned his head sideways to the right, then to the left.

The screen was showing the view from the smokie. It was doing reconnaissance. It flew through the forest, trees rushing past in a blur. Soon, the trees thinned then disappeared, giving way to rolling hills of green and yellow. Clear of the trees and branches, the smokie shot into the air, thousands of feet, giving a vast bird's eye view of the ground below. Red boulders were scattered across the hills below, and those slowly took over the ground until all that was below were countless boulders crushed and tumbled over one another.

The ocean came into view, dark green waves splashing over rocks, leaving tide pools that glistened in the sunlight. Rising higher still, the smokie continued forward until the other continent rose out of the water. The engineered tunnels connected it to the natural stone towers in a beautiful maze through which thousands of four-legged creatures travelled.

The Singer holding the screen began to hum, providing a deep, tense soundtrack to what was about to happen.

Amid the tunnels and towers, the biotech beasts were being brought outside and forced to brawl. The Smokie flew in and landed atop a stone pillar, peering over the edge. A massive half horse, half reptile had its jaws clenched down on the neck of a creature that looked similar to a sloth, but in one swift movement it ripped the bottom half of the horse's jaw off, stabbed a claw in each of its eyes, and slammed it into the ground. The four-leggers clicked and chattered as if, Tashon thought, amused by the spectacle.

Then, without warning, a blaring siren sounded, and every four-legger snapped its head directly at the smokie.

The sloth, though wingless, rose into the air and rocketed toward the smokie, its body growing bigger on the screen until it crackled and went black.

This other Frame, different than others
Its melody awake, alive
Two melodies, two windows
One frame
Another piece not foretold by Mother
So much that none expected, none planned for
These Frames, not saviors as we imagined them to be
They live, exist, complexly outside what was foretold.
Mother, forgive us the question, could you have been wrong?
Will our family remain asleep, silent, unmoving?
Mother?

Chapter 16

The weight of terror and dread fell onto Abe's shoulders, onto everyone's. He looked around, feeling the silence. Feeling the weight of the decision he'd already made to go to the land of the four-leggers. What he had seen didn't deter him from going, but he was now afraid that the visit to their land would be far more violent than he had hoped.

Gathered in their own circle, the Singers quietly communicated. Most likely they were discussing a plan, and Abe realized he should be doing the same. He quickly gathered Rosa, Winona, Tashon, Ballas, Johann, and Smith. Others stood off to the side, listening to the conversation, eyes still dazed from what they had witnessed.

"We can't just show up there expecting to communicate with them," Abe said.

"I agree," Ballas replied. "Though I was hoping we would have that option."

"So what's the plan, then?" Winona asked.

"First, I think I should join you," Johann said.

Abe shot a glance at the older man, shocked by the offer, but before he could respond, Tashon spoke.

"Your military experience could be useful," he said. "But once we get there, what's the plan? You saw how quickly they spotted and destroyed the smokie. That could be us."

"You're right," Smith said. "Doing this is a risk, and it could kill all of you."

Smith looked at his son as he finished the sentence, and Abe felt a pang of guilt. If he were to die, would his dad be able to handle that loss?

"But," Smith continued. "I have faith in all of you."

"I do too," Rosa said. "And I have an idea. Tashon, do you think that you could bring others into the Fourth with you?"

"I, uh, maybe. With practice. Today was the first time I've done it."

"Right, but we, or at least you, could go to the Fourth and get into their land unseen."

Abe smiled. "That is a good idea. But what would he—or us—do once we got there?"

The group went silent, pondering the thought.

"Take a bomb with us?" Rosa said.

Smith shook his head.

"Maybe, but we'd have to make one first. And I don't think any of us are comfortable committing genocide."

"I never said genocide, Farmer. Though I'm not against it."

Ballas scoffed. "You would willingly destroy an entire species? It is very unlikely they are all evil. From an ethical—and a scientific—standpoint, we cannot do that. We now know, without doubt, that there are at least two intelligent species besides our own. And you would destroy one entirely?"

"Not saying I will." Rosa stepped toward Ballas. "Only said I'm not against the idea. But if we all decide not to destroy them, I'll honor that."

"Good."

Silence again. Abe expected Rosa to mumble something under her breath or call Ballas a coward, but she remained quiet.

"Okay," Abe said. "I agree we shouldn't kill all of them. We know nothing about their culture, their government, their values. Nothing. But we do know, because of Tashon, that these... Crawlers are planning to attack us."

"No," Theresa joined the discussion. "We assume they are. Tashon says he knows, because of his Fourth sight, that they will attack us. None of us can corroborate that. All we know for certain is what we saw on the Singer screen. How do we know that what we saw was an act of aggression? Maybe the Singers were breaking a treaty by sending their smokie there. We. Don't. Know."

"Cut the shit," Rosa said. "Yesterday, you were saying we should be cautious around the Singers, a species that has proven to be nothing by kind and docile. And now you're saying we should give these Crawlers the benefit of the doubt?"

"What I'm saying is this: everything we've recently come to understand about Aethera is from the Singers, a species with which we can't clearly communicate. My concern is that they are using their language to manipulate our emotions into doing their dirty work."

"What about what Tashon has learned of Aethera from the Fourth?"

"Yes, the visions of Tashon who, for all we know, is simply sick in the head," Theresa said calmly. "No offense, Tashon."

"Right," he said.

A pit formed in Abe's stomach. He'd never questioned Tashon's ability. Never thought what Tashon said he'd learned from the Fourth could be false, simply the delusions of one whose mind had been derailed when the beast's tentacle pierced it.

"Watch your damn mouth," Rosa seethed.

"Hey." Smith rose a hand. "That won't help. Either way, we know that there is another intelligent species on Aethera, and that they possess biotech that could massacre all of us, if they choose to do so."

More silence as the group let that sink in. Abe's heart pounded, feeling that the decision they made in that moment would impact humanity's future on Aethera in unknowable ways.

"Then what the hell do we do?" Winona threw her hands into the air.

Abe closed his eyes, trying to force a solution to come, but none would. They could stay, hope that the Crawlers would do nothing, that Tashon was wrong. Or go to the Crawlers, try to communicate with them, to form a relationship that would benefit all species of Aethera. Or assume that Tashon was right and go on the offensive. Figure out some way to infiltrate the Crawlers' land and destroy their weapons, possibly killing innocents in the process.

"Whatever we do," Ballas said. "We need to make sure we're on the same page as the Singers. We don't want to jeopardize that relationship."

"And how the hell do we do that?" Winona asked.

"Images have been the most effective so far," Tashon said. "That's how I got them here."

"Yeah, Tash. But how can we come up with a plan of attack with them? It needs to be thought out, detailed. And then executed."

"Right," Johann said. "And we need a layout of the Crawlers' land. Their tunnels, their structures. As in depth as we can. And how can we do that without getting closer?"

"Maybe the Singers have another type of tech that could do that," Winona said. "Or maybe they already have one, or even already know it."

"That would be helpful," Smith said, scratching his head.

"Right, and the one who murdered the Crawlers' leader would have had to know the layout beforehand to have gotten close enough to do it."

"Wait. These are all questions that need to be answered," Ballas said. "But first. Do we even know if one of the Singers want to go with us? Or if they would even support us going?"

Everyone nodded in agreement.

Theresa walked away from the group.

"I guess that's the first question that needs to be answered," Smith said with a nod.

"Yeah, but we need to move quick," Tashon said. "I got the feeling that whatever the Crawlers are planning is going to happen soon."

"Okay," Johann said. "Tashon, Ballas, Abe. Go connect with the Singers. Rosa, Winona with me. Let's talk to everyone. Calm some nerves, get some opinions."

Abe smiled and turned with the other two to walk to the Singers. He would spend all day with the Singers if he could, even though he couldn't understand them. The melodies that flowed from them were mesmerizing, intoxicating. But that also would make it even more difficult for the two species to fully comprehend each other. The Singers reached notes no human could and, for all Abe knew, those notes could be crucial to fully explaining the ideas they needed to discuss.

They approached the Singers, who opened up their circle for the newcomers. Neither humans nor singers made a sound. Abe looked to Tashon, then Ballas. Both seemed to be lost in thought, obviously unsure of how to begin. Abe lowered himself to the ground and sat with his legs crossed, the same way they had earlier in the caves. The Singers sat down, then Tashon and Ballas.

"We need to come up with a plan," Abe said, making eye contact with each of the Singers.

"They won't understand that," Ballas said.

"It's better than staying quiet."

"Maybe," Tashon said. "But the Singers at least have an idea of what's going on with the Crawlers. Let's give them a chance to try to communicate."

Abe agreed, surprised he hadn't thought of it himself. The Singers obviously trusted the humans and wanted to communicate too. At least, Abe hoped. Theresa's fears of the Singers manipulating them kept creeping into his mind, threatening to ruin the new relationship with the Singers. But he told himself, again, that the Singers had no ill intentions.

Tashon placed a cube on the ground, made the map of Aethera appear, and zoomed it in so it showed only the continent of the Crawlers.

And they waited, the Singers staring at the image, a note or two occasionally leaving their lips. It was obvious to Abe that the Singers at least knew that something was going on with the Crawlers. But how would they react? That's the answer Abe wanted. Would they retreat into their cave, wait and see what happened? Or would they see the importance of trying to stop it? Or maybe they didn't even think there was a threat, though Abe doubted it.

The Singer with braided hair lifted her palms out and produced an image between her wires. It was a still shot from the smokie's reconnaissance footage when it was standing on top of the stone pillar. It showed a vast layout of the Crawlers' domain. Abe assumed it wasn't all their land, but it showed plenty for them to at least begin planning. In the center was a large, spherical building the color of copper. There was a line of Crawlers walking out of it, one biotech creature for every five Crawlers. They lead them toward the circle that the sloth and reptile horse had been fighting in, and Abe wondered if they continued to pit the creatures against each other after the smokie was destroyed, or if they went to plan their massacre on the Singers.

"This could be really helpful," Tashon said. "Ballas, what do you think they're trying to tell us, though?"

"No way to know for sure." Ballas stood up. "They could simply be trying to share information about the Crawlers. Or, yes, they could be trying to make a plan of attack with us."

Abe thought for a moment.

"Tashon, let me see the cube. I have an idea."

Tashon fished it out of his pocket and placed it softly in Abe's hand.

Abe placed the cube down, flipped through it until small images of him, Tashon, and Ballas floated in the air. He carefully slid the cube under the image between the Singer's hands so that the pictures of the three humans occupied the land of the Crawlers.

Ballas chuckled and Tashon nodded his head in approval.

Without turning their eyes away from the images, the Singers exchanged notes back and forth for over five minutes. Highs and lows, staccatos and vibratos, and everything in between. Abe found it beautiful, and could have listened to it all day if they weren't trying to communicate with the Singers a way to stop their destruction.

They continued their singing as the scarred Singer walked to Abe, sat inches away from him, and stared. The Singer slowly lifted his hands up, placed them on Abe's shoulders. Abe's entire body tensed as the coolness of the Singer's skin sunk into his own. But when the Singer began to whisper a new melody, Abe's body relaxed, and the Singer gently directed him to stand in the middle of the group, then walked a few steps away from him.

One singer stood on each side of Abe, each a few feet away. Both turned their palms up and extended their wires to form one large, cubic image that encompassed Abe. He stood in the middle of the brawl between the biotech creatures, surrounded by Crawlers. He felt, for a moment, that he had been transported to the Crawlers' land. He looked around at the Singers, then at Ballas.

"I think they're making certain they understand us," Ballas said as he joined Abe in the center of the projected image. "Tashon."

Tashon joined them. Abe again looked at the Singers, but none of them moved. They needed at least one Singer, and some type of Singer transport, to go with them. It was possible the Singers knew the language of the Crawlers, and there was no human transportation that would make it across the ocean.

"None of them are inside the image," Abe said.

"Maybe none of them want to go," Ballas suggested. "It is the species that tried to murder all of them."

"But if they're not willing to send at least one with us...." Abe paused, unsure if he should finish his thought. "Maybe Theresa is right. They're just manipulating us to do what's best for them."

"They're not," Tashon said firmly.

"And if they are, so what?" Ballas shrugged. "If the Crawlers attack the Singers, we're going to get caught in the crossfire. Right now, stopping the Crawlers is just as good for us as it is for the Singers."

Abe knew Ballas was right, hoped that Tashon was, too. He simultaneously believed and doubted Tashon's ability and didn't know what to make of that. The hope that it was true constantly battled the fear that it was false, and the fact that the Singers didn't seem interested in joining them on their journey was only escalating his fear. He took a deep breath, turned around, and walked to the Singer with the scar. Pushing the tinge of fear aside, he grabbed the Singer's shoulders, making sure to not break eye contact. Then, gently, he tried to guide the Singer into the image. The Singer did not—would not—move, letting out a high-pitched note that made Abe drop his arms and step away.

Abe blinked, looked at his feet, then at the Singer. He had no idea how he had moved those few feet, no recollection of letting go of the Singer's shoulders. The fear rose yet again, bubbling inside him, nearly drowning out any hope that he felt.

The Singer had not only refused to join them, he had also made Abe release him without moving a single muscle. He had controlled Abe with his voice alone.

Chapter 17

Tashon blinked and looked at Abe, whose confusion and fear was unmistakable.

"Abe?"

"I-I didn't move away. The Singer—"

Abe walked farther away from the Singer until he stood next to Tashon.

"Abe, what are you saying?"

"He controlled me. Made me move away."

"Maybe," Ballas said. "I'm trying to look at this positively, Abe. Maybe it was just a firm no. They are refusing to go with us."

"But if he could control me like that, what else could they make me—us—do?"

Tashon could hear the fear in his voice, see the trembling of his hands. But Tashon still did not believe the Singers held any ulterior motives. The ethereal Singer appeared above him, and he closed his eyes to hone all his attention on her. He hoped she would put words into his mind like Laos did, but knew she could not, and it confused him why there were still language barriers in the Fourth. He took a breath, waited for images or memories to overtake his mind.

The Singer and Laos stood side by side, a sense of understanding and joy radiating from both. Vibrant wind circled around them. Tashon gazed at the companionship between them, and was convinced that one day the humans and Singers in the Third would be connected the same way.

Then his mind, his entire vision, was overcome with nothing but bright white. He felt like he was falling, or perhaps floating. The white slowly faded. He stood on Aetheran ground amid the thin black trees he had been among just the day before, only Tashon knew that he was looking at the landscape from a millennia before humans landed in Aethera, centuries before the great Singer city was destroyed.

The trees were ablaze in flames. Thousands of Singers and Crawlers attacked each other, rage seething from every creature in the fight. Singers clubbed Crawlers to death with sticks. Crawlers stoned

Singers until their bodies went limp. Blood dripped from everyone, soaking the ground beneath their feet. The Singers spoke in sharp clicks, yelled in guttural rumbles. No notes, no melodies swam from their lips.

After what felt like hours, maybe even days, all the Crawlers succumbed to death. The Singers left alive collapsed to the blood-soaked earth, exhaustion overcoming their rage. Rain fell, soaking the exhausted Singers. Some gasped, struggling to breathe. Others pressed hands on wounds that would not stop bleeding. And others still, somehow, were free from injury. It was these who sat in silence, staring at the carnage around them, caused by their own hands.

One of them, a woman with flowing white hair, stood up, standing as tall as she could, her short, thick frame covered in torn, draping rags. She coughed, gurgled, coughed again. Moved forward, stumbling through the rain-soaked, bloodied earth. Her eyes looked at each and every dead body. Each dead because of the rage of both species. She opened her mouth and screamed out one, high-pitched vibrato note that held strong for minutes. As the sound burst from her lungs, the rage visibly rushed off her body in flowing waves of dust.

Hours later, the rage dissipated. The Singer dropped her gaze, staring at the crushed, beaten, bloodied bodies around her. Three low notes came slowly from her mouth in an alternating pattern. Guilt. Regret. Disgust. Guilt. Regret. Disgust. Guilt.Regret.Disgust. Guilt.Regret.Disgust.Guilt.Regret.Disgust.GuiltRegretDisgust.

Over and over and over until, one by one, each surviving Singer stood and joined the song, each adding their own notes until the air was filled with a ground-shaking chorus drenched in sorrow and remorse.

The rain slowly dissipated, a hard, cold wind taking its place. Yet the Singers continued their chorus as the sun rose, set and rose again, the wind growing more swift and chill by the hour.

The sun set again. A vibrant moon rose into the sky. A cloudless night, bright enough to still see the bodies littering the ground. Slowly, almost imperceptibly, the melody shifted from one of pain to one of purpose, resolve. The Singer who had begun the chorus grabbed a large stick, still dark from the dried blood of countless Crawlers.

She stabbed the stick into the ground and began digging, her melody now strong, firm. The hole, eventually, was big enough to fit the body of a Crawler. When it was finished, two other Singers rolled the nearest Crawler body into to the fresh grave, and filled it in.

With the dirt and that first grave pounded flat, the surviving Singers started digging holes and burying bodies. Tashon watched, silently, as the Singers emoted their melody of sorrow and penance. The rain returned as they filled the grave of the last Crawler, but they did not stop.

Their chorus shifted from the notes steeped in sorrow and atonement to one of shame and depression. Hundreds of their people were dead. They were to blame. Tashon wondered what the Singers had done to initiate the violence, but his vision gave no such answer. He simply observed as two Singers hefted one Singer body into their arms, waited for the others to do the same. Then, in single file, the Singers carried their dead through the forest of black trees, for what must have been at least five miles, to the edge of a wide river. They gently laid each corpse on its bank, then walked back through the howling wind and beating rain to get another one.

Hours and hours of walking and carrying dead weight through thick mud and freezing rain until the row at the edge of the river stretched hundreds of yards across. Again, the melody shifted, this time to one of simple and pure sadness at the loss of so many of their kind. One Singer stood behind each body. In exact synchronization, the bodies were pushed into the river, washed away from the land and—Tashon felt this strongly—the forefront of the Singers' thoughts.

They returned to the Crawler grave sites and sat in a large circle on the wet ground. The melody stopped, the falling of the rain the only sound around. Each Singer's gaze was focused down, as if staring at their own feet. The Singer who had begun the melody days earlier let out one short note. For the first time, Tashon understood this note with an exact English equivalent: change. The Singer wanted to change their ways. She stood, picked up a bloodied stick from the ground and threw it as far as she could. It soared out of sight. She let out a string of screaming notes that Tashon felt in his bones.

Never. Again.

All of the Singers rose and sent their bloodied sticks flying away, the same screaming promise echoing from their throats.

Never. Again.

And from that day on, not one Singer took the life of another living creature. Not until the assassination of the Crawler leader hundreds of years later. Even when the Crawlers reacted to that murder with exponential aggression, the Singers still did not act out of hate or violence. They simply retreated peacefully into their caves, keeping the promise that had been made centuries before.

And now the humans came along and expected the Singers to send one of their own into the heartland of their enemy where they may have no choice but to break that promise.

Tashon shook his head and sat on the ground, eyes closed.

"Tashon," Abe's voice came to him faintly, as if from a distance. "Tashon, you okay?"

Tashon opened his eyes. He was back in the Third, sitting on the ground in the middle of the same floating image. He pushed himself to his feet and glanced at the Singers who stood outside the projection.

"Yeah." He shrugged. "We're not going to get any of the Singers to come with us."

"How do you know?" Abe asked.

"It's... well, I'll tell you later."

"But we need one of them," Ballas said. "At least. We don't understand the geography here. Probably wouldn't be able to pilot any of their transports, either. If they let us use one without them around."

"I get that, Ballas. But I don't think they will. And I'm not going to ask any of them to."

If we were to break our contract of life,
Our melodies would cease, go silent
Mother said it would be so,
Mother was proven right,
For we saw it with our outlier
Who stopped the moving of the Head of our Neighbors
Her melody left her,
Leaving only –
Silence.
Silence that seeped out of her, darkened Family's melody.
Ate at Mother until her Melody was forever silenced,
Gone forever.

Chapter 18

Abe stared at Tashon, trying to think of a response but nothing came. Tashon wouldn't ask a Singer to join them? That had been the plan less than an hour earlier, but now Tashon was opposed to it.

"Why?" Abe asked.

"Why?" Tashon blinked as he repeated the word. "What do you mean, why?"

Abe looked at Ballas, who shrugged and shook his head.

"What is it," Ballas said slowly, "that makes you think we should not ask a Singer to go with us?"

"That battle," Tashon said, obviously confused. "Between the Singers and the Crawlers."

"What battle?" Ballas asked.

Tashon looked at Abe, then Ballas, then back at Abe. His eyes pleaded with Abe to understand what he was saying.

Abe shook his head, taking a step closer to Tashon. "Tash, what the hell is going on?"

Tashon looked around, gazing at everything but Abe's face, seemingly lost in confused thought. His fingers snapped softly against his legs.

A sense of worry came into Abe. Something was wrong with Tashon.

"Oh," Tashon stopped moving his eyes around and fixed them on his own feet. "Oh, right."

"Tash?"

"Sorry, I saw... was shown something in the Fourth. And you were right next to me in the Third and... I don't know. My mind told me you saw it too."

Abe started to ask Tashon if he was okay, but Ballas spoke first.

"What did you see?"

"A violent battle between the Singers and Crawlers. Centuries ago." Tashon explained, as best he could, everything he saw, and everything he felt it meant. "We can't ask them to break that promise. Only one Singer has since that promise hundreds of years ago."

"Or so you were told," Ballas said as he scratched his face.

"You sound like Theresa."

"No, no. I just find it unlikely. A species that, as a collective whole, has made and kept a pact of non-violence for centuries? That promise would have been passed down to future generations, and the younger generations never questioned it? Except one?"

Tashon nodded.

Abe began to realize some of the simple things that they should know about the Singers, but didn't. "But, Ballas, we don't know how long a Singer can live."

Tashon smiled.

Ballas laughed in surprise. "True, Abe. Good point. So, perhaps the Singers here in front of us were survivors of that battle. Damn, can you imagine? To live for centuries. I would die for that."

Abe laughed. "You'd die to live longer?"

"Funny," Ballas said. "But, really, if they're refusing to go because of a moral and cultural requirement, I don't think there's going to be convincing any of them."

Abe shook his head. He knew the journey would be much easier with a Singer by their side. And just because a Singer joined them, it didn't mean the Singer would have to kill. The Singer would be their guide, their aid.

"But I'm not asking or expecting them to kill for us. Just send at least one of them with us."

"But we may end up killing Crawlers," Tashon said. "And they're not stupid. They see that. I don't think they want any part in violence."

Abe looked at each of the Singers around them. He wanted their help, their guidance. Felt that the humans needed it. But how could he tell them that? Ask them to get, at the least, to the shore of the Crawler's land. They wouldn't have to kill. Wouldn't even have to see a Crawler if they didn't want to. He thought back to when he yelled at them about those they couldn't save. They had answered with an apology, right? So they could understand him to some extent, he decided.

He turned and looked directly at the Singer that had controlled him. "Please."

He thought of his mom, of Sylvia and Jonstin. Let the tears pool in his eyes and run down his cheeks. For them to understand, he thought, he must be as emotive as possible.

"Please, we need your help. We can't get to the Crawlers ourselves. We don't know enough about anything here. We can't lose more of us. We can't."

Abe's head dropped at the thought of losing anyone else, even if they would still exist in the Fourth, which he wasn't sure they would. And even if they did, the emptiness he felt at the absence of his mom, of Sylvia, of Jonstin, was too much. He was afraid he'd be swallowed up entirely if that emptiness grew any bigger. He wiped his tears and looked up at the Singers.

"We are going to stop the Crawlers. With or without your help, but please, one of you, come. If there's any violence to be done we'll... I'll do it."

Abe hoped they understood him or, at the very least, felt the meaning behind his words. But he also wondered if what Tashon saw was real, was truth. Wondered whether Tashon even saw it and, if he did see it, whether he interpreted the scene correctly. It still seemed unlikely that an entire species would make such a pact, but what else did Abe have to go on? Nothing. Just the words of someone he'd known for years, suddenly capable of interacting with the Fourth in ways that should have been impossible. If he could do that, why not also have visions that explained the behavior of the Singers, or warn them of an impending attack from across the sea?

The Singers forming the screen closed their hands and the image disappeared, leaving the three humans alone in a circle of Singers. The Singers slowly walked together until they formed a line in front of Abe, Tashon and Ballas. Abe waited for them to sing, or move, or show another image, but they simply stood silently.

Johann's voice called from behind, asking if a plan had been decided.

Abe turned around.

A small crowd had gathered, all eagerly awaiting an answer to Johann's question.

"It appears," Ballas said. "That us humans will be making the journey alone."

Johann nodded, a look of concern quickly crossing his face.

"All right. We better spend the rest of the day preparing for the trip, and head out in the morning."

Tashon and Ballas agreed. They joined Johann and the rest of the crowd, and walked back to the ship.

Abe stayed behind, turning back to the Singers. "Please."

After nearly ten more minutes of silence, Abe headed back to the ship, the first wave of fear about the journey washing over him with each step. What if they couldn't stop the Crawlers? Or, what if they weren't planning anything, but by them going, they set off a chain of events that led to war? Or, his worst fear: what if the Singers were controlling them, and the humans were just puppets being sent to do their will? But if Abe was convinced it was also his own will, did it matter?

He rubbed his forehead, trying to push back the doubt and confusion.

It didn't work.

But as he walked back to the ship, a smokie appeared at his side, as if answering his pleas for companionship on the journey.

We have stayed
Far from Neighbors
To preserve our Melody,
Abstained from aggression
To do the same.
But these new Frames burn to free us from threat of Neighbors,
Would assuredly, willingly, silence any Neighbor to protect us.
To protect us, yet don't know us.
That choice, I feel, shows a savior in these Frames
That I cannot ignore.
I burn to aid them on their quest,
To not stand still or stay silent as they go to wake my Family.
Will I break my pact, will I harm a Neighbor?
I do not know.

Chapter 19

With everything packed and ready to go out with the group in the morning, Smith sat on top of the ship with Abe, Johann and Tashon. Stars that had become familiar shone above them in the night sky.

"You sure you're all ready?"

All three said they were.

"I'm just nervous," Johann said. "About that trip across the ocean."

"Why?" Abe asked.

"You really think the smokies are going to go with us? The Singers won't even consider the idea."

"Each of us who's going"—Tashon leaned forward as he spoke—"has had a smokie by our side since we spoke with the Singers. And we saw before that, the Singers control the smokies. I think them sending smokies with us is the best they can do."

"You think, or were shown?" Smith asked.

"Think. But after what the smokies did to help you out in the desert, it's not impossible."

"Agreed," Smith said.

He looked at Abe, at his son, knowing all too well he wouldn't see the boy for weeks or longer. Or never again. But he wouldn't—couldn't—stop him from going. He knew Abe needed to go, though he didn't know why. Just something he knew, a fact he felt in his bones.

Smith had heard other fathers talk about when their kid was born, or the first steps their toddler took. But when Smith thought about Abe, he always went back to just after Abe turned seven.

In the ship's farming sector, Smith was puzzling over a row of carrots that crumbled every time he tried to pull them out of the soil. A door swung open and Abe ran to him, arms spread out for a hug.

"I learned something, Dad," young Abe said as they hugged.

"Yeah? What's that?"

"The great Ship of Nations," he began, his voice monotone, as if reciting from memory. "Would not have been able to leave Earth had it not been for Chief Farmer Smith joining its citizens. Chief Smith ensures that all on our fine home have healthy, balanced diets."

Abe stopped and stared into his dad's eyes, a wide grin on his face.

Smith couldn't remember what he said to Abe, was never certain where Abe had learned to say it. But he always remembered the realization as he looked into seven-year-old Abe's eyes. To Abe, Smith was a hero, the entire reason the Ship of Nations was successful. And from that moment on, Smith did everything he could to live up to his son's vision of him.

He smiled, looked at his son, about to embark on a journey of unknown dangers to protect all living on Aethera.

"You ready for this, Abe?" he asked again.

"Yes," Abe spoke without hesitation. "I have Tashon with me. Winona. And Rosa and Johann. Those two are badasses. They can fight, if they need to. And I will too."

Smith smiled at his son's confidence, but knew he would worry anyway.

"Abe," Tashon said, adjusting awkwardly in his seat. "What you said to the Singers, about you committing acts of violence if you need to. I know it might be necessary. But be careful. Don't kill unless you have to. I killed on the ship, you know that. And doing that nearly destroyed me."

"But he won't be killing humans," Johann noted.

"I don't think that will change the effect it has on his mind, though."

"Maybe."

Smith closed his eyes, his gut turning that they were even having such a conversation with his sixteen-year-old son. He hoped Abe wouldn't have to kill anyone, including a Crawler. But he also knew that it might be inevitable. He would just have to trust that, when it came to it, Abe would make the right choice. Though Smith didn't even know what the right choice would be.

"Don't worry, Abe," Johann said. "If someone has to kill, Rosa or I will take care of it. And only if we have to. Goodnight."

Johann turned and walked back into the ship, followed by Tashon, leaving father and son alone to stare at the deep night sky. They sat in silence, Smith knowing Abe should rest up too, but wishing the night could go on forever. Yet, knowing his son was leaving the next day was far better than waking up to find him gone, or dead. Would it have been better to know the night before Evalee's death that it would be his last time sleeping by her side?

He shrugged at the thought, letting it leave his mind as soon as it entered. Because what good did it do to ponder on how a tragedy could have happened differently? He was just happy to have that night with Abe, and hoped that his son would return alive.

"Thanks, Dad. For letting me do this."

"Yeah, son." Smith inhaled deeply, trying to steady his voice. "I think it's the right thing."

"You sure?"

"I think so."

"I'm convinced, then," Abe said with a smile.

Smith smiled back. "I'm impressed with what you're doing, Abe."

"Thanks," Abe said. "It's something I think Mom would have done. Trying to communicate with the Singers and Crawlers to avoid death or war."

"She was good at that. I think she'd be happy that you're doing this. Just—" Smith paused.

"Just don't die like she did?"

"Right."

"I don't think I will."

Smith stood and so did Abe. They hugged and walked, slowly, back to their living chamber. Abe somehow fell asleep as soon as he dropped onto the couch. Smith sat at the small eating table, unwilling to close his eyes. He truly expected Abe to be okay. Successful, even. But with the pain of his other losses still fresh in his memory, he spent the night praying to whatever God might exist in the Fourth that his son would return to him.

Chapter 20

Sleep was lost to Tashon. He lay alone in a small living chamber, considering what role he would need to play. Would he need to return to the Fourth like Rosa suggested? Or, more terrifying, would he end up killing again?

He sat up and groaned, the thought of taking another life churning his gut. Even though they weren't human, the Crawlers were an intelligent species. They had lives. A culture.

"But you weren't wrong to kill me, Tashon."

"Shut up!"

Tashon stood. The speed of his breaths increased. He knew Laos didn't blame Tashon for killing him. Even knew that killing Laos was, in some ways, necessary to save those on the ship. But what scared Tashon, what really kept him awake, was how easily the killing had happened. He put no thought into driving that blade into Laos's skull. No time to consider whether there was a better way. The knife was in his hand, a terrorist walked through a doorway, and seconds later Tashon was pulling his blade out of a dead man's head.

"Calm down."

Laos was right. It wouldn't do any good to let his mind get sucked into that hole again. He needed to learn to calm himself, to quiet his mind. He sat on the floor, crossed his legs and closed his eyes. Looked down on himself from the Fourth. With that piece of his mind, he stretched down to the Third and lifted his body off the ground, slowly. He rose higher, floating in the air, the invisible tether pulling him closer and closer to the Fourth.

A flash of white light, a pounding headache, and he was in the Fourth again.

"Didn't take as long as last time," Laos said.

"Still kills my head," Tashon replied as bile filled his throat. "And my stomach."

He clenched his jaw and swallowed it back down.

"It's much closer now," Laos said.

Tashon stood and looked around. The green light he had seen before, flashing in the distance, now seemed to be maybe a dozen yards off. The light itself floated high amid the swirling wind, hovering over a rotating mass of interconnected fourth-dimensional spheres. Tashon felt the structure pull at him, to come see what secrets hid beneath the green light. The intricate movements of each sphere, sliding in and out of perfectly formed slots, was mesmerizing. He didn't know whether he should run to it or stare at it from afar, swallowed by its beauty.

"What is it?"

"I've asked every soul I've seen. At least the ones who will talk to me."

"And?"

"Most consider it some kind of holy place."

"Holy place?"

"A temple. A sanctuary. A few called it the Higher Spheres." Laos paused, his attention drawn somewhere else. "Look," he said.

A lone soul, its light a few shades darker than Laos's, sped against the wind toward the spherical holy place. The closer it got, the fiercer the wind pushed against it. A few times it was pushed, losing some of the distance it had gained. But it pushed on, slowly gaining ground. Inch by inch, minute by minute. Tashon had no idea who the soul was, why it was fighting so hard to reach its destination, but despite the forces pushing against it, the soul moved on.

It was almost upon the spheres, then everything under the green light went still. A cube-like opening appeared in the sphere nearest the soul. It flew in without hesitation, and the opening vanished. The spheres resumed spinning, faster than before, creating a loud whirring noise. The entire structure lifted higher into the air and, with loud claps and sparks, blinked out of sight, sending forth waves of multicolored particles in every direction.

One of the waves rushed through, past and over Tashon, pushing him backward and lifting him up. A paper man slowly blown around by a kaleidoscope wind, twirling around in six different directions. He tried to touch a surface, any surface, but could find nothing to stop himself. He tried to find Laos. All he could see was the wind of the Fourth and the thousands of tiny particles that pushed him farther away from where he'd entered the Fourth. If he kept going, he could end up above a completely different planet than the one he'd just been on.

The wave changed directions, gradually and graceful lifting him higher into the air. Despite the slowness of the force pushing on him, through him and around him, he had no control over his body. Arm, legs, toes and fingers moved independently from each other, and Tashon felt they were moving in ways that should not be physically possible. But when he tried to catch a glimpse of any one of his appendages, they were only a vibrational blur. The wave shifted again, resuming its sideways course.

Tashon's shoulder pressed softly into a warm surface and his forward momentum stopped. He slid down whatever had stopped him until he landed on the ground and fell onto his knees. He peered through the foggy ground of the Fourth. The wave must have been moving even slower than he thought, as he was still above Aethera, though below him was an empty continent he'd only seen on maps. He tried to push himself up, but his shoulder gave out and his face hit the ground. He grabbed his shoulder. It was wet with blood.

"Damn it," he whispered and turned to look at what he had run into.

A large structure with thousands of faces, thousands of angles, thousands of sharp edges loomed high above him. He looked down at his shoulder. His sleeve was ripped to shreds, his arm covered in dozens of cuts. Beside him, the structure twisted and all of the sharp edges disappeared. It shrunk down until it stood a few heads taller than Tashon. He looked at it. A smooth, twisted form that, despite its lack of eyes, stared at Tashon. It felt to Tashon as if something invisible spread out from the being and enveloped him. Something that told the being everything about Tashon. His history, his pains, his joys, his knowledge, his confusion. In an instant, the being knew all of this and more.

The being enlarged, then shrunk again, expelling a warm fog that floated to Tashon's arm and sunk into his wounds. Any pain that he had felt went away, and within seconds, the wounds on his arm closed, dried blood on his skin the only hint that there had been anything wrong.

"You do not belong here," the being said. *"Not yet. Do not return until it is your time."*

The being was not angry. But Tashon knew that if he returned to the Fourth again before he died, something bad could happen. That it could destroy. A twisting arm stretched out from the being, wrapped around Tashon and threw him. He sailed straight through the air in a smooth arc, crashed through the ground of the Fourth, and landed softly on the couch of his living quarters.

PART TWO

Chapter 21

The six explorers arose early, kept their goodbyes short and were walking north away from the ship as the rising sun sent rays through the branches. A soft mist hung in the morning air. Tashon kept a quick, steady pace with the others, doing what he could to focus on the journey that lay ahead, fighting the desire to rise back into the Fourth and see what other mysteries lay in the higher plane. He traded thoughts with Laos.

"Can we really protect ourselves from the Crawlers?"

"Who can know for sure?"

"Are they even really a threat, or are we being manipulated?"

"Yes, from what I've seen, they're a threat."

"What about that being I saw? What do you know about it?"

"Nothing. I didn't see it, remember?"

Tashon looked at his companions. Ballas moved in his skip-like walk, a smile plastered on his face. Abe walked by Winona, the two passing the time sharing memories from their time on the ship. Johann and Rosa walked on either side of the group, their eyes moving back and forth as they kept vigilant watch on their surroundings.

Tashon hadn't told anyone what he'd seen the night before in the Fourth. He wasn't even sure he had seen it. Wasn't sure it had actually happened, despite his sleeve being ripped to shreds that morning. And what would he tell them? They would want to know what it meant, the effect it would have on their lives and their understanding of the universe. But he had no idea what any of it meant. And if he didn't know, everyone would discuss what it meant for the rest of the journey. He just wanted to forget about it, at least for a time.

A smokie walked closely by his side. Nanotech watchdogs the only sign that the Singers supported what the humans were trying to do. Was the native species manipulating the humans into doing their dirty work? Or did they truly think the humans were for the job? Or, Tashon thought, they rationalized sending the humans off on their own so that the Singers could retain their promise of non-violence. But whatever the explanation, Tashon did know that going to the Crawlers was the path they had to follow.

A long path. A long walk.

"Abe," Tashon called. "Didn't you say the smokies flew you across the desert?"

"Yeah."

"Then why aren't they flying us through the forest?"

"I was wondering the same thing," Rosa said.

Abe shrugged, as if he weren't bothered by the miles-long walk ahead of them. "Flying must take more energy," he said. "They probably just don't have enough power to fly us all the way, so they're saving it for the ocean."

Winona smiled. "Makes sense."

The others agreed and they moved on in silence. One mile turned to two, to five, the trees growing thicker as they moved forward. Soon, they walked in a single line, weaving in and out of the pulsing trees, Aethera's raw energy pumping under their bark, through their veins.

"Why do you think the trees pulse like this?" Abe asked.

"They're alive." Rosa chuckled to herself.

"All plants are alive," Ballas said as he slid between two trees. "These just behave differently than others that have been discovered."

"But why?"

Tashon didn't understand the question. Had they already forgotten the history the Singers had given them of their species? He remembered it clearly. The Singers had shown the image of the liquid energy source that ran beneath the trees, pulsed into their veins.

"You know why," he said, the confusion clear in his voice.

The others stopped walking to look at him, and Tashon caught a glimpse of alarm on Abe's face.

Abe stepped to his side. "Tashon, did you see why in the Fourth?"

Tashon looked at Abe, for a moment not understanding what Abe meant. But when it dawned on him, he wanted to scream. Abe and Ballas had been there, had been shown the same history of the Singers that Tashon had, right? It seemed obvious that they hadn't been, that Tashon was the only one who knew any of it. But his mind screamed at him that the others were with him, that he hadn't been alone in the Fourth.

"Yeah, yeah, sorry," Tashon said. "The Singers' energy source runs beneath the forest, and somehow pumps in and out of the trees."

"At some point I hope we learn how that works," Ballas said.

Tashon nodded, and the rest of the group quickly forgot about Tashon's simple mistake. But Tashon couldn't let it go, nervous that his connection to the Fourth was too much for his third-dimensional mind to handle. But, he tried to tell himself, at least it was only messing with his memories and not his ability to live and survive in the Third. If only he could stop thinking it was going to get worse. Could stop worrying that other beings roamed the Fourth, others less benevolent than the one he had encountered.

They entered a small clearing. The ground was covered with a wispy blue-green grass none of them had seen before. A thin line of sweat slid down the side of Tashon's face as he leaned down to touch it. Each blade of grass was stiff yet smooth. Tashon pinched one between his fingers and easily snapped it in half. A cloud of pink powder burst out from the grass, slowly expanding until it dissipated, leaving behind a sweet scent that seemed vaguely alcoholic.

"Ballas," Tashon nodded to the older man.

"Right," Ballas said as he pulled a small tube from his pocket.

He grabbed the blade of grass from Tashon and placed it inside the tube. Then he pulled out a cube, bigger than the standard ones, and twisted the tube into its side.

"Give it a minute," he said.

Johann and Rosa dropped their bags on the ground. The others followed suit and sat down as the smokies positioned themselves on the outer edges.

"I get why we're doing this," Winona said. "But what the hell are we going to do once we get there?"

"I'm still hoping we can figure out how to communicate with them," Ballas shrugged.

"Right," Abe agreed. "And avoid starting a war."

Rosa shook her head.

"But based on what Tashon saw, and what the Crawlers did to that smokie, that's not going to work."

"I think Rosa's right," Johann said. "I don't want to be thrust into another war. But war seems to be the way of the universe."

"Not the way of the Singers," Tashon said.

"I still can't fully comprehend that," Ballas said. "It's unprecedented."

"But how are we going to stop them?" Winona asked. "What the hell are we going to do?"

Rosa shrugged. "We won't get there for at least a week. Plenty of time to figure that out."

"Let's start figuring it out now," Winona said. "We're pretty sure the smokies will take us across the water. What do we do once we step onto their land? You saw what they did to that smokie."

"What I'm hoping"—Rosa looked at Tashon—"is that our prophet will be able to use the Fourth to get into wherever he needs to be."

Everyone looked at Tashon. He averted his gaze and saw a lone moth fluttering through the branches. Why did Rosa put so much faith in him? And, even if he did make to the center of the Crawler civilization, he wouldn't have the capacity to do anything. He nearly passed out returning to the Third the last time he did it. More importantly, he wasn't meant to go to the Fourth again, not until it was time for him to die.

"By himself?" Abe asked. "Maybe you could bring someone with you?"

"Maybe," was all Tashon could say.

The others continued to discuss options, but Tashon didn't hear what they were saying. A part of him knew he might be the only way for them to safely get into the Crawlers' territory, but what then? Take a bomb with him, make it a suicide mission? If he even made it out of the Fourth again. Going back there could be suicide too.

It wasn't that long ago that he'd seriously considered suicide, but that urge had since left him, for the most part. He rubbed his eyes and turned his attention back to the conversation, refusing to let his mind crawl back into that cave.

"I still think," Ballas was saying. "That we should at least attempt non-violence first. Calmly approach their territory, show no signs of aggression."

"But, Ballas," Johann said, "you know that they could interpret our movements in a way we can't expect. What we think is peaceful, they could see as aggressive."

"Right, it's possible. But if we hurt one of them on sight, they'll retaliate. I've no doubt about that."

Tashon thought about his role in all of it and was painfully aware that no one else could do what he could. And he knew he wanted to play a part in preserving lives, human and Singer alike. Above him, Laos pushed forth encouragement.

"Maybe, while you all approach on foot," he said quietly, "I can be in the Fourth. Keeping an eye out. And while they're focused on you, I can try to find the right place to drop in."

"That's the start of a plan, at least," Winona said.

The cube in Ballas's hand beeped.

"All good." Ballas nodded. "Nutritious, even."

He took the tube off the cube, pulled the piece of grass out, and placed it on his tongue. It crunched softly between his teeth, and he smiled.

"It's sweet, almost like a fruit."

With a chuckle, he bent down and broke off five more pieces, sending up more clouds of pink. He passed them out.

Tashon grabbed his piece and twirled it between his fingers, then lifted it to his nose. The grass itself smelled sweeter than the dust from inside them, a citrus-like scent but different from anything he'd smelled from the ship's farm. With a deep breath, he put it in his mouth and bit down. A warm juice squished out, water-like in consistency. He swallowed it, and a soothing warmth flushed through his body. He immediately felt awake, alert.

"You feel that?" Ballas laughed and did a heel kick. "That's good stuff. Great."

"What about—I don't know—side effects?" Winona asked, still holding the plant in her hand. "I'm not eating it."

She opened her hand and the blade floated to the ground.

"I don't think I want to either," Abe said, sliding it into his pocket. "Maybe later."

"Okay, okay. You'll be like a control. See if we start acting any different than you." Ballas nodded, smiling, then shuffled his feet back and forth.

"Right. We have a few hours of light still. Grab a sip of water and a food bar and let's get going." Johann hefted his pack on and started walking.

The rest followed, Tashon trailing at the back of the line, a smile on his face as the warm comfort from the grass continued to run through his veins. He ripped a handful of the grass out of the ground and put it in his pocket.

Chapter 22

"Smith, do you really think it's a good idea to grow our society here into one that values mercy above all else?"

Smith looked at Theresa, squinting at the sun behind her. They sat at the edge of the clearing outside the ship. Some sat around them, listening to the conversation. All the survivors had been discussing the ideas of mercy and justice since they heard about Johann's fictional tribe.

"I do. Wouldn't that have solved a lot of the problems we had on Earth?"

"I think it would have only created different problems."

"Like what?"

"People taking advantage of it. We can try to nurture that sense of kindness and mercy, but there will be those who use such mercy to get off easy."

"And that's what we, or judges, would do. If someone is a repeat offender, there can be protocols put in place."

"But how?" a man to Smith's left asked. "How are we—how can we—engrain such mercy and kindness into future generations? It's human nature to screw up."

"You're not wrong." Smith laughed. "But I think that's the point. We do screw up, all of us. But if you think about it, shouldn't that mean that we all owe each other a bit of grace?"

Theresa nodded. "And I think that point of what you're saying is good. But what I don't want is for future generations to end up like the Singers."

"Unwilling to take a life?"

"Unable to protect ourselves."

She was concerned for the future generations of Aethera, then. She wanted to ensure their safety, their survival. And Smith, of course, wanted the same. He looked at the farm on the other side of the clearing, watched a young girl pull a fresh carrot out of the soil, brush it off and take a bite.

"Okay, I agree with that point. But we also don't want to end up like the Crawlers, who nearly murdered an entire species because of the actions of one."

"Allegedly," Theresa said. "I still don't trust them. For all we know, those are coffins and they all died of a disease. Or, they are stasis chambers, and they're in annual hibernation and they're just using us to take care of an enemy nation."

"This again?" a woman standing behind Smith asked. "It was standard on Earth, for a time, that a person is innocent until proven guilty."

"But that was for a single person accused of a crime," someone said. "Not a species that could be manipulating us into starting a war."

"But we should still apply the same benefit of the doubt, whether it a single person or a group of people."

"The Singers aren't people," Theresa said.

Smith paused, surprised by her harshness. Why was she so fearful of the Singers?

"They're not human," he said after a moment. "But I think we should still consider them people."

Some called agreement to Smith's words while others did not. Smith thought it was out of fear, though he couldn't know for sure.

Theresa sighed and shook her head. She didn't respond.

"The Singers and Crawlers are here. Unless you're telling me you want to commit genocide twice, we need to learn how to live with them." Smith paused to let a thought form in his mind. "Aethera's future is not just human."

The crowd that had gathered began to take seats, quietly talking among themselves. Theresa's, and his, opinions were not the only ones that mattered.

"What thoughts do the rest of you have?"

"We do need to make sure we're protected," an older man said.

"But we need to realize Aethera is not just a human planet," another said.

"And we can't force people to be kind and merciful. People will get angry, steal and seek revenge. But I like the idea of creating a legal system that encourages mercy and kindness."

"Okay," Theresa said. "Within our... community, we can work to encourage that kindness and mercy. We can work on putting that into writing. Smith?"

"Yes. Thank you, Theresa. And I agree that we do need to protect ourselves. But what does that look like?"

"Right," a woman holding a child spoke up. "I don't feel protected right now. The Crawlers could send one of their creatures for us at any minute."

"Yeah, how can we protect ourselves against that?" someone asked.

Silence. Clouds rolled into view above the trees, heavy with rain.

Smith felt the worry and the fear of those around him, his shoulders heavy with it. The Crawlers, and their engineered creatures, were unlike anything he'd seen. If they showed up, they'd all be left defenseless.

The only weapon they had that worked was a small engine bomb that must have been built by one of the terrorists. It was strong enough to probably destroy a few of the Crawlers' creatures. But, unknown to the rest of her group, Rosa had taken it with her. Just in case.

Smith thought of everything they learned about the Singers, the Crawlers and Aethera. He imagined again the beetles destroying the Singer city.

"The mountains," he said.

Theresa looked at him, head tilted to the side in confusion. "The red mountains?"

"Right. In the video, when the beetles attacked the Singer city, none of them went into the caves. I don't think any of them even tried. And when they tried to get Abe, me and Jonstin in the desert, they didn't even get close to the mountains."

"I don't know, Smith," Theresa said.

"What?" someone asked.

Theresa shook her head. "He's thinking that we should move into the caves."

"But the beetles haven't shown up on this side of the mountains, either," someone said.

"Yeah," another agreed. "Maybe for some reason the Crawlers can't enter the caves or the forest."

"Then why were the Singers so worried when Tashon told them the Crawlers were coming here?" Smith asked.

Silence. The wind picked up, sending rogue drops of rain from the clouds onto Smith's face. The group stood and turned to the ship, talking as they walked.

"But if the Crawlers couldn't enter the caves," Theresa said. "Then the Singers still shouldn't have been worried."

Smith shrugged and scratched his head. There was no clear decision to make or path to take. The Crawlers were likely a threat to the humans. But what could any of them do against such a threat? Or, what if, in reality, they were no threat at all? Smith hated to think it, but Tashon could be wrong. True, everyone had seen what the Crawler-created creatures did to the smokie. But for all Smith—or anyone else—knew, the smokie's presence was breaking some unknown treaty and the destruction of it was a security measure on the part of the Crawlers. Or a warning: do not enter our land.

And if that were the case, Abe and the others could be killed before even trying to stop a threat that might not even exist.

As he stepped inside the ship, the rain came down in sheets and he hoped again, always, that Abe and Tashon would make it back.

Chapter 23

As soon as the rain started to fall, Abe and his companions took shelter under a cluster of thick branches. But the water fell heavy and thick. They were soaked within moments, Abe shivering in minutes. Through half-closed eyes, he watched the smokies form a circle around the group. Slowly, the smokies stretched and spread into each other, forming a black circle that rose and closed above the group, enclosing them in an almost pitch-black dome.

"Woo, I love these things," Ballas said, shaking the water out of his hair.

No one else spoke, but Abe felt their agreement in their contented sighs and hums. A soft blue light filled the dome, a gentle warmth emanating from the smokie walls. Abe pulled his dripping jacket and shirt off and his body soon stopped shaking. He sat down and crossed his legs. Winona and Ballas joined him while the others stood, arms pulled tight against their chests.

She looked at Abe, smiled and put her head on his shoulder. Abe twitched, startled by the contact. He'd known Winona since they were kids, spent time together growing up on the ship. But over the past few weeks, they'd spent more time around each other than they had in years living on the ship.

She was the only other sixteen-year-old among the survivors. The destruction of the colony ship had left her fatherless and motherless. And in a month, they had grown to be close friends simply because they shared a similar trauma.

"I'm still not sure how I feel about calling them smokies," she said calmly.

Abe coughed in surprise and let out a small laugh. "Too late to change it," he said.

"Who died and made you Adam?" she asked.

"What?"

"Adam," she said. "The first man on Earth. God let him name the animals."

"Oh, right." Abe nodded. "I didn't realize you were so religious."

"Not really." She shrugged. "Just a story I remember. I like stories."

Abe smiled. "Yeah, me too."

"That's why I first wanted to explore Aethera. I wanted to be a part of the story. A part of the adventure."

Abe smiled, surprised by the simple excitement she felt at being on a grand journey. Her eyes full of a childlike wonder, eager to see what there was to see.

Rain softly tapped above them. Abe had read that people found the sound of rain soothing on Earth. Stories and poems about the homey comfort of hearing rain pitter-patter on their rooftops.

Abe had never lived on Earth, and the idea made no sense to him, his only other experience with weather, the hailstorm that killed Sylvia. The sound of drops on the smokie dome filled him with an anxious dread that he didn't think he could shake. He told himself the smokies were strong enough to protect them from the rain. But what if the rain turned to hail?

Outside, the wind picked up speed and Abe imagined a large chunk of hail colliding through the smokies' barrier and slamming into his head, killing him instantly, splattering Winona with his blood. He looked up. The dome was stable, secure, no cracks or holes to be found.

"How's everyone feeling?" Johann said as he passed out food bars.

Ballas smiled. "Excited."

Rosa nodded. "Me too. I feel like we're part of something historic that will be written in the history books."

"Careful you don't get a big head," Tashon said.

Rosa nodded and laughed. "No, I'm just trying to appreciate the... enormity of what we're doing," she said.

"It is immense," Ballas said, his hands drumming on his crossed legs. "How these next days go will directly affect how the future of humanity on Aethera will look."

"Damn, Ballas," Winona said. "Thanks for the pressure."

Abe laughed and considered reaching for her hand, but didn't. It wasn't a romantic desire, but one to show he was grateful for her support and friendship. To tell her he was there for her, too.

"But he's not wrong," Tashon said. "This could destroy us or save us."

Abe sighed and rubbed his eyes. Following Tashon's path, without seeing it or knowing it for himself, was exhausting. Confusing.

"You okay, Abe?" Tashon asked.

"I don't know." Abe turned to Tashon. "Are you sure about this?"

Tashon closed his eyes, then opened them again.

Abe had known Tashon for years, had never had any reason to doubt him. But Tashon's hesitation to speak made Abe think that Tashon might not even be sure they were doing the right thing. Outside, the wind roared and rain pelted the dome harder still, the sound echoing off the dark wall. Abe rested his head on Winona's.

Everyone looked at Tashon, waiting for his response.

He clicked his tongue. Cleared his throat. "I've seen everything I told you," he said. "And, trust me, I've wondered if I'm just crazy."

He paused and looked at the group, a small glimmer of doubt passing across his. "But I've seen it all. And I did move through the Fourth on my own. That part's real. And everything I've seen, what we're doing, it just feels right." Tashon sighed. "The Crawlers are there, that's not a question."

"So what is the question?" Rosa asked. "Why are you doubting yourself, Tash?"

"I just hope I'm interpreting what I saw the right way."

Abe nodded.

"But we have to do something," Winona said. "And from what we know, the Crawlers created the beetles that almost killed Smith and took Abe's arm."

"Exactly," Johann said. "Everything we do know about the Crawlers show that they create biotech with violent potential, possibly violent intent. Would you agree, Ballas?"

"Unfortunately, yes."

"They destroyed that smokie as soon as they saw it," Abe said. "How do we make sure that doesn't happen to us?"

"The Crawlers have bad blood with the Singers." Ballas stood, bounced on the balls of his feet, and then sat back down. "And the Crawlers are definitely an intelligent species. I would hope they at least give us a chance and don't kill us right away."

Abe thought about it, and it made sense. But then he remembered the conversations he'd had with Ballas. What if the Crawler culture, opposite of the Singers, tended toward violence as their first choice of action?

"But if we don't go, they could attack us and the Singers," Winona said.

"No. If we don't go, they will," Rosa said. "Tashon was told that the Crawlers are mounting an attack, and I have full faith in what Tashon has seen and said. Full faith in what we're doing."

"Okay," Abe said.

For the time being, he'd try to have the hope Rosa did. He did believe Tashon, to an extent. And wanted to believe him the way Rosa did, because then he would fully believe his mom was somewhere in the Fourth.

But doubt was a train of thought not easily derailed.

"Good time to get some rest," Ballas said as he fell onto his back and closed his eyes.

"Yes," Johann said. "I'll stay up, keep an eye out. Don't trust the smokies with everything."

Abe lay down on his back. Next to him, Winona rolled onto her side and placed her hand on his arm, just above his stump. His body twitched again, but he kept his eyes closed.

Despite the pounding of the rain and the howling of the wind and the doubt running through his mind, he fell asleep.

***

Abe stood in an empty tunnel deep within the red mountains. The floating white lights blinked on and off, each to its own rhythm, creating a chaotic strobe that made it hard for him to see what was happening. He placed his only hand on the wall and walked. The voice of a Singer, deep and rumbling, echoed off the walls. A door appeared in front of Abe. He stopped. His hand grew heavy and he looked down, a gun held tightly in his grip. One like what he'd seen in the Earth history books. The voice of the Singer grew louder.

He looked back at the door. Knew who he'd find on the other side. Knew what he had to do to them. If he didn't, Aleron's monster would return and destroy the third dimension entirely. It was a fact that he felt with every piece of his being. And so he would do what he had to do.

The singing rang in his ears as he kicked the door open. With emotionless speed and accuracy, he let the bullets fly. Each went through a head. Each splattered blood and brain matter on the walls. Each dropped a body to the ground.

Each a body he had once cared for. Tashon. Rosa. Winona. Johann. Ballas. His dad.

Each collapsed to the ground, blood spreading out from the holes in their heads until the floor was entirely covered in deep, wet red. The act done, the singing stopped. Abe's vision blurred, refocused. He saw the bodies. Saw his dad. Ran to him, lifted his head into his lap. Cried. Screamed.

And sat up, wide awake. He looked around. A dream. He'd been dreaming. There was no way, he told himself, that the Singers were capable of that kind of control. And if they were, the humans were already lost. And if they could, or wanted to, they already would have. Just a paranoid-fueled dream, he told himself. The light in the dome had dimmed, and he could barely make out Winona's shadow lying next to him. He sat up and rubbed his eyes.

He was the only one awake. The others lay on their backs or sides, resting, sleeping, perhaps dreaming. But he could tell sleep would not come back to him easily. He focused on his breathing, listened to the sounds of nature roaring. Wondered how humanity had been lucky enough to survive their first centuries on Earth without being destroyed by storm, or fire, or flood.

Sylvia hadn't been that lucky.

He pushed the thought away.

Outside, the time between drops hitting the dome slowly widened, the wind calming until Abe was surrounded by silence. He stood and stretched with a sigh, realizing he needed to relieve himself. It was too cramped in the dome for him to leave a puddle of piss on the ground, but after a few minutes of waiting he knew he wouldn't last. He walked to the wall of the dome, pressed his palm to it, and a hole just big enough for him to walk through opened.

It was night outside. The branches above obscured most of the light from above. Abe walked to the nearest tree, but before he had the chance to empty his bladder, footsteps from deeper in the forest sped toward him.

Chapter 24

Smith lay on the couch Abe had slept on for the past three weeks, eyes open, mind full of worries, both relevant and needless. Were Abe and the others all right? Did they get hit by the storm? Was Evalee hurt that he was moving on? Would Evalee be bothered if he found someone else? What if he was voted out of being a leader? What if he wasn't? Which one of the two did he want?

He sat up, stretching his back until it cracked, stood and then walked to the small fridge. It didn't keep anything cold anymore, but he still used it to store bottled drinks. He found only one bottle in it, a half empty yellow soda with a faded label. Abe must have had some, put it back to save for later. With a cough, Smith closed the fridge, leaving the drink untouched.

The sound of voices echoed down the ship's massive hallway. Loud, excited and passionate. Being with people sounded better than trying to sleep in vain. He walked slowly toward the voices, stretching his arms above his head, behind his back.

A large group was gathered in one of the ship's common areas. Some sitting, others standing. Everyone focused intently on the conversation. Smith stopped just outside the group, listening.

"... need to work out what integration will look like," a young woman was saying.

"What do you mean by integration?"

"We're talking about what our society is going to look like, what our government will look like, our laws, even our religion and spirituality. But we're not the first intelligent species on this planet. Not even the second."

Smith nodded to himself, feeling slightly stupid that he hadn't considered it himself. As he took a few steps forward, the young woman looked at him.

She smiled. "Chief Smith."

"You bring up a good point," he said. "I can't remember your name, though."

"Minow," she said.

"Right, Minow." Smith sat down. "So, how are we going to integrate with the Singers? Or the Crawlers, if they end up not wanting to kill us."

"The biggest issue is communication," a man named Jhal said. "We've been lucky to have videos and images with the Singers. That's helped. But what about true communication? Or even translation?"

"And maybe that's not possible," Minow said. "Which means integrating with them will look different than when races and nationalities first integrated on Earth."

Smith nodded.

"Okay, then what do we do?"

"Chief?"

Smith looked around at everyone gathered, impressed and happy they had begun this discussion by themselves. "I have no idea," he said. "What the future of Aethera will, or should, look like. What do we do, can we do?"

"I think we should first ask what we're doing." Jhal looked around the room. "We've been doing well, I think, with the Singers. Finding them answered a lot of questions about Aethera."

"You think it's going well," another man said. Smith was fairly sure his name was Diel. "But we still don't know if them sending six of us—alone—to the Crawlers was a good idea."

"The mind control theory?" Minow rolled her eyes.

"No. Emotional control," Diel replied. "Which is probably more dangerous."

Jhal shook his head. "But the Singers have shown no aggression."

"Not in the way a human would be aggressive," a girl across the room said. Ballas's sister, Pruta. "But perhaps they've done things that, to them, show aggression."

"So we really don't know if anything we're doing is right, or will help us build our future here?" Minow sighed, obviously frustrated.

Smith looked around the room, faces furrowed in confusion, drooped in worry. He thought of a conversation he had with Evalee, years ago, back on Earth. "Occam's razor," he said.

"You think that applies here?" Pruta asked.

"Yes," Smith said. "To me, it does. The Singers have done nothing to hurt us. Their smokies even saved a lot of us, more than once. The easiest way to explain that is that they don't want to hurt us."

"But, again, that's by human logic," Diel said. "And we've all felt how their singing, or talking, can make us feel. And we've all seen how emotion can strongly encourage us to do things. Stupid things. Violent things."

"I talked to each of the six before they left." Smith looked directly at Diel. "There weren't Singers there. We weren't feeling anything that was... uh, put on us by the Singers. They were still committed to go, to stop the Crawlers."

"But that was more because of what Tashon says he saw in the Fourth than anything else," Jhal said. "We don't even know if what he saw was real. I mean, to join Diel's side for a minute, if the Singers here are manipulating us, couldn't a Singer in the Fourth do the same with Tashon?"

Smith sighed and shook his head. There was no clear, right choice. But to him, it seemed better to make choices out of hope, not fear, just as Johann had said. But what if his hope was placed in something false, or in someone insane? Was hope placed in something unseeable still hope, or blind faith? Was there a difference? Someone new walked into the circle. He turned his head, and Theresa sat down a few chairs away from him.

"Look, I understand your worries. Hell, I probably caused some of them." She nodded to Smith. "But this has already been discussed. We're not going to hurt or kill them. We move forward, cautiously."

"And do our best to communicate," Smith said. "And, what was that word, Minow?"

"Integrate. We need to figure out how our race will integrate with theirs. And with the Crawlers."

"So what do we do now?" Smith asked.

"Now, and in the next few weeks," Minow said.

"Honestly," Pruta said. "It's gone better than it could have. No violence yet."

"Remember, they are pacifists," Smith said.

"Supposedly." Diel stood and stretched. "They could just be passive-aggressive."

Smith and the others laughed.

"Goodnight, all. Wife must be wondering where I am." Diel waved his hand and walked down the dimly lit hall to his quarters.

"If they are passive-aggressive," Jhal said, "they're more human than we thought."

He earned a few laughs, but not as many as Diel. The idea of a passive-aggressive species with the ability to manipulate emotions was, in some ways, more terrifying than the Crawlers. If the Crawlers started a war, it would be obvious. But an entire species fighting an emotionally-charged, aggressively passive war? To Smith, it seemed far worse than traditional war.

"Minow, what do you say we do?" Smith asked.

"Me? I.... We keep building what we have. The farm, our defenses, our community. Include the Singers as much as we can."

She stopped and looked at Smith. He could tell she had more to say, so he waited.

"We need to get a group together that can work on direct translation," she said. "I think we need a few who speak multiple languages, and some who are musical. There's a man, Yeance, who studied musical theory back on Earth. Before he moved into physics. The sooner we can actually talk with the Singers, the better."

"Good," Smith said. "Can you put that group together?"

"Yes, chief." She smiled, and turned to walk away.

"Minow, wait. How many languages do you speak?"

"Seven."

"Damn. Good, you head the group too."

Minow's eyebrows shot up, then lowered. "Thank you, Chief Smith. Goodnight."

The group slowly dispersed, eventually leaving Smith and Theresa by themselves.

"Do you think humans will ever actually be able to speak Singer?" Theresa asked.

"I don't know," Smith said.

"I know I've been difficult, Smith."

Smith smiled. "Very true."

"I'm just terrified we're going to make the wrong calls, mess everything up before it gets started."

"Yeah. I once heard someone say that a lot of world leaders in history had the same fear. I worry about it, too."

"There's just no obvious right answers."

"I've been thinking the same thing. But...." Smith looked around at the now empty chairs. "All these people. They were up in the middle of the night, talking about what to do. The people want to do the right thing, too. It's not just us."

"Not the people, remember?"

"Yeah, that's right. Our people, then."

"Our people," she said.

Chapter 25

Tashon awoke suddenly, the sound of someone calling his name making him jump to his feet. He looked around the dome, wondering for a moment if the voice had only been a dream. Then he saw it: a small opening in the dark wall, through which he saw the forest and the outline of someone illuminated by the moonlight.

"Tashon!" Abe called.

Tashon ran out of the dome, and stopped when Abe lifted his hand out.

"Sh," Abe whispered.

Heavy footsteps approached from the trees to their right. Both turned. Tashon tried to keep his breathing slow, but the pounding of his heart made it difficult. The crunching on the ground grew closer. A light appeared from behind a tree. Soft, white blue. Tashon was ready to run as a figure stepped out from behind a tree. It held one hand out, palm up, a blue light glowing above it.A Singer.

"Damn it, Mohawk," Abe said as he tried to catch his breath.

Tashon laughed.

The Singer, unaware of anything humorous, stood still and placed his free hand over his mouth. Abe copied the motion, and Tashon followed along. Apparently, the Singers had interpreted that motion as a form of greeting.

The rest of the group emerged from the dome.

"What's going on?" Ballas said sleepily, eyes half closed.

"One of the Singers decided to join us," Tashon said.

Ballas rubbed his eyes and shook his head. "Woo, damn," he said. "Now that's some good news to wake up to."

Tashon agreed with the statement but couldn't help wondering why the Singer had decided to come. The other four had been strongly against any of them joining the humans. Had they changed their minds, or had Mohawk gone rogue and snuck away?

"I thought you said they wouldn't come," Abe said, doubt laced over each word.

"I didn't think they would. I mean, they do have a pact of pacifism. But he could still uphold that pact, even with us."

"Then why didn't they just send one of them in the first place?" Abe asked.

"I got the feeling," Ballas said. "That they felt if one of them came with us, they wouldn't be able to avoid violence."

"That doesn't boost my confidence," Winona said, her voice still slow with sleep.

"Yeah, but I think Ballas is right," Rosa said. "The Crawler beast destroyed the smokie as soon as it saw it. If they react to us the same way, we're going to have to do some fighting."

"If they react in the exact same way, we're dead," Winona said.

"Yes, but I don't think they will." Ballas yawned.

Everyone looked at him, waiting for him to explain, but he didn't. He simply stood there, looking at the Singer.

Tashon followed his gaze. The Singer waited patiently and, Tashon thought, it had to know the humans were talking about it. Did the Singer feel awkward? Could it feel awkward?

"Ballas?"

"Right. So, I don't think the Crawlers will destroy us right away. I'm guessing they're aware of our existence. And they are intelligent, as far as we can tell. I think they'll at least give us a chance."

"But," Rosa said. "Tashon had a Fourth vision that showed they're mounting an attack against us."

Tashon cringed at the word 'vision,' still uncomfortable with Rosa's claim that he was some type of prophet.

"No, what Tashon saw is that the Crawlers have massive biotech creatures that could destroy us, *if* they mounted an attack," Ballas said. "He felt that what he saw meant they're mounting an attack."

Rosa started to argue, but Tashon stopped her.

"That's a fair point, actually," Tashon said. "Who knows, Ballas? Maybe I did interpret what I saw wrong. Hope I did. Either way, we're going to the Crawlers. And now we have a Singer with us."

Ballas smiled. "Yes, we do."

They all turned to the Singer. He walked slowly toward the dome of smokies, a simple tune of short notes escaping his lips. The smokies, reacting to the melody, pulled apart from each other and formed a sideways line, each one looking north toward their destination. The sun peaked over the trees, large streams of light split and scattered through the branches, creating dozens of slivers of light that dotted the forest floor. A soft fog filled the air as the sun's warmth hit the damp earth.

The Singer, Mohawk, walked past the smokies and let out one long, deep note. The smokies spread out to form a circle around the group. Mohawk looked back at the humans, sang a word or a sentence, or perhaps even gave a speech, but all Tashon knew was that Mohawk was ready and excited for the journey. That excitement seeped into Tashon's skin, pumped through his veins.

"Let's go then," Tashon called.

The others responded by cheering and falling into line behind Mohawk and Tashon, the joy of the journey palpable in the air. Tashon leapt over a root in the ground, a smile on his face. They were going to the land of the Crawlers, and they were going to save the Singers and the humans from destruction. They would succeed, Tashon was sure of it. He saw the group from above, saw how relaxed each of his companions was. Ballas, as always, skipped as he walked, a wide smile on his face. Winona and Abe walked side by side, talking and laughing, Abe seeming more carefree than Tashon had ever seen him. Johann and Rosa hummed and sang together, unencumbered by talk of what was to come.

He pulled his focus back to the Third, his eyes drinking in the beauty of the land around him. Mohawk's singing continued in the background as Tashon noticed vibrant details about the forest he'd never seen or even considered. The way the flowers on the trees gently pulsed in syncopation with the beating of the trees. Or how, randomly, and somehow always timed perfectly for him to see it, the flowers would breathe out small clouds of pink-orange pollen that lazily floated up into the sky. Tiny ant-like creatures, a soft green, spiraled up a tree so perfectly in line with each other that it looked as though they were ascending a spiral staircase to some unknown destination in the treetop.

On they walked as the Singer continued his melody, not a care or doubt in the world. And why should they doubt? They were in the fresh morning air of a beautiful forest, sunlight dripping down the bark of trees, warming the ground below their feet, on their way to successfully stop a war.

But after moments or perhaps hours, a question arose in Tashon's mind: had he been this hopeful, this carefree, when they began the journey just the day before? Had he felt so positive they would succeed before Mohawk showed up?

He stopped walking. Ballas ran into him and happily swore.

"You okay, Tash?" someone asked.

He didn't respond, cast his eyes to the sky in search of the sun. When he found it, he figured about four hours had passed since they started following Mohawk further into the woods. Four hours, and all he could remember was that he'd been blissfully hiking amid the trees. He looked at Mohawk, who had stopped walking. The smokies stood still, ever staring north.

"We've been walking for hours," Tashon said.

"Huh?"

"What?"

Everyone shared glances, looked back at Tashon. Abe's eyes were wide. He was obviously afraid of what had been happening.

"The Singer?" Johann said.

"I think so," Tashon replied.

"Damn it," Abe said. "I thought you said we could trust them."

"Who says we can't?" Rosa questioned.

"What? The Singer's melody just took over our thoughts the entire morning!"

"Did he hurt us? Make us do anything that we weren't already planning to do?"

Abe looked at her silently. Tashon thought she did make a good point, but there was no way to know what the Singer's intentions were. He glanced at their guide, who stood a few yards ahead, his head tilted up to the sky, surrounded by sitting smokies.

"The singing impacted our mood," Ballas said. "Not our actions. And helped me, maybe all of us, feel more aware, more alive. Doesn't human music do the same? Maybe not as intensely, but maybe he was just trying to calm our nerves. And his."

"Maybe," Tashon said.

"It makes sense to me," Rosa said.

"I don't know." Abe rubbed his face.

"Me neither," Winona said. "It's like he... drugged us with his singing. I don't like that."

"And back at the ship, the one *made me* move away from it without even touching me." Abe's voice trembled slightly.

"I know, Abe." Tashon sighed. "I know. Look, if you don't trust them, you and Winona can head back to the ship. And anyone else who wants to."

"No," Abe said. "I want to do this. And I trust you, and you say the Singers are okay."

"Okay," Johann said. "I don't know if we can trust the Singers either. But the Crawlers are out there, and we need to do something about that. Make friendly or take them on if we have to."

"But how can we work with him if we don't trust him?" Winona asked.

"He hasn't hurt us yet," Johann said. "And that's our first good sign."

"And it only lasts while he's singing," Ballas said.

"Exactly." Johann nodded. "Plus, we're aware of it now. Next time he starts singing, pay attention to your thoughts. Your feelings. See if you can direct them. Maybe he's not controlling what we think or feel. Just influencing it."

"So, if his singing makes us happy and peaceful, try to fill our mind with thoughts of chaos and depression instead?" Ballas chuckled.

"Something like that," Johann said, finding no humor in Ballas's remark.

They began walking again. Soon, the Singer resumed his melody, and they continued blissfully on their journey.

Chapter 26

Abe walked through the thinning trees with the rest of his group, not a doubt or care in his mind. The sun was nearly in the middle of the sky, sending warm rays onto his face. As he walked, the soft earth cushioned his feet with each step. He looked at Winona and smiled. Everything felt right.

Except, hadn't he been feeling something different the night before? He thought of where they were going. The Crawlers. They were going to stop a war.

What had Johann been saying? To, what, question his feelings?

Right. They were going to try to stop a war. To try. He had to force the word into his mind, something in him wanting to push out any notion that they wouldn't be successful. They might not be successful.

Slowly, his doubts and fears began to return. He had to force each one back into his conscious mind.

Tashon might be wrong.

The Singers might not be as peaceful as they seemed.

The Crawlers could destroy them as soon as they arrived at their shores.

They might not even make it across the ocean.

Abe's shoulders sagged. It felt odd to force himself to see potential failures, to find reasons to doubt. He slowly blinked and inhaled deeply, exhaled. Listened to the notes of the Singer, and a sense of hope returned to him. But not so much as to eradicate all of his doubts. It felt that, for that moment, he had found a balance between hope and doubt.

"Winona," he said, glancing over at her.

"I'm here," she said.

"Are you nervous about what might happen?"

"Yeah." She looked at the others. "Tashon? Johann?"

"Yeah, I think I'm thinking clear," Tashon said. "Just wondering if the Crawlers are really doing what we think they are."

"That's a good sign," Johann said. "So now we know they can't force us to think or feel certain things."

"Which makes me think even more the Singer is just trying to help us," Rosa said. "Calm us. Encourage us."

"And it most likely doesn't know the exact effect it's having on us," Ballas said. "How could it?"

Abe realized they were right. What was the point of fearing the worst? He would remain skeptical to a degree—he decided skepticism in small doses would benefit everyone. But hope would, too.

"Let's keep going," he said. "I want to get as far as possible before it gets dark."

Tashon lowered his voice. "Abe? You sure?"

"Yeah. I am. We can break out of the... trance that the singing puts us in. And something has to be done about the Crawlers."

"Peaceful contact or they kill us all," Ballas said.

"Or we stop them," Rosa said.

"Let's stop guessing what might happen when we get there," Johann said. "And just be prepared to fight. Rosa, tell them."

"If it comes to it, I have a bomb in my pack."

"Damn it, Rosa!" Ballas yelled. "We should not show up on an intelligent species' doorstep with a bomb."

"We should when that species could murder every single one of us in a day."

"And," Johann said. "We're only using it if all other options fail."

"Tashon saw that we need to stop them from mounting an attack," Rosa said. "So that's what we're going to do."

"Stop the shit, Rosa," Abe said. "Tashon's my friend too. And yeah, he can go into the Fourth. But he's not God. Or a prophet."

Rosa seethed. Johann put a hand on her shoulder, and she took a breath.

"Then why the hell did you even come?"

"I was going out to explore Aethera anyway," he said. "And I decided to still come because, if there is a danger to us, I want to help. But we can't take everything Tashon says as completely true. I do believe a lot of it, especially that my mom is up in the Fourth. But we can't take anything we hear, see or feel at face value."

"I'm not even sure I believe all of it," Tashon said. "But thanks for believing it enough to come with me."

They nodded to each other, and without further discussion, resumed walking.

The Singer took a break from his melody, leaving Abe to fend off the doubt and fear himself. Tashon could be wrong. But Tashon had already been right about a lot. The Crawlers were real, and they had massive, violent biotech creatures. Both of those were confirmed by the Singers. And Tashon could travel, of his own will, in and out of the Fourth. That alone showed he had something special. A skill that could be crucial if they ended up fighting the Crawlers and their creatures.

The trees quickly began thinning out, and a field of rolling green and yellow hills appeared ahead of them. Abe's heart raced, the excitement of exploration taking center stage in his mind for the first time since they set out. Somewhere new, where human feet had never walked.

Mohawk stopped at the tree line. The group spread out to his side, staring at the beauty in front of them. Undulating hills covered in thick, blue-green grass swayed in a gentle breeze. Golden bushes, waist high and a dozen feet across, were scattered across the landscape, some splashed with a thick orange liquid. A small, furry animal darted through the grass in the distance.

Abe lifted a foot and lowered it to the green grass. Just before it touched down, the Singer screeched one loud note, freezing Abe. He gently pulled his foot back and waited, silently. The nearest bush trembled, shook as if something big were hiding in it. Abe breathed slowly, excited yet terrified that he might see what a large Aetheran creature looked like.

The entire bush lifted above the ground, wavered back and forth. Underneath, Abe caught glimpses of dozens of short legs that lifted the weight of a massive golden beast. Its body folded in half, turning a white, domed head to Abe and his companions. The opaque, faceless head rotated. Slowly at first, then as it got quicker it began to glow. Pulse, brighter and brighter, until one bright flash blinded Abe for the briefest moment. But when he could see again, it was gone, leaving a shallow dent in the grass.

"Beautiful," Ballas whispered.

Abe silently nodded. No words came to mind, his thoughts overtaken by repeated images of the spiraling head. Mesmerizing, beautiful and frightening. A creature he hoped to see again yet feared he would come upon at the wrong time.

"You think it's completely organic?" Winona asked.

Abe shrugged, shaking his head.

The Singer made three distinct notes and walked into the field. The others followed, the seven of them walking through the soft grass side by side. Mohawk kept a slow pace, his eyes calmly scanning back and forth.

"Do you think those things are dangerous?" Abe whispered.

"Mohawk seems to think so," Ballas answered. "But that one ran away from us, so I don't know."

Mohawk chirped two high-pitched notes that made Abe shut his mouth, feeling that if he spoke again something terrible would happen. As they continued, more golden bushes popped into view. Some as small as a human child, others twice the size of the bush that had blinded them. Each time they neared one, Mohawk let out the same loud note and everyone stopped. Wait for the bush to move, close their eyes against the flash, open them, and the bush would be gone.

They crested small hills, descended into shallow valleys. Passed bush after bush, disturbed each away from its resting place. As the sun sank lower, the air grew chill.

Before long, Abe recognized the Singer notes that meant "stop," "be quiet" and "go." And once he understood them, he no longer felt forced to obey them. Once he understood them, he was free to choose how to respond. The emotional power behind the notes, or words, seemed to be a tool to facilitate quicker understanding of the melodious language. Abe's fear of being controlled by the Singers began to fade, though they did not disappear.

They neared another bush. This one smaller, a few feet across and as high as Abe's knees. The seven waited, but the bush stayed still. A new note left Mohawk's mouth, and Abe felt the urge to wait, and watch.

Mohawk stepped carefully toward the unmoving bush, one hand stretched out in front of him. With each step the Singer took, Abe expected the bush to explode out of its spot and attack, but it remained still. Then, in one swift movement, Mohawk grabbed a stick of the bush with each hand, lifted the creature into the air and dropped it on its back, exposing the belly.

The skin was black and rough, with a checkered pattern that reminded Abe of the soles of his boots. The animal remained still. Mohawk opened up his right palm and one wire flipped out of it. With his other hand, he pulled the wire out, leaving behind a small, bloodless hole. He clicked his tongue and electricity sparked from the tip of the wire. Using it like a scalpel, he pushed it into a corner of one the squares and traced the shape as he cut. The cut finished, he pulled on the square, bringing out a white, wet piece of flesh. He took a bite of one of the corners and set it in the grass.

He quickly removed six more identical pieces of meat, lining them up beside the first. He placed the wire back into the hole in his hand. As it folded back into his skin, he pulled a large vial out of a pocket. The vial contained some type of powder, and Mohawk dumped some of it into each symmetrical hole he had left in the creature's belly.

A new string of notes from the Singer told Abe and the others to sit down. They did, and Mohawk handed each of them a chunk of meat, then joined them on the grass. It was slick and sticky, and thick juices slowly dropped through Abe's finger onto the ground. Mohawk took a few bites of his, but stopped when he saw the humans weren't eating.

"Ballas," Abe said. "You test it yet?"

"Oh, right." He tore a chunk off the cube and placed it in the same tube he had used to test the blade of grass.

Abe lifted it to his nose. It smelled delicious, a mix of salt and honey. Though, of course, he'd never had real honey in his life. As a kid in the ship, he loved the imitation honey his mom bought him, though each time she did he'd have to hear about how it didn't even come close to the honey that came from the bees on Earth. He wondered if Aethera had its own, bioengineered version of bees. Perhaps it did, and they deposited their honey into the belly of the bush creatures, creating meaty chunks of honeycomb.

"Good," Ballas said, lifting it to his mouth and taking a large bite.

Rosa and Johann quickly sank their teeth in, juice squirting out under the pressure of their jaws. Both silently chewed. Abe held a corner in his mouth and bit down. His teeth broke through a crisp skin and sank into soft, moist flesh. It was sweet, salty, the most delicious thing he'd eaten since falling to Aethera. He smiled. His human companions looked content, almost peaceful. He hoped the Singer was too.

"My dad loved meat," Winona said.

"We didn't have meat on the ship," Abe said, slowing chewing the new food.

"And he talked about that every day." She laughed. "My mom cooked imitation meat, but he always complained about how it didn't compare."

Abe smiled. "My mom was a vegetarian years before boarding the ship."

"My dad hunted every weekend. He and my mom never bought meat. He told hunting stories for hours."

Abe smiled, then looked at Winona. "Is that why you wanted to—what did you say?—be a part of this story?"

"I think so," she said. "Partly, at least. Also, we're the only two our age who survived."

"Yeah." Abe nodded.

There had only been a few others their age in the ship, so Abe and Winona had known them well. With the loss of his mom, and Jonstin and Sylvia, though, Abe realized he'd hardly thought about the friends he'd lost. Kids he'd learned with, ate with, played with. If he didn't have his dad, he'd feel even more alone than he already had been. *Am I really the one living person she feels closest to?* Abe wondered.

"I just wanted someone to be around who I could talk to easily." She shrugged.

"I'm glad you came," Abe said.

He took another bite and his mind wandered away from the moment, considering how historians would view the journey they were on. The brilliant start of humanity's grand existence on Aethera? The start of a war that all but wiped humanity off the planet, leaving them enslaved to the Crawlers for generations? The only thing he knew for sure was that he would see the journey through to its end.

"Woo, that's good." Ballas laughed and licked his fingers.

They finished eating in silence, the sun slowly sinking into the horizon. Abe was at peace, excited about his life. Nervous. Scared, even, about what might happen. But there he was, watching the sun set, eating the most delicious meat he'd ever had. He looked at Winona and smiled. She smiled back. His mom had always talked about how she couldn't wait for him to find love. But what was love? And did finding it even matter in the face of a potentially lethal intelligent species?

Mohawk whistled and clapped his hands. The smokies converged around the group and covered them in a half dome, the opening facing the setting sun. They sat silently, watching the light slowly fade away. Winona squeezed Abe's elbow, just above his stump, and rested her head on his shoulder. He smiled and took a deep breath. *It might not be love,* he thought. It might not have been anything more than Winona looking for comfort. Whatever it was, Abe tried to push aside his worries and enjoy the warmth of her hand, the rhythm of her breathing.

Chapter 27

"We've been able to figure out some of the basics of their language," Minow told Smith and Theresa. "At least, we can understand what some of the simpler notes or note arrangements mean. Their greeting, their notes for food, for tree. Each one has a distinct note that seems to be their form of a name."

"So you're beginning to understand them. Can you speak or... sing, I guess, any of those notes?" Smith asked.

"No," Yeance said. "That's a big part of the problem. See, I trained my voice for years, even after I moved to a career in physics. But none of us can mimic their notes. Their vocal cords must be designed entirely different than ours."

"Right," Minow said. "I think we'll eventually be able to understand them. But not speak their language."

Smith nodded. It was better than nothing, and if the Singers were able to understand humans and the humans cold understand the Singers, they would still be able to effectively communicate with them.

"Did you find out where the fifth one went?" Theresa asked.

"We can barely make out their notes for a handful of words," Yeance said. "If they did tell us, we wouldn't understand it."

"Do you think they can understand anything you say?" Smith asked.

"That's harder to tell," Yeance said. "They don't react to things the way we do. I think they're starting to, though. They've begun looking at me, or Minow, when we're speaking."

"But no reaction to what you're saying?" Theresa said.

"Not that we can see," Minow said.

"At least it's something," Smith said. "I'll come with you tomorrow. I want to see if we can figure out if those are stasis chambers or coffins."

"I want to know that, too," Theresa said. "Are we dealing with an endangered species, or an entire society?"

"Right." Smith stood and stretched. "The answer will impact how we build our future on Aethera."

Two of the Singers walked through the trees toward the caves. The one with the blonde braids and the other with thin white hair. Smith walked toward them, deciding then was as good a time as any to try to get some answers. He jogged to catch up with them, Minow and Theresa close behind.

The Singers greeted them by covering their mouths. Smith, Minow and Theresa did the same.

"We want to see the sleeping ones," Smith said.

The Singer with the braided blonde hair shot a blank stare at Smith as soon as he spoke. She sang one note, then quickly walked toward the caves.

Smith was filled with an urge to chase after her.

Minow gasped. "I think she just said 'yes.'"

"You mean she understood me?"

"I think so. Let's see where she leads us."

"Are we sure we want to have hundreds more Singers around?" Theresa asked.

"As long as they're not a threat to us, then yes," Smith said.

They quickly made their way through the forest, Smith nearly running to keep up with the two Singers.

"And we're sure they're not a threat?" Theresa asked.

"What do you think, Minow?" Smith deferred.

"Well, we can't be completely sure. But I really think the Singers are going to be an asset to human life on Aethera. They've done nothing that makes me feel threatened by them."

"Yeah," Theresa said. "I know. But they just—I don't know—scare me still. I don't want it to turn out that they're manipulating us and we all end up dead or enslaved."

"So you're scared of the Singers or scared you'll make the wrong choice?" Minow asked.

"Both."

They reached the entrance to the caves. A smokie swung the door open and they jogged down the red hallways, past the floating lights, directly to the stasis chambers. Or were they coffins? The Singers stopped at the center of the floor.

"Well, damn," Smith said. "They understood me."

"Now what?" Theresa asked.

Smith looked at Minow, then gave her a nod and a smile.

She took a few steps closer to the Singers. "Are they"—she indicated the chambers in the walls—"dead? Or sleeping?"

Both Singers made the same note at the same time.

"Do you know what that means?" Theresa asked, an excitement growing in her that Smith hadn't seen before.

"Yes," Minow said.

"And?"

"It means 'yes.' 'Yes' was their answer."

"Doesn't make sense." Theresa said.

"But maybe it does," Smith replied. "Humans have often referred to death as an endless sleep, or similar phrases. What if they don't differentiate between the two?"

"But why?"

"The easiest explanation would be a spiritual one. They believe in some type of an afterlife, so death is simply a different type of sleeping."

"But how would we know if that's what they believe?" Theresa asked, squinting her eyes shut.

Smith shrugged.

"We couldn't," Minow said. "At least not with what little we understand of their language. And culture."

Smith walked to one of the supposed stasis chambers and placed his hand on it. He looked at the Singers.

"What is this?" Smith asked.

The white-haired Singer sang a short string of notes. The response made Smith feel somewhat tired, but it was otherwise void of emotional connection. Smith looked at Minow, who shrugged and shook her head. Smith looked back at the Singer, who joined him by the stasis chamber. She made a fist, pushed it gently into the surface, and a box slid open with a soft puff of air. Inside, another Singer. The top of its head was bald, its face covered in stubble. A thin tube, connected to the center of the Singer's chest, stretched down past his feet and connected to the wall. A stream of liquid moved back and forth inside the tube as the Singer's chest moved up and down.

"Alive," he called.

"Really?" Minow said, the excitement obvious in her voice.

"Are you sure?" Theresa asked, the worry obvious in hers.

"Look," he said, moving out of the way.

The two women stepped forward and peered into the open box, their eyes wide. Smith took the moment to glance at the Singers who seemed slightly excited about what was happening. They weren't smiling, but they seemed to be standing taller, more proud.

"Why?" Minow asked.

Smith turned back to her, raising his eyebrows.

"Why are only five awake? Why keep the rest in stasis?"

"It doesn't make sense," Theresa said.

Smith looked back to the Singers. The two of them stood silently. Were they waiting for something?

"Why?" Smith asked them, stretching his hand wide to indicate all the stasis chambers. "Why?"

Both began singing in deep, vibrating tones that filled Smith with a fearful dread.

They lifted their palms, projected the image Abe had described to Smith: the great Singer city, brought to ruins by the Crawlers' beetles. As they continued to sing, the terror draped over Smith like a blanket. He sat down. The Singers closed their hands, and ceased their singing.

"They're terrified," Smith said.

"They think the Crawlers will attack again"—Minow wiped tears from her eyes—"if they realize how many Singers survived."

"So they're just going to leave them like this and let us take care of the Crawlers?" Theresa said. "That's not good with me. They could wake them up and have an army to fight the Crawlers. Instead, our people are out there, trying to mediate a species war we have nothing to do with."

She had a fair point, Smith thought. Why should it be left to the humans to solve the problems? To ensure peace? He knew it happened on Earth between countries all the time. Russia stepped in to prevent the United States and Mexico from blowing up North America. Human history was full of examples of entire countries doing what Smith's son was on his way to do. And Smith couldn't remember a time when any of the countries involved refused to fight. He tried to think of it the way Ballas would.

"But," he began, speaking as the thoughts came to him, "if the Singers were a neighboring human nation under threat from the other side of their borders and we were, I don't know, Australia. A world superpower. Would we really let genocide be committed?"

"Of course not," Minow said.

"But in that situation, there were always those willing to fight to protect their people," Theresa said. "But the Singers are doing nothing. They wouldn't even send just one of their own with our people."

"I know, Theresa. I know. But we can't...." Smith paused, considering how Ballas would explain it. "We shouldn't judge on human understanding."

"But we are human!" Theresa tossed her hands up. "We understand based on what we've gone through as humans."

"But we can at least try to understand the Singers' perspective," Minow said quietly. "Especially since we're going to share this planet with them."

Theresa huffed.

Smith understood her frustration, but he also knew getting upset about the Singers' actions wouldn't get them far.

"Minow's right," he said. "And, based on what Tashon saw, the Singers do have a deep rooted cultural pact to avoid violence. It's almost religious. Spiritual. On Earth, if there was a nation of pacifists being slaughtered, would you not have expected your nation to intervene?"

"I... maybe... probably. But the Singers are not being actively attacked."

"But it seems—or, at least, the Singers believe—that the Crawlers will attack if they discover all of these Singers alive."

"And if that doesn't convince you," Minow said. "Abe and the others aren't going to the Crawlers just for the Singers. The Crawlers could kill all of us, too."

We five were one –
Now we are four, and one.
He has left his Family.
His absence quiets the melody of us all
But does not silence it.
Shadows of doubt have come over us all,
Yet we know to whom we sing.
We sing to Mother, we remember Mother.
Despite the omissions in her foretelling,
We put our hope in her songs.
Was it doubt that made him go?
Perhaps, but something more is hiding quietly within him.

Chapter 28

Mohawk stood to the side of the smokie dome, asleep, chin touching his chest. The humans whispered quietly.

"Your ability to go into the Fourth might be crucial, Tashon," Rosa said.

"Yeah." Tashon nodded. "I went back the night before we left."

Everyone stared at him, waiting to hear what he saw. He told them, deciding not to say that it could be detrimental to him if he returned to the higher dimension. If he did, he knew none of them would let him return. But it was likely that returning would be the only way to beat the Crawlers.

"You met a god," Rosa said, eyes wide.

Tashon nearly gasped. He hadn't considered that possibility. "I... maybe," he said. "It could just be a... higher being with a deeper understanding of how the universe works. How to manipulate molecules in a way that healed me."

"Couldn't that be one definition of a god?" Ballas asked.

"Was it like the spirits that you've seen? Like Laos, or my mom?" Abe asked.

"No. I think it was natural to the Fourth," Tashon said.

"Why?" Johann asked, his fingers ever moving through his beard.

"It didn't feel like the spirits there." Tashon shrugged. "It was different. Stronger. More in place there."

"What does this mean?" Winona asked. "About how we understand the universe?"

"That the universe was created by something." Rosa smiled. "There is a creator."

"That's not necessarily true," Abe said. "There is no actual proof that this being Tashon saw is a god. Or that a being like that could even create worlds, or intelligent life."

"But it does make the theory of a creator more possible," Winona said.

"That it does," Johann said.

"Why all the skepticism?" Rosa asked, her voice rising. "This is an amazing, beautiful discovery! There are beings higher than us. More intelligent. More skilled. Maybe even more perfect. Tashon met a god! Maybe you don't like that word, but what else describes what that being did? Its form cut him, and for all we know, could have killed him. But, instead, it changed form and healed him. A being that can destroy and heal."

"It is amazing. And I think we all agree on that," Ballas said.

"Yeah, of course," Abe said. "It is amazing. Everything we've learned from Tashon has been life changing."

Tashon smiled. He hadn't realized how much Abe's doubt had been affecting him, and to hear that Tashon's discoveries had helped Abe—that meant more than Tashon would have imagined.

"So you believe Tashon now?" Rosa asked Abe.

"At least some of it," Abe said. "Mostly that the Fourth is an afterlife. People have always said 'oh, they're in a better place' or 'you'll see them in heaven one day.' But that always seemed like BS to me. Yeah, I've always hoped it were possible. But the afterlife being in the Fourth just makes sense to me. It's—I don't know—scientifically spiritual?

"And the rest of it, like I've said. I just don't know if we're interpreting what Tashon has seen in the right way. I don't like calling whatever that is a god because we don't know what it is. Why give it a name and meaning before we have all the facts?"

"That's fair," Tashon said.

"Maybe it's not a god," Rosa said. "At least not *the* God."

Tashon looked at her, raised his eyebrows, and looked away. If she believed in God, in a creator, did she see him as God's prophet? As his spokesperson, like some believed Muhammad or Jesus to be? He thought of his history lessons on the ship. Both of those prophets, most prophets, in fact, taught the importance of peace and kindness. But throughout Earth's history, humans had used the Bible or the Quran or some other religious text as an excuse to commit acts of severe violence. Acts that Jesus and Muhammad would have never condoned, yet some viewed Christianity and Islam, or religion in general, as violent and oppressive.

Tashon didn't want that to be his legacy. If history were to view him as a prophet, he did not want to give anyone any reason to use his life or teachings to excuse violence.

"Do you believe in God, Rosa?" he asked.

"I do," Rosa said quietly, seriously. "I was raised in a Protestant Neo-Taoist family."

Tashon would have thought she was joking if she didn't look so solemn about the statement.

"Really?" Ballas said. "You're definitely not practicing, though."

"No," Rosa said. "I could never get control of my anger. You all saw me break Cosima's wrist. But I do believe that there is a creator. I do believe in God."

"What's Protestant Neo-Taoism?" Winona asked.

"A fascinating religion, really," Ballas said. "An intriguing blend of Western and Eastern theologies. It's a religion that promotes individual enlightenment by combining the teachings of Jesus, from the Bible, with the search for inner peace described in Taoist texts.

"It teaches the importance of ridding oneself of worldly desires and negative emotions, such as anger." He nodded to Rosa. "In order to bring oneself into alignment with the teachings of Jesus. Taoism by itself teaches that cleansing one's body and mind of such things would enable one to return to Earlier Heaven. Standard Christianity teaches that, by truly following the teachings of Jesus, one would live with Jesus after death.

"But what I believe Rosa's family taught her was—" He stopped and looked at Rosa.

"To them, all things were created by Jesus," She said. "And they believe that Jesus resides in Earlier Heaven, a place where only those who have truly discarded hate, anger and worldly desires can go. For them, returning to Jesus and returning to Earlier Heaven are one and the same. And they combine the teachings of Jesus with the Taoist practices of internal alchemy to achieve their goal of returning."

"So," Tashon said. "Do you believe God is Jesus?"

"No." Rosa shook her head. "But I do believe that God, or the creator, does desire peace for all of his creations. And I believe that everyone who has been viewed as a prophet or sage—Jesus, Buddha, Muhammad—was given light and understanding from the creator."

Tashon smiled, but inside his heart sank. Rosa believed that Tashon's insight into the Fourth was a gift from God. She really was putting him in the same category as Buddha and Muhammad. And knowing that terrified him.

The dome went quiet.

Abe yawned, stretched and then lay down in the grass. The others followed and before long all Tashon could hear was the whistling snores of Rosa and Johann.

He closed his eyes and found Laos hovering above him.

"Do you think my ability to interact with the Fourth is a gift from God?"

"Maybe, Tashon."

Tashon's mind wandered. He saw the moths fluttering in circles, jumping between dimensions. In the Fourth, they danced around Laos. In the Third, they spun above the dome.

"Laos?"

"Yes?"

"Do you think there is a Creator out there?"

"I don't have any idea."

"Do you talk to the other souls up there?"

"Sometimes."

"Can you ask them?"

"Yes."

Laos left him.

Tashon watched the moths and, just before he fell asleep, he caught another glimpse of the blinking green light.

Chapter 29

The stars shone brightly in the night sky. A cold wind passed by Smith's face as he sat on top of the ship.

"It's been getting colder," Yeance said.

"Yeah," Smith said. "I liked the cold on Earth. But I don't know about here. No power heating."

"What about in the cave?" Minow asked.

Smith shrugged. "It's not a bad idea. But I don't know how everyone feels about moving into the caves. I know Theresa's against it."

Yeance pulled his arms tight across his chest. "It would be warmer, and most likely safer."

"Do you really think we can trust the Singers?" someone asked from behind them.

She walked up slowly, her body softly shivering.

"Theresa." Smith smiled. "Just talking about you."

She sat down and looked each of them in the eye.

Smith thought he saw a hint of sadness in her eyes, or maybe fear.

"I do think we can trust them," Yeance said. "And most everyone does at this point."

Theresa nodded.

"We should try to ask them if we can move into the caves," Minow said. "The ship's not going to stay warm. And one end is a massive hole. It won't keep any Crawlers out."

"I don't think they'd mind at all." Yeance took his coat off and handed it to Theresa, who was shivering. "We can figure out a way to ask them."

"I like the idea. Theresa?" Smith looked at his fellow leader.

"I don't like everything about them," she said. "But, you know, the caves would be warmer. And we could defend ourselves better if the Crawlers attacked. But they still scare me."

"Why?" Minow asked. "They've done nothing to hurt us."

"I know," Theresa said, obviously frustrated. "But I don't feel comfortable around them, don't trust how they can toy with our emotions."

"You're afraid of them controlling us to do their will, using our emotions?" Yeance raised his eyebrows.

"Terrified, if I'm honest. I don't like being out of control."

Smith laughed, then apologized when Theresa glared at him.

"It's just that, I think we already knew that," Smith said. "But, tell me, have they made you do anything against your will?"

"No," she admitted.

"And we are considering going to the caves," Smith said. "No Singer has given us that idea."

Theresa nodded. "It just doesn't make sense to me that five of our own decided to risk their lives to go to the Crawlers." She pressed her fingers against her forehead.

Smith sighed. She didn't understand self-sacrifice, then. At least not to the extreme that Abe and the others were taking. Or did she, and the idea just scared her? Perhaps she just placed more value on human life than Singer life, which made more sense to Smith. But that kind of thinking would not help them build a future on Aethera.

"But do you agree that we should let our people decide whether we go to the caves?" he asked, looking directly at Theresa.

"Putting it to a vote?"

"Right," Smith said.

"Okay." She nodded. "If that's what the vote decides, I can respect it."

"Okay, then." Yeance stood. "Goodnight."

"I'm heading inside, too." Minow gave Theresa a short hug and walked off.

Smith and Theresa sat in silence. The wind picked up and a row of dark clouds appeared to the north, reminding Smith of the storm that had taken Sylvia. He let himself miss her for a few minutes, remembering her kindness and her strength, then pushed the thought aside.

Theresa opened her mouth to speak, closed it, opened it and then closed it again.

"Weren't you against us moving into the caves?" Smith asked her.

"I was. Still unsure of it, unsure of the Singers. But I asked around today, too. And who am I to tell our people they're wrong, if they vote to go to the caves? And let's be honest, I think most of them will. Most of them are starting to like the Singers. Trust them. And who am I to tell them not to? So much violence on Earth happened because we naturally distrusted groups or races or species that we didn't understand."

"That's very true," Smith said.

Theresa smiled at him. He looked back at the stars, considering what she had said. Happy that she had said it, that she was coming around. He thought of all the war and bloodshed on Earth. Would they really be able to avoid the same tragedies on Aethera, with three different species sharing the planet? It seemed impossible, especially with the threat the Crawlers presented. Or were they judging that species too quickly, too?

"Theresa, do you think we're too quickly distrusting the Crawlers?"

"What? I don't— " She paused. "Oh."

"Right. We're distrusting them because of what the Singers showed us. And I do think the Singers are telling the truth about what the Crawlers did to them. But we don't know how long ago that was. What if the Crawlers aren't as violent now?"

"Smith." Theresa shook her head. "You saw the biotech weapons they have. Saw what they did to that smokie."

"I know," he said, shivering against the cold. "I know. But we've been here for weeks, and they've done nothing. And the smokie was on their land, their territory. It could have simply been defense."

"Okay, it could be," Theresa said.

"And it's obvious they're intelligent and advanced," Smith said. "I'm sure they know that we're here, and that those five Singers are too."

Theresa raised her eyebrows. "Yeah?"

Smith nodded. "Yeah."

"But they could just be keeping an eye on all of us, ready to strike if it seems like we're a threat to them."

"Right," Smith agreed. "If true, that means they don't see us as a threat."

"Yet. Do you think they'll see it as a threat when Johann and the others show up in their land?"

Smith sighed. He'd had the same thought, of course. The Crawlers could very well perceive the humans showing up on their doorstep as a threat and kill them all in an instant. "Maybe. But we're forgetting the whole reason they're going to the Crawlers in the first place."

"Tashon?" Theresa said.

"Tashon." Smith nodded. "He saw from the Fourth that they are a threat, and he knew that going there was the right thing to do."

"What the hell are they going to do when they get there?"

"Tashon will see the next step to take," Smith said, his voice quiet.

"That's where you're putting your faith?" Theresa asked, obviously skeptical.

"Where else is there to put it?"

Chapter 30

Abe awoke to the sound of Mohawk whistling and the smokies pulling apart from the dome, returning to their standard form. Winona was asleep on his chest, her arm wrapped tight around his torso. He wished he could stay there on the soft grass forever, and he instantly felt guilty for that desire. Who was he to want such peace when the human future on Aethera was so uncertain?

"Time to go," he said, shaking Winona awake.

"Yeah, okay," she said, sitting up and stretching.

Everyone stood up, yawning or wiping sleep from their eyes. Mohawk walked to the bush creature that had fed them the night before and crouched beside it. The holes from the meat they had eaten were gone, replaced with new flesh. The Singer slid his hands underneath the creature, turned it back to its feet, and patted its side. The white dome of its face lit up and spun, and the creature ran off.

Abe shook his head in amazement as the others muttered startled or excited profanities.

Ballas laughed loudly and clapped his hands, his amazement at the wonders of Aethera reminding Abe more and more of a child.

The humans ate a quick breakfast of food bars. The Singer ate nothing, and they were soon on their way. Hours passed. Abe assumed the sun was following its usual trajectory across the sky, but dark clouds overhead hid it from view.

They continued up and down the hills of grass as cold wind came at them from the west, growing stronger as the day went on. The Singer was silent that day, no notes or songs to uplift spirits.

The clouds grew darker still, and a chill began to set in Abe's bones. As he carefully stepped down a short hill, he pulled a coat out of his pack and pulled it on.

He realized he missed Mohawk's singing.

"What's on your mind?" Winona asked as she took hold of his hand.

"I was kinda wishing the Singer would manipulate us into thinking everything was wonderful again."

"I know." Winona smiled. "But I think he's focused on something else."

Abe looked closely at Mohawk. At first, it seemed he was just walking. But then he noticed the Singer's hands, clenching into fists, then opening straight, releasing a wire, then closing into fists again.

"Is he nervous?" Abe asked.

"I think so," Winona said. "And I was in front of him for a bit. His eyes are constantly moving back and forth, like he's watching out for something."

"But what?"

"No idea. But it is weird that those bush creatures are gone," she said.

"Yes it is," Johann said. "Especially because we've passed plenty of fresh dents in the grass. Means a lot of them left in a hurry."

"Left, or ran away?" Abe asked.

"Exactly," Johann said.

Winona squeezed Abe's hand tighter. He squeezed back, and on they walked. Time moved on, their feet moved forward, the sky grew ever darker. They continued through rolling green hills still void of any other signs of life. Mohawk remained on edge, ever watchful, but no harm came to them.

The wind changed directions and whipped mercilessly into their faces. A snowflake fell to the ground and melted. Then two, then thousands of soft white flakes fell from the sky, thrown into their faces. Mohawk stopped and whistled at the smokies, who moved to form another dome around them.

But before the black dogs finished, something large rushed past. A loud bang echoed through Abe's skull after it passed.

"A sonic boom," Johann yelled.

Whatever it was, it moved faster than the speed of sound. They all stood still, eyes searching for a glimpse of the machine or creature. It sped past again, closer. The force that erupted from it was larger this time, sending the black dust of the smokies out, the blackness hanging in the air like bubbles. The metal rods that formed the frame of the smokies fell to the ground and scattered across the snow.

Something to the left of them screamed. Abe turned. A creature stood, staring at them. It didn't look like it came from the Crawlers or the Singers. It was something entirely new.

It stood proudly, its neck stretched high into the air, taller than any of them. Its gray eyes stared down at them from a beaked head. The neck connected to a bulbous feathered body from which extended two thin legs that seemed to be pure muscle. It had no arms, no wings.

Abe shivered. His nose ran, and he could feel the fluid freezing to his upper lip. But he dare not move to wipe it off. The creature seemed to be waiting for any reason to pounce.

The Singer sang a few notes. Ones that Abe had learned meant "don't move."

"No shit," Rosa said. "But what the hell do we do?"

Mohawk whistled. The clouds of smokie dust did not respond. They hovered in the air, unmoved by the storm. The snow began sticking to the ground, soon covering the earth in a thin blanket of white.

The breath of the creature was visible in the cold, the puffs of white air floating out of its single nostril. Mohawk put one foot forward. In an instant, he dove to the ground, rolled, snagged a metal smokie rod and threw it at one of the black dust bubbles. As it sailed toward its target, the creature shot forward in a blur. Everyone jumped in a different direction as another sonic boom shook the ground, the air. Abe hit the ground hard, unable to catch his fall with his one hand. The rod Mohawk had thrown landed next to him.

Then he heard someone scream.

He sat up, whipped his head around. Ballas was on his knees, his hand clutched over the right side of his face. Blood seeped from between his fingers. Abe moved to help him, but the old man held his other hand out and gently shook his head.

The creature that towered above them stood still again, the red from Ballas's face dripping down and off the point of its beak.

Abe looked at the smokie rod laying next to him. Mohawk had been trying to get it into one of the smokie clouds, hadn't he? If the smokie rod reconnected with the nanotech, would the smokies begin functioning again? Slowly, Abe slid his fingers across the snow, stretching nearly as far as he could before he wrapped the rod in his fist. It was warm, and pulsed within his grip. He pulled it to his chest. His eyes locked with Ballas, and the two nodded.

Ballas screamed. The creature jerked its head toward him. Abe threw the rod at the nearest patch of black. The body of the creature vibrated. Ballas kept screaming and the rod continued its flight. The creature flashed forward. Ballas's scream was cut short as it broke the sound barrier yet again. Blue electricity sparked in the smoke as the rod hit its target.

Streams of black shot out of the cloud and encircled the creature's body. It vibrated, tried to move, but the Singer nanotech held it in place.

Abe, Johann, Rosa and Winona ran and picked up rods and threw them into the remaining masses of smokie essence. And Ballas, Abe realized, did nothing. Was nowhere to be seen.

"Where the hell is Ballas?" he screamed.

Two rods lit up two more clouds, and strands of black wrapped around the struggling animal.

"I don't see him!" Winona called back to Abe.

The creature vibrated faster, sending ripples across the deepening snow. The black holding the creature hostage bulged outward. A section shot off of and landed in the snow near a pile of rods. The dust and rods rose, and a lone smokie stood, facing the creature.

"Dammit, Ballas, where are you?" Rosa called.

The supersonic creature struggled even more. Johann pulled one long knife from his coat and charged the animal. He neared it, rolled, stood and made a deep cut on the back of one leg, sunk the blade into the other. The animal screeched and kicked Johann. He flew back a few feet and landed with a soft thud in the snow.

The animal screeched again. Its body trembled, and the rest of the smoke containing it exploded off its body, scattering the white ground with black specks.

Hastily, the sole smokie ran past its downed nanotech companions, pulling each out of the snow like a magnet. The smokie grew bigger, adding each dot of black to its legs, body and head until it was one massive dog the same height as the beaked creature.

The two stood yards apart. The creature stretched its neck and lifted its head as high as it could. The smokie remained still as its foe began, again, to tremble and shake. Then the creature shot forward, stumbled on its injured legs, regained its balance. It moved quickly for its injuries, though below supersonic speeds. Abe hoped Johann's attack had done enough damage to thwart the creature as he watched it and the smokie charge toward each other.

Silently, the two connected. The smokie's front legs went up, the creature's head whipped backward and slammed down into its attacker. Blue lines of light came to life inside the smokie. Its assailant's body pulsed, its feather's sticking out from its body. Electricity crackled. The ground shook. The two combatants blew apart in a quiet explosion of black dust, meat chunks and shattered metal rods.

As the shrapnel settled, Abe saw Ballas in the distance, face down in the snow.

"Ballas!" he called as he broke into a run.

Abe and Tashon got to him at the same time. The snow around his head and neck was soaked in red. They slowly rolled him into to his back.

"Shit."

"Damn it."

The skin on the right side of Ballas's face was gone, leaving sections of bone and muscle exposed to the elements. Dried blood ran down his face from a wound hidden in his hair.

Rosa joined them, crouched down by Ballas and pushed two fingers against his neck.

"Still breathing," she said. "Barely. He won't last long."

Chapter 31

Tashon looked down at Ballas, then looked up at the white nothing that surrounded them.

"We don't have anything that can help him?" he asked.

"We have bandages, some antibiotics, and some pain killers." Rosa shrugged. "Not enough for something this serious."

"Maybe Mohawk can help him," Abe said, doubt lacing his tone.

Tashon sighed, knowing it wasn't likely. He knew, instantly, that he would be the one to help Ballas. He didn't know how, but he knew he didn't want the man to die. Knew the man didn't deserve it. Was convinced it wasn't Ballas's time to rise to the Fourth.

Mohawk joined the group and squatted next to Rosa, looking intently at Ballas's injuries. After a deep breath, the Singer began a soft and whispering melody. It floated through the falling snow, struck Tashon in the gut, filled him with a painful sorrow. It began to weigh Tashon down, but he fought it—he was not ready to face such grief again. He could help Ballas, he knew it.

"Rosa," Tashon said. "They would be able to save him if we were at the ship, right?"

"Yeah." Rosa looked at Tashon. "But we're dozens of miles from the ship."

"I know," Tashon said.

He knelt down in the snow, slid an arm under Ballas's shoulders and lifted him to a sitting position. Then he closed his eyes, pushed away as much of the Third as he could.

Laos's voice echoed in Tashon's mind. *"I don't think this is a good idea."*

"Shut up."

Tashon focused all his attention on that part of him that remained in the Fourth, let it pull him in. He clutched tightly onto Ballas. His mind strained with the added weight, his stomach churned and his lungs tightened. He slowly pulled away from the Third. Someone yelled at him. Abe, or maybe Johann. He had no idea what they said, didn't care. He couldn't let Ballas die.

White filled his entire vision. The gravity of the Third fell away, he floated freely for a moment. Then all went black. He slammed onto a cold, hard surface, his vision still nothing but black. But the way the air felt on his face told him he was in the Fourth.

"Laos?" he said loudly.

"Right here. Can't you see me?"

"No." Tashon shook his head, and pain seared through his skull, into his eyes. "Wait."

Black faded to gray, to white, until he could see again. His eyes burned. He struggled to breathe.

"I told you it was a bad idea," Laos said.

"I said" —Tashon leaned over and vomited— "shut up."

"Okay," Laos said.

Tashon waited for the pain in his head, the wheezing of his lungs and the turning of his stomach to stop. All three persisted. He wiped moisture from his eyes and sat up. Ballas lay on his side, face squished into the ground, still unconscious. With a grunt of commitment, Tashon gripped Ballas underneath his armpits and stood. He weighed less than he would have in the Third, but it still wouldn't be easy.

"Why kill yourself trying to save him?"

Tashon ignored Laos as he walked backward, dragging Ballas across the Fourth. He took one step, then five, then ten. Stopped, hurled more bile, and looked below into the Third. He was still over the snow-covered, grassy plains. How many more steps until he reached the ship? His head spun, but he took another step.

One turned to two, two became five and five turned to fifteen. He closed his eyes, tried to focus on breathing, on walking, on not vomiting. Sixteen. Seventeen. Eighteen. Nine— He backed into something hard.

"Ugh," he said, dropping Ballas.

He turned around. The wall in front of him curved upward and sideways and downward. Curves that formed one sphere, then another, then twenty more. He craned his neck to look up. High above was the flashing green light.

"The Higher Spheres," he whispered, then coughed.

"Haven't seen them since last time you were up here," Laos said.

Tashon hadn't realized Laos had followed along. "The Higher Spheres," he said again, wearily. "The Higher Spheres are in my way. Too long to walk around."

He looked back into the Third and found he was standing above the yellow forest, just past where it merged into the plains.

"I'd say halfway there, Ballas." He grinned, then frowned. "If these damn spheres would move."

Tashon's head spun and his legs trembled. He leaned over, dry heaves taking over, and then collapsed to his knees with both hands on the surface of the sphere. It radiated wisdom. Understanding.

He longed to go in, feeling that if he did, everything would become clear to him.

"Didn't one of these spheres open?" Tashon asked.

He felt Laos's concern at the idea, but ignored it. Next to Tashon, Ballas lay still, breathing shallowly. If they didn't make it to the ship soon, Ballas would be gone. Tashon would not let that happen. He'd already taken Laos's life, caused the deaths of hundreds of others when he didn't stop Aleron on the ship.

"But I've forgiven you," Laos said. "Don't kill yourself trying to make up for that."

Tashon responded by forcing himself to his feet. A piercing pain shot though his head.

"Damn it," he said.

"Go back to the Third," Laos said.

Tashon didn't respond.

He needed the spheres to open for him. Needed to go through them to get above the ship and save Ballas's life. The pain, the dizziness, the nausea, the exhaustion—none of it mattered to Tashon in that moment. He looked down at Ballas. His breathing had slowed, become shallower.

And his right foot was missing. Tashon rubbed his eyes and looked again. No, Ballas's foot was still there. But it had sunk through the ground and back into the Third, a lone foot dangling amid the yellow trees.

The Fourth was rejecting Ballas.

"No," Tashon whispered.

He pulled on Ballas as hard as he could, hefted him onto his shoulder so that no part of Ballas touched the ground of the Fourth. But his foot remained in the yellow forest.

"Damn it, no." Tashon turned back to the spheres and looked up at the green light. "I need to save him."

The spheres were unmoved.

"Tashon," Laos said.

Tashon shook his head, pounded a fist on the sphere, willing it to open to him. It paid no heed.

"Tashon," Laos repeated. "Look."

Lazily, Tashon turned his head. In the distance, a form sped toward the Higher Spheres. *Just like the time before,* Tashon thought. *And that time, the spheres had opened up to the being.*

The being got closer. A hole to Tashon's left began to appear. He moved toward it. The spheres might not be opening for him, but they were opening.

And he was going in.

Chapter 32

Tashon and Ballas flickered out of the Third. Abe stared at the blood Ballas left behind, the falling snow slowly turning red to white. The sky darkened. They would need to settle down for the night before long.

He looked at the debris scattered around them. Johann and Rosa examined the damage, and it looked like every smokie rod had been shattered. If the smokies didn't work, they wouldn't survive the freezing night.

"What's he doing?" Winona asked.

He followed her gaze and saw Mohawk walking through the wreckage, collecting feathers from the beaked animal.

"No idea," Abe answered.

She stepped closer to him, grabbed his hand, and rested her head on his shoulder.

"It's going to be a cold night," she said.

"Freezing," Abe agreed.

"Think we'll make it to the Crawlers?" she asked calmly, as if the answer didn't matter.

He stopped to think. "I do."

"And when we get there?"

A laugh leapt from Abe's throat. He shook his head. "No idea," he admitted. "It just depends."

"On what?"

"Whether the Crawlers kill us on sight or take a chance to understand us."

"Wonderful," she said, and Abe sensed a smile on her lips.

"It'll be something," he said.

Mohawk sang at them to join. Abe pulled his hand back to himself, and everyone gathered together. The Singer had collected the feathers into a pile. He sang one note, and Abe knew immediately Mohawk was asking that everyone watch closely.

He took a feather in each hand, took a few steps backward, and stuck the stem of each into the snow. From those two feathers, he drew a circle in the ground, then handed a feather to Abe. Two notes encouraging Abe and the others to complete the circle of feathers. They grabbed their feathers and began their task. Mohawk walked away.

"Why are we doing this?" Abe asked, pushing a feather into the snow.

"He asked us to," Rosa said. "Tashon has faith in the Singers, so I do too."

"No, what's the purpose?" Abe shook his head, annoyed by her constant proclamations of faith.

"Probably a more primitive form of protection," Johann said. "Built something similar back on Earth, after our camp was burned down by the enemy. But we had a fire to keep us warm, to keep predators away. Don't see how we're going to do that."

"Seems like Mohawk has a plan," Winona said. "He's protected us so far. Why would he stop?"

"I don't think he would stop willingly," Johann shrugged. "But what if he can't protect us?"

"Have some hope," Rosa said calmly.

Abe sighed. Rosa's constant talk of faith and hope grated on him, but he couldn't help but notice she seemed more at peace than anyone else.

The snow fell slower, but it didn't stop. They worked on in silence. Just before the circle was complete and as the sky went completely dark, Mohawk joined them with a bag full of meat from the animal that destroyed the smokies. He dropped it in the snow, placed two more feathers, and they were fully enclosed in a circle of feathers.

Abe looked at the meat. Raw, not like what they'd eaten from the bush creature. It would have to be cooked to be safe for humans to eat.

"Seems like he knows what he's doing," Winona said.

"Yeah," Abe nodded. "He knows how to survive out here."

"But it's getting colder," she said, and stepped closer to him.

He wrapped his arm around her shoulder and pulled her in, the warmth of her body spreading to his own. She wrapped both arms around his torso. No words to speak came to him, so they stood silently. Johann and Rosa probably spoke, but Abe didn't hear them. He looked to the dark sky, watched the flakes fall gently, quickly.

After a few minutes, Mohawk walked to the edge of the circle.

Abe pulled his arm off Winona, grabbed her hand and they walked to see what the Singer was doing.

Mohawk looked at them. His lips didn't curve up, but something in his eyes told Abe that he was smiling at them.

Mohawk chanted a deep melody and lifted his left hand ceremoniously to the nearest feather. The wires, no longer a surprise to Abe, popped out of Mohawk's palm, brushing the edge of the feather. The chanting continued, got louder, faster. A blue line of electricity sparked between the wires. The edge of the feather lit up with a small green flame.

The fire spread across the feather, slowly covering it until the flames reached outward and lit the feathers on either side. It continued its path, and soon the five of them were encircled by burning green.

"Beautiful," Winona said.

"Yeah," Abe replied. "And warm."

"What chemical burns green?" Rosa asked.

Johann shrugged. "I probably learned that once."

"Copper will do it," Winona said excitedly. "But it could also be boron or barium. Possibly tellurium. I don't know what's most common on Aethera."

Abe grinned and chuckled.

"I like chemistry," she said.

"Yeah, sounds like it," Rosa said with a smile.

"I'm hungry," Johann said as he stretched and walked to the bag of meat. "Think we can eat this?"

"Damn it," Rosa said. "Ballas has the field tester on him."

"Looks like beef." Johann picked up a piece and sniffed it. "Smells fine. I'll just cook it."

"We have food bars," Abe said.

"And you'd rather have that than fresh meat?"

Jonstin picked up a broken metal rod, stuck it in the ground near the flames and skewered the meat on top of it.

"Does look better than a bar," Abe admitted.

Mohawk followed Johann's example and set his own piece of meat up to cook.

"See, it's fine," Johann said.

"For him," Winona shook her head. "His physiology is different than ours. Just because he can safely eat doesn't mean we can."

"After everything that's happened...." Johann ran a hand through his beard. "I think it's likely to be good."

"If you sleep through the night without puking or getting the shits, I'll have some for breakfast," Abe said. "I'd rather just sleep by the flames right now, anyway."

"Agreed," Winona said.

"What the hell, I'll try it," Rosa said.

Abe and Winona lay down, side by side, at the edge of the circle opposite the cooking food. The heat coming off the burning feathers would be enough to keep them warm, but the wind still whipped into the circle from above.

Winona rolled onto her side, wrapped an arm around Abe's chest, and pulled herself into his side. Abe tried to wrap his arm around her shoulders, then realized she was on the side of his severed arm. For the first time since he'd lost it, Abe wished to have it back.

"My parents would have loved it here," Winona said. "Even with all the loss, they would have loved to be a part of the discoveries here."

"My mom, too," Abe said. "That's why I chose to be part of the group to leave the ship."

"Me, too." She paused, then said quietly, "And because you were going."

"Yeah?" was the only thing Abe could think to say.

"You've been the nicest person to me," Winona said. "I just didn't want to be at the ship without my friend."

Abe smiled. "I'm glad you came."

He kissed the top of her head. Felt the urge to kiss her more, to pull her on top of him, to feel every part of her. He slowed his breathing, not wanting to ruin the moment and instead watched the snow fall in the flickering flames as they slowly drifted off to sleep.

A happy voice pulled Abe out of sleep. "I didn't get the shits."

"What?" Abe mumbled as he opened his eyes.

"Didn't get the shits," Johann said again. "Slept like a baby."

Abe sat up and shielded his eyes against the rising sun. Winona sat across the circle, eating a steaming piece of fresh meat.

Winona waved Abe over. "Made you one, Abe."

"Thanks," he said as he stood and stretched. "Glad you didn't get the shits, Johann."

"Told you that meat would be good," Johann replied. "You two eat and let's get going."

Abe sat next to Winona and took a bite of food. It was crispy, drier than the other meat, but surpassed his usual food bar without question.

"You sleep good?" Winona asked with a smile.

Abe returned her smile. "Yeah. You?"

"Yeah."

A few feet away, Mohawk opened a small screen in one of his hands. He sang a phrase and the screen blinked on. A face appeared on it. The bald Singer, a scar across his head. Mohawk lifted a broken rod to his face and said something to Scar. The two spoke quickly, harshly, and for the first time, the Singer language filled Abe with a sense of anger.

The other Singers were not happy Mohawk left them.

Chapter 33

Smith sat on a white bench in the main cavern of the red caves, trying to catch his breath. They had spent most of the morning lugging supplies from the ship to the cave, and the large space was filled with humans and things from a different world.

A coming together of the species. Smith wondered what a city would look like hundreds of years in Aethera's future. A blending of human and Singer cultures, technology and aesthetics. And, perhaps, some Crawlers would be there too. A city built to accommodate each species in their own required ways that created the same opportunities for happiness despite genetics.

He could hope.

The four Singers meandered around the crowd of humans, both species trying to communicate with the other. The hardest part, to Smith, was that the Singers never had any facial expressions or physical reactions to what the humans said. No laughs, no gasps, no shrugging or shaking their heads. They weren't near as easy to read as humans.

A Singer, the one with thin white hair, sat next to Smith. It sang a short string of notes that, according to Yeance, was a type of greeting.

"Hello," he said.

Three more notes from the Singer that made Smith feel safe, at peace. He was sure it was the Singer's way of saying something similar to 'welcome to our home.'

"Thank you," he nodded. "For helping us."

Smith felt grateful again that the Singers' language carried its meaning with the force of emotion—it made understanding them easier than it should have been. And the evolution that created such a language filled him with wonder. If humans understood and felt the intent behind each other's words, so many struggles could be avoided.

The Singer's hand began to glow a bright blue. He looked at it, stood and met the other three Singers in the center of the room. Each with a glowing hand.

Two Singers, the one with thinning hair and the one with braids, stood facing each other. They flipped open their hand wires and a large screen formed between the two of them. In between them, facing the center of the screen, was the scarred Singer.

The screen flickered, and another face appeared—the Singer with a mohawk, the one who had disappeared. Immediately, Scar let out a phrase of notes that Smith could feel were full of anger and hurt.

The Singers exchanged heated melodies for a few minutes, then the room filled with silence. Smith and the other humans exchanged uncomfortable looks but said nothing. Scar reached into a pocket of his pants and pulled out a book. A physical book made with real pages. Smith raised his eyebrows and shook his head in surprise.

With a few solemn notes, Scar held the book in front of his face and flipped through the yellow pages. On the screen, Mohawk responded firmly and resolutely. Whatever Scar has said, Mohawk was not swayed.

Mohawk then held up a small piece of metal, a broken smokie rod, and sang a short phrase that filled Smith with sympathy. Mohawk was pleading for help.

The Singer with the braids joined Scar and responded to Mohawk.

Scar replied firmly to her.

She responded in kind and left the room.

"Winona, look. Is that...?" Abe's voice came from the screen.

Smith jumped to his feet just as his son's face appeared next to Mohawk.

"He's talking to the other Singers," Abe said.

"Abe," Smith called as he ran to join Scar.

Abe smiled. "Dad."

"You okay out there?"

"Mostly, yeah." Abe shrugged. "Are Tashon and Ballas with you?"

Smith looked around, confused. "No. They... they're with you."

Abe shook his head. "Ballas got beat up pretty bad. Tashon took him into the Fourth to get him back to the ship."

"Shit," Smith said. "We're all in the caves." He turned away from the screen. "You heard Abe. Get some people to the ship."

In seconds, a small group was jogging out toward the ship. Smith looked back at Abe.

"Looks like we found our lost Singer," he said.

"Yeah." Abe chuckled. "Honestly, we'd be dead if he hadn't come."

Smith's stomach sank. "Really?"

He knew Abe would face danger, but knowing Ballas was almost dead and hearing that they'd all been close to death terrified Smith.

"I'm okay, Dad," Abe said. "Has the snow hit you?"

Smith shook his head.

"I hope you see it," Abe said. "It's damn beautiful."

"Me too," Smith nodded.

"Good thing we planted seeds that'll survive that kind of cold," Abe said.

Smith nodded. "Very good. Mom's pink peach trees are coming in beautifully, too."

Abe smiled at the memories the trees brought, but was quickly brought back to the present.

"We need to get going," Johann's voice said off-screen. "We'll see you soon, Smith."

"See you, Dad."

"Bye, Smith," Rosa and Winona said at once.

Mohawk and Scar exchanged a few more notes, and the screen turned off.

Chapter 34

Tashon, Ballas on his shoulder, jumped into the opening in the Higher Spheres right behind the flying soul. The hole closed behind him silently, leaving him blinded in an area filled with light. He rubbed his eyes with his free hand. As he waited for his eyes to adjust, he noticed that he wasn't standing on anything. He couldn't see, but it felt as if he were floating.

His sight came back one color at a time. A stripe of blue above his head, a swirl of an unknown Fourth color to his right. Colors turned to shapes, shapes turned to objects. A floor-less space full of floating, flying forms of thousands of species spanned out before him.

Souls of species he had never even imagined could exist, moving, speaking and interacting. Some loitered peacefully about. Others sped by as if on a crucial errand. Tashon tried to discern what each would have looked like in the Third, but it was impossible.

There were souls made strictly of straight lines. Souls that were simply one bulbous shape. Or a single line, stacked on top of itself over and over, each time at a slightly steeper angle, forming a mesmerizing being that transfixed Tashon.

None of them seemed to notice Tashon, except for the moths that appeared in front of him and danced circles around him and Ballas.

He looked down at his feet. The space extended down, filled with more souls, more forms that Tashon could barely comprehend. He could not see the Third.

Ballas weighed down on him, and he needed to keep moving. But how to walk without a surface to push against? And where was he supposed to go? All he saw was a vastness filled with concourses of the unfathomable. No landmarks, no goal in sight.

"Forward, then," he whispered to himself.

He moved a leg forward and placed it in front of him. It stopped at the same height as his other foot, as though he were on a level surface. He pushed off to take another step, shot up and forward at a steep angle, his body doing somersaults between the colors and shapes and souls.

Still, none paid him any attention. The moths stayed right in front of him, swirling in graceful circles.

He slowed and came to a stop next to a mass of small, interlocking elliptical objects that collectively made up a single being. It made noises at another being, this one a flat plane that hung vertically in the air, waves of colors running across its surface. The elliptical form bounced up and down a few times, spun in a circle and then took off.

Tashon looked at the colorful surface in front of him. Knew that it was indeed alive, intelligent, aware.

"I'm lost and tired," Tashon said. "And he's dying."

The living surface tilted to face Tashon directly. Multiple lines of light shot out of it and moved along Tashon's body. He could feel the lights reaching underneath his skin, analyzing every part of him. In amazement, Tashon realized the being was trying to understand Tashon. It, perhaps, had no idea what Tashon was, the same way Tashon had no idea what it was. The lights retreated.

"We're human." Tashon adjusted his grip on Ballas. "The, uh, third-dimension versions."

Lights swirled and blinked on the surface. The most comforting color Tashon had ever seen shot out of the flat being and disappeared in the distance. The surface floated away, but the line of color remained.

Tashon's stomach twisted. He doubled over and dry heaved. He moved Ballas, cradling him in his arm like an infant.

"Follow it, Ballas?" he whispered.

The moths flapped toward the path of color and encircled it.

"I think so, too."

Adjusting his angle to match the path of the light, Tashon pushed off again. He was positioned at a shallow angle, looking in the direction that he considered "up." Ballas moved his head slightly, coughed, and went limp again.

"I'll save you," Tashon said.

The line that Tashon followed seemed to pull on him, refusing to let his momentum slow. Or perhaps it was the moths that kept him moving as they swam through the air in front of him. He liked to think it was the moths.

Time passed, though Tashon had no idea how much. He lifted his head to get a better view, but still saw no end to the trail he followed. His head pounded harder and louder, his ears ringing against the pain. He moved past dozens more beings, but never saw any one of them long enough to understand what they might be. The pressure in his head grew, spread to his eyes, his cheeks, his jaw. Exhaustion swept over him, and he knew that he couldn't be in the Fourth much longer.

He closed his eyes.

He was back on the fully functioning Ship of Nations, standing on the top floor, staring out the windows into a dark void. Next to him was an alien creature, paper thin and short. It was telling him a joke. Something about a writing instrument and industrial grade adhesive. Tashon could make no sense of it but laughed at what seemed like the punchline.

He opened his eyes. With blurry vision, he tracked the line. Still no end in sight. He thought of trying to stop but didn't have the energy. He closed his eyes again.

He was floating on his back in the Aetheran ocean, gentle waves bobbing him up and down. Something gurgled next to him. He turned his face to look. Rosa lay in the water, face down and motionless. Panicked, Tashon turned vertical in the water and flipped her body over. Her face was wrinkled from being in the water for too long, but she seemed to be breathing. Then something wrapped around Tashon's ankle and pulled him into the water. He instinctually screamed, and water filled his lungs.

He gasped. His eyes burst open. Ahead, Tashon saw something directly in the line's path, past the moths. It did not look like the line continued past it. As he neared it, he slowed down and came to a stop next to a mountainous being he did not recognize, but somehow felt familiar to him. The moths flew around it, and then returned to Tashon.

The mountain spun, disconnected into a thousand pieces, and reconnected into a shape Tashon knew. It was the same god-like being that had hurt him, healed him, and sent him out of the Fourth. Tashon looked closely at it and felt that, in some ways, it resembled a human, its form like that of Laos. But not an exact match.

"Here again?" It questioned calmly. *"Did you not understand it was not your time? Did you not know coming back would cause you harm?"*

Tashon nodded. He looked down at Ballas.

"You came to save him. I cannot heal him. He has no connection to this place."

"I know."

The being examined Tashon. *"I see. Travel through this plane is far quicker than down there. You risked your life to save him?"*

Tashon nodded again.

"He can be saved. But he will not be whole."

Tashon looked at Ballas. His entire leg, up to the hip, was gone. No blood, no wound. Just gone.

The being lifted Ballas out of Tashon's arms and lobbed him off into the distance, then did the same to Tashon. He barrel-rolled past colors and beings, slid through the barrier of the Higher Spheres, sunk into the ground of the Fourth and slapped onto cold Aetheran ground just outside the ship.

He groaned, rolling onto his hands and knees. He vomited slippery bile into the dirt, and then fell onto his side next to a shallowly breathing Ballas.

"Help," Tashon tried to scream, but it came out as a whisper.

Still, footsteps rushed toward them, and Tashon knew they were saved. He closed his eyes.

"Tashon, what happened?"

"Can you hear me?"

"Ballas! His leg... we need to stop the bleeding."

Tashon tried to tell them there was no blood, but he was too tired. He drifted off into dark, dreamless sleep.

Chapter 35

Abe, Winona, Johann, Rosa and Mohawk had spent the morning silently leaving trails of footprints in the snow as they moved ever closer to their destination. Clouds formed in front of Abe's face each time he exhaled, but the consistent movement and the rays of sunlight kept him warm.

It would be another cold night. In preparation, they had each folded and stuffed as many feathers into their bags as possible. Enough to last at least a few nights. And by that point, Abe hoped the help Mohawk had begged for would arrive. Hoped that the scarred Singer felt the depths of the plea the way Abe had.

But that thought raised a question. He turned to Winona. "Do you think the Singers are as emotionally affected by their language as we are?"

She smiled, her eyes lighting up at the question. Abe had learned that she relished discussing the unknowns of the world around them. He loved that about her.

"It's possible," she said. "But even if the intensity of the effect were the same between humans and Singers, the Singers would still react differently than we do."

"Why's that?"

"They've spoken the language their entire lives." She shrugged. "I'd assume they had ways to prevent themselves from being emotionally manipulated."

"That does make sense," Abe said.

Ahead, the white was broken up by a scattering of large red boulders.

"And we get closer still," Rosa said.

"Careful," Johann said. "Those rocks could turn around and explode into hundreds of venomous snakes that chase us down."

"Shut up, Johann," Rosa said. "Snakes are cold-blooded."

"On Earth," Abe said. "On Earth, they were cold-blooded."

Rosa rolled her eyes.

Winona laughed, and Abe was surprised at how happy that sound made him feel.

Johann cleared his throat. "Really, though. We need to watch out."

They stopped in the shadow of the first boulder. Mohawk took off his pack, dropped it in the snow, and quickly ascended the rock. Once there, he sat and pulled a book out of his pocket.

"Is that...?" Winona whispered.

"A book," Abe said.

"Damn," Rosa said.

"Amazing." Johann smiled. "I like them more every day."

Mohawk flipped the pages back and forth, and then settled on a specific passage. He propped the book on the rock, gingerly holding it open with two fingers. His other hand rested in his lap.

The Singer's shoulders tensed as his eyes scanned the page. He lifted his gaze to the horizon, opened his mouth, and enveloped the still air with a fervent melody. Each note carried a different meaning, a distinct feeling that was lost to Abe. He felt Mohawk's passion, his regret and his hope, his goals and fears. But Abe could place no discernible meaning on those feelings, did not know what it was the Singer feared or hoped for. He told Winona this, and her response filled him at once with shock and clarity.

"Why can't the emotion be the meaning?" Winona asked.

The melody continued, the notes reaching high pitches that somehow remained smooth, the diving down so deep that the rock Mohawk sat on seemed to tremble. Abe kept feeling everything Mohawk's singing projected, but this time was not controlled by them. More than anything, Abe was filled with wonder at the sheer beauty a single being could create.

Abe sat down, leaned against the rock, and let out a contented sigh. The others joined him, Winona right by his side. They sat silently, letting the Singer fill the air around them with the waves of its language.

Not once did Mohawk stop as the sun descended in the sky, as Abe and Johann made a half circle of feathers beside the boulder and lit them with matches found in Winona's pack. Did not stop as stars appeared above them, as the moon rose higher in the dark sky. Did not submit to silence or succumb to fatigue as Johann, Rosa and Winona drifted off to sleep.

Sleep did not come to Abe, nor did he want it to. He wanted to hear Mohawk's entire oration, and felt that someone should be awake to keep him company. So Abe listened, eyes and ears open, letting his thoughts wander where they may.

Tashon and Ballas, he imagined, had made it back to the ship safely. But how had their trip through the Fourth gone? He knew being up there took its toll on Tashon, and he figured it had to be worse on Ballas. But, for some reason, he felt they would be okay. Maybe it was Mohawk's singing. Or Rosa's faith was rubbing off on him.

He looked at Rosa, her head leaned back against the rock, her mouth open, drool running down her chin. Was what she believed true? If there was an afterlife—Abe believed there was—did that mean that God, or a god, existed? And did that make Tashon a prophet or a visionary?

Maybe it did. Based on all he'd seen, it made sense that the Crawlers were mounting an attack. But one question lingered in his mind, causing him to doubt: if that were true, why hadn't they attacked already?

As the hours went on, Mohawk's melody did not cease. Exhaustion eventually got the best of Abe, and he fell asleep, the impassioned notes of Mohawk ringing in his mind.

By sunrise, the group was back on their feet, continuing north to the ocean. Abe didn't know when Mohawk finished his reading or, perhaps, his prayer. But the Singer had been silent all morning.

Rosa and Winona spent time discussing whether Mohawk had been singing or praying or reading poetry. But they soon settled into a quiet routine of walking, eating and sleeping. Each mile they walked the land filled with more boulders and rocks. Within two days, the only surface to walk on was red stone, sections of it covered in slick ice.

"I thought Tashon would be back by now," Rosa said, carefully stepping over a patch of ice.

"Yeah," Johann said. "He'll be okay. What worries me is that we don't have any smokies. How the hell are we going to get across the water?"

"But don't we agree that Mohawk was asking the other Singers for help?" Abe asked.

"Yeah, I think he asked," Rosa agreed.

"But it didn't sound like they wanted to send help," Johann said.

"Then what the hell are we going to do?" Abe asked.

"We've gone too far to turn back," Winona said.

"I don't think Mohawk would want to, either," Abe said. "He seems set on doing this."

"And we should be too," Rosa said.

"Rosa," Johann said. "I love the faith you've found, but we also can't keep moving forward blindly."

"Exactly," Abe said. "But it is at least possible that the Singers send some kind of help. More smokies, or some other tech. I'm not saying it's impossible."

"But it's going to take time for help to reach us," Winona said.

Johann nodded. "So we should at least give help a chance to get here."

"And if nothing else, we'll at least see the ocean," Abe said.

They fell back into silence as their legs continued propelling them forward. Despite the fear that they could fail, Abe still held on to a sense of wonder about their journey that he didn't want to lose. If he did, he knew the fear would overwhelm and cripple him.

"I lived by the ocean," Rosa said. "Back on Earth."

"Yeah?" Abe said, knowing she wanted to tell more.

"Yeah. It was in Chile. My dad was the main Protestant Neo-Taoist master in our area. We lived with him, my mom and I, in a small cave near the beach."

"A cave?" Abe shook his head. He knew from his studies on the ship that Chile, along with most countries on Earth, had sufficient infrastructure for everyone to have some type of home, regardless of financial status.

"Yes, a cave," Rosa said. "Part of that belief system involves keeping your desires for worldly things at bay. My father lived a humble life, free of materialism and fine foods. He even went celibate after my mom died."

She paused for a moment, and looked around with a smile.

"Yes, a cave by the ocean. As a teenager I hated it. Never got a real shower, nowhere to charge any tabs. No money to buy tabs, actually.

"But that view every morning. Couldn't beat that view." She inhaled and a large smile cracked her lips apart.

"Do you miss Earth?" Winona asked.

Rosa glanced at Johann and they both chuckled.

"On the ship, I missed the fresh air and the smell of the ocean," Rosa answered. "I missed all the natural and raw beauty of Earth. But not what our species did to it."

"And what we did to each other," Johann said. "I don't regret fighting in the military, did what I thought was right. But that it got bad enough for any of us to have to kill?" Johann shook his head.

"But do you think that's part of human nature?" Abe asked. "Can it be escaped? The Ship of Nations was trying to escape it, but it happened right on the ship. Killing, death."

"I don't know," Johann said. "I like to think it can be weeded out of us. But, here we are, going to stop a potential attack. And we might end up killing to save our species. And the Singers."

"Does that make us hypocrites?" Winona asked.

"I—" Johann stopped walking and scratched his chin. "I don't think so. We wish the universe worked differently, but we do our best to live in it the way it is."

"Do you think we can change the way it works?" Abe asked.

"If anyone can," Rosa said, "it would be Tashon."

Mohawk stopped walking, making a seat out of a rock. He pulled out a handful of dried meat and passed it out to everyone in the group. This time, none of them questioned if it was safe to eat, each quickly sating their hunger.

As they chewed, Abe thought about what Rosa had said. Tashon could do things no other human ever could, but how would that give him the capacity to change human nature? Then he thought of Jonstin. How he had been arrogant and self-centered.

"Jonstin changed," he said aloud.

"What?" Johann said through a full mouth.

"I think Tashon"—Abe paused—"or any of us, really, can encourage others to change. Jonstin was a self-centered prick, but then he died saving my life."

"But...?" Winona said, pushing her shoulder against his.

"But can we really make a completely peaceful world?"

Rosa sighed. "I don't think so," she said. "I'll admit that. But can't we at least make Aethera better than Earth?"

Chapter 36

Tashon and Ballas sat in a small room within the caves. It had been hours since Tashon was overcome by nausea and dizziness, and he was ready to get back to Abe and the others. But he feared another trip through the Fourth would kill him.

Ballas slept, the stump where his leg used to be covered in white bandages tinted red with blood. Ballas had lost no blood in the Fourth, but as soon as he was back in the Third, blood started draining from the wound. Tashon had no explanation for it, but knew it had probably saved Ballas's life.

Most of Ballas's face was covered in bandages, too. It would be weeks, at least, before the wounds could be open to the air. Tashon sighed. Ballas's understanding of foreign cultures would have been invaluable when they met the Crawlers, but now he wouldn't be at the crucial introductions.

Tashon might not be, either.

He closed his eyes and looked down at himself and Ballas from the Fourth. A few seconds, and the dizziness started to creep back into his mind. He opened his eyes and sighed. He might not have been able to go to the Fourth, but that didn't stop him from obsessing about it.

The images of all he saw in the Higher Spheres constantly rolled through his mind. The being that he crashed into, the being that helped him out of the Higher Spheres. Was it—or he or she—indeed some kind of god? That being felt similar to a human, but it wasn't. Unless it was a higher form of a human. Higher than the Fourth. Perhaps that's why that place was called the Higher Spheres.

And then there was the flat being that had sent Tashon along the path of color. It would make sense for it to send a human to its own god. If that's indeed what it was. Maybe it was just an even higher form of a human soul, with a deeper and broader understanding of the universe. Like Ballas had said, though, could that not be one way to define a god?

Someone knocked gently on the door, then opened it without waiting for an answer. Smith stuck his head in.

"One of the other Singers is going out to help the others," he said.

Tashon jumped to his feet. The blood rushed to his head. He waited for it to pass and then walked out the door.

"I'm going," he said.

"You're feeling good enough to go?" Smith asked as they walked down a hall to the main room.

"Yes," Tashon lied.

He needed to be there, no matter the cost. If things went bad with the Crawlers, he could use his connection to the Fourth to help them.

From the Fourth, Laos told him to let it be, to not risk his life anymore.

"Shut up," Abe said aloud, in the Third.

"What?" Smith asked.

"Oh, nothing," Tashon shook his head and rubbed his eyes.

For a moment, he had thought he was fully in the Fourth. Was his connection to the higher dimension impacting his mind? He told himself it wasn't, that it was just because he'd spent so much time in the Fourth and that it would soon pass.

"It won't," Laos said.

Tashon opened his mouth to respond, but caught himself. He was in the Third. In the Third.

They walked into the large main room. The Singer with the braids was lifting a square, metal box with straps onto her back. He walked to Braids, covered his mouth with his hand as she did the same.

"See ya, Smith," he said, not wanting to make a long goodbye.

None of the other Singers were there to see Braids off.

The Singer walked off at a brisk pace, and Tashon followed. They walked out into the yellow forest, the ground white with a thin layer of snow. The moths rested motionless on a nearby tree, and Tashon found himself hoping the creatures would stay with him.

Braids put the metal box on the ground, whispered a few quiet notes, and pressed a button on the container. Each side folded out with a squeak that made Tashon think the box hadn't been opened in a long time. The metal folded out flat into six distinct, connected squares. Each square held one full set of smokie rods resting in white slots, outlined in softly glowing green light.

She grabbed two large rods, gave one to Tashon, and sang a string of notes. Slits opened in the two rods, releasing the now familiar black clouds of nanotech. The nanotech spread and began to take shape just as the other three Singers burst out of the caves.

They shouted upset notes at her, their despair filling the air. They plead with Braids not to go, but she stayed silent, ignoring their pleas.

The nanotech slid under Tashon's feet and lifted him into the air. He fell to a sitting position in a half dome of black. He looked to Braids, who was in a half dome of her own. But she kept her balance and stayed standing as the nanotech rose higher and flew north.

Braids stood firmly in the flying disc, paying no heed to the impassioned cries of her peers. She didn't care what they said. She was helping Mohawk. Another note whistled from her lips, and their speed increased. Before the sun had gone down, they were out of the yellow forest.

Braids spoke her notes, and the nanotech slowed and landed in the snow. A nearby bush creature stood, lit its face, and scurried off. Tashon and Braids stepped onto the ground. The nanotech sucked back into the rods and Braids placed them into her pack. They were surrounded by the green light, and the Singer pulled out four smaller rods.

"It's to keep a charge," Tashon said. "Why didn't Mohawk use this?"

Braids looked at him and replied with notes he didn't understand. He thought about it, and realized the Singers had sent the smokies with the humans, but nothing more. For some reason, the Singers didn't want to send anything but the smokies with the humans. And Mohawk had, Tashon thought, quietly snuck away, and thus took nothing extra. But Braids had been more bold about her rebellion. Had done what she wanted, perhaps what she thought was right, and took what she needed to accomplish her goal. Tashon wasn't sure if that should be admired or feared.

He looked to the setting sun, then back at the forest to see how far they'd traveled. The speed they were going, they would catch up to the others within a day or two. Braids let out another string of notes. The black smoke poured out of the rods and enclosed the two in a warm cube.

In the Fourth, a familiar form Tashon had not seen in days appeared next to Laos. Tashon smiled, closed his eyes, and greeted the higher Singer who had shown him so much of her people.

She looked at him, an invisible smile radiating from her being. Images from her consciousness slid into his mind.

He stood on a muddy, rocky beach with his human and Singer companions. Behind them, the wide ocean. In front, three caves and a narrow canyon. The pillars of sandy rocks that stretched high above them told him they were at the threshold of Crawler territory.

The group discussed which path to take, and settled on the farthest cave to the right. They quickly made their way across the beach, into the tunnel, and out of the sunlight. The path curved left and right, up and down. A grinding echoed from farther in the tunnel. The group stopped. An indiscernible shadow leapt from the darkness. Blood splattered from Mohawk's head, then from Rosa's. Both bodies collapsed as the beast landed on the other side of the tunnel, turned, and ripped out the throats of Abe and Winona. Braids lit the electric light in her hands, and the creature came into full view.

A biotech creature, crablike and dark gray, standing upright on two legs. Blood from its first four victims dripped off its pinchers. It screeched at the light, charged and took off Braids's arms at the shoulders. Braids turned to run but was too slow. It cut her in two at mid-torso, and then quickly did the same to Johann. It turned to Tashon and dashed at him.

Tashon opened his eyes. His heart pounded. In the Third, Braids slept peacefully in the corner. In the Fourth, he looked at Laos and the unnamed Singer.

"Okay," Tashon said. "Don't go down that tunnel."

The Singer wanted to show him more, but that night focusing all of his energy on the Fourth drained what little energy he had. He closed his eyes and fell into a sleep full of dreams. Dreams of genetically-engineered monsters murdering him and his friends.

Chapter 37

On the distant horizon, gray sky met green water as Abe and his group neared the ocean. Snowflakes floated gently from the sky. A light fog hung in the crisp air. The sun would be setting soon, and exhaustion had swept over the party. No one talked. No one sang. No one worked to discern a possible solution to the problem of crossing the ocean.

Abe held tightly onto Winona's hand, slowly taking step after step. They were set on reaching the ocean. For the time being, that was their main goal. A goal that Abe wasn't ready to reach because, once they did, their journey would come to an end far too early. And what then? Turn around, head back to the ship, having done nothing to protect humans or Singers? Attempt to swim across the ocean? If pressed, Abe knew he would likely say he preferred the latter. He wondered what that said about him. Brave? Stubborn? Stupid? Suicidal?

He looked down at his feet. The snow was deeper, settling over the iced rock, making it less slick, providing less opportunity to slip and snap an ankle. Or break his wrist trying to catch himself, leaving his one hand useless. Winona said his name, but he barely heard her.

"Abe," she said. "Abe, look."

He stopped moving and looked up. A few dozen feet ahead, the ground disappeared. Rosa, Johann and Mohawk stood at the edge. When Abe and Winona caught up to them, both gasped. They found themselves at the top of a cliff that fell thousands of feet below onto a long, wide beach. Scattered across the cliff face were scores of waterfalls pouring out of holes in the stone. Some roaring white, some slower streams the same green as the ocean. Each ended in a vast maze of pools and streams that wove back and forth until, eventually, reaching the ocean. Trees with leaves of nearly every color lined the streams, circling the pools.

Abe looked down at the closest waterfall. It was at least fifty feet wide, yet far from the biggest that poured from the cliff. Dark, pointed shapes moved with it, falling faster than the water itself. *Or,* Abe thought, *perhaps they were more Aetheran creatures, propelling themselves through the water*. He wished he had a camera to document all the creatures they'd seen. And all the ones he hoped to see.

Then he looked back up at the ocean, remembered that their destination lay across that vast water.

"What now?" he asked, and looked at Rosa.

She looked at Abe, then out at the ocean. A look of doubt passed over her face but quickly disappeared.

She smiled. "Wait," she said with a shrug.

"For help that might not come?" Abe asked.

Johann raised his eyebrows. "Are you saying you want to go back?"

Abe shook his head. Of course he didn't want to go back. He didn't want to wait, either. They had been making progress. What Tashon said he had seen was panning out, and started to make the smallest bit of sense to Abe. But now it was all gone again. All just a possibility that Rosa still clung to as fact.

"There's far worse places to wait," Winona said as she stared down at the waterfalls.

Johann smiled. "Far warmer places, too."

He pulled a feather out of his bag and tried to stab it into the ground, but the snow had iced over and the stem broke in two. Without hesitation, he pulled two more feathers out and stood the three up, each leaning into the others. Mohawk lit the feathers with his electric palm, faced the ocean and sat down.

"I only have one feather left in my bag," Winona said.

"Me, too," Abe said, dropping his pack on the ground. "Rosa?"

"Two," she said and sat down.

Johann looked in his pack, back at the others. "I'm out," he said. "Looks like we have fire for a couple more nights."

Everyone answered silently by nodding and looking at their surroundings. The only wood in sight were the trees thousands of feet below them. And without smokies, there was no way they would take down another one of those supersonic creatures and harvest its feathers.

Clouds rolled over the setting sun, casting them in darkness sooner than Abe would have liked. They sat backs to the fire, eyes to the water.

Mohawk pulled out his book, opened it and stared silently at the markings on the page.

The humans glanced at each other, waiting for the singing to begin.

The Singer remained silent.

A chill wind came in from the ocean. Abe shivered, but said

nothing. For some reason, it did not feel like a time for words. Winona squeezed his hand, let go and then slid over to sit directly next to the silent Singer. She didn't look at him, didn't touch him, sitting there in a way that could have been awkward, but wasn't.

She opened her mouth and began to sing. A soft yet firm voice immediately full of pain and understanding. The melody was familiar, but the words were entirely new to Abe.

These times are hard,
These times come fast,
These times of fear,
How can they last?

These times of dark,
At times so slow,
These times of doubt,
Oh, on they go.

They plod, they run,
Stand up, lie down,
They beat our hope
Into the ground.

She closed her mouth and gently hummed. Abe could tell she felt sad, but he saw hope in her eyes that didn't match the tone or words of her song. Something told him that, somehow, she understood what Mohawk was feeling and she was attempting to communicate that she understood, that he was not alone. She inhaled and resumed her singing, this time in a booming vibrato that filled the air, sank into the rocks and rose to the clouds.

This time of pain,
This time of cold,
Still on we go,
We'll never fold.

Or so we say,
But nights like this,
We close our eyes
And pray Death we'll kiss.

I think. She was up all night with the Singers. She said ıme with every note— or word, I guess we could say. A wnpour, hail, snow. All the same word, each time evoking lenotes the specific meaning."

.iled again and shook his head. Saddened that Evalee share in the discovery. Hopeful, most of the time, that ad an eye on Abe. And the hope helped him enjoy the e imagined Evalee watching it all unfold from the Fourth.

ıer words of ours are you certain they understand?" he

." Yeance exhaled loudly. "Mostly, we've used words ral world. Tree, cloud, sky, dirt, rock."

out human or Singer? What do they call their species?

eance nodded. "It's just that, uh...."

Yeance said, turning to the Singers. "Singer."

Hair placed a hand in the center of her stomach and let . Two short, one long. Those three notes filled Smith with e and well-being. He felt strong, sure of his path. Knew that the choice of strict pacifism was the one true way.

g passed.

y humble species," Smith noted.

ıans are?" Yeance responded.

ir," Smith said. "The Singers who left, though. I would ew of their own species would impact the emotions ıose notes."

t likely. Their views of what a Singer is seem to differ

y of communicating must make lying impossible," Smith

dded. "Yes, yes it would."

Smith said to the Singers.

two quick notes. Smith immediately felt at once hopeful onfused yet certain. Full of kindness and rage, dark and

the feelings lingered far longer than with the previous Ie remembered much of the good he'd done in his life. e bad. He felt as though everything might come crashing ıim, but also knew that he couldn't simply stay still. But,

Tears trickled down her cheeks, and she choked on a sob.

But why so sad,
So full of fear?
Look all around,
See, there's beauty here.

So, yes, we'll go
Out in in the cold,
We'll face the fear,
We will not fold.

We may still doubt,
We may still fear.
Still full of pain,
And held-back tears.

But on we go.
On we go.

She closed her mouth and resumed humming.

Mohawk turned his face to her, closed his eyes nearly all the way, leaving the smallest slit of vision.

Abe had no idea what it meant, but it was the greatest physical reaction he'd seen a Singer make. And that seemed significant to Abe.

Winona's humming slowed, quieted and then stopped.

Mohawk turned to face the fire and looked back at his book.

Everyone followed suit and formed a circle around the burning leaves.

Abe sat with his legs crossed.

Winona lay down on her side and rested her head in Abe's lap.

"I think I've heard that before," Abe said as he stared into the green flames. "But not those words."

"My mom...." She sighed. "My mom hummed that tune to me when I couldn't sleep. The words—those words—just came to me."

Abe looked down at her.

"You mean that was all just"—Abe paused—"made up on the spot?"

She shrugged and smiled, then closed her eyes. Abe shook his head and realized that, besides his parents, Winona was the one person he cared for the most.

My Family, I am sure, is lost to me
Or I to them. Lost and, I feel,
Willingly forgotten.
And I cannot, do not, blame them.
I turned against our pact, against our Family,
Against Mother.
But Mother has not left me.
I still hear her melody
In the air, in the clouds, in the rocks,
In these new Frames.
I am lost to my Family, but these new Frames.
These two, young Frames hear me.
The one, he fought exhaustion to be with me as I sang to Mother.
The other, she communicated with a melody
As pure as any I've heard from my Family.
Perhaps they are as grand as Mother foretold.

Chapt

"Music," Yeance said as Smith s
They were in a corner of the r
them as both species worked to und
"Music?" Smith said.
"Music, song, melody. A main p
"Yeah, agreed," Smith said.
He thought of Fritz the night t
few minutes singing with him had
than all their other interactions co
made sense.
"Tree," Yeance said to the Singe
The Singer with thin white h
learned meant "tree." But the not
equivalent. They made Smith feel
Singer specifically meant a tree in
same two notes. But, somehow, s
nervous, chaotic and cold. A tree in
The feeling quickly passed, a
said.
Yeance nodded, smiling.
Smith clicked his tongue and s
ceiling of the cave. He thought of b
time using the same sounds. He co
two, but something had to be differ
He looked at Yeance. "Did they
"Exactly. I've had them do it
notes for tree are identical."
"Then how?" Smith asked.
"No idea."
"Does Minow know about this
"She's the one who figured it o
"Right," Smith said. "Where is

"Resting,
they do the s
soft rain, a do
a feeling that
Smith sm
wasn't here t
she at least h
discovery as h
"What o
asked Yeance
"Not sur
about the nat
"What a
Ours?"
"Yeah," Y
"What?"
"Listen,"
Thinning
out three note
a sense of pri
with certainty
The feelin
"Not a ve
"And hu
"That's f
think their v
connected to t
"Yes, mo
significantly."
"Their wa
said calmly.
Yeance no
"Human,
Scar sang
and terrified,
light.
This time
Singer notes.
And most of t
down around

Tears trickled down her cheeks, and she choked on a sob.

But why so sad,
So full of fear?
Look all around,
See, there's beauty here.

So, yes, we'll go
Out in in the cold,
We'll face the fear,
We will not fold.

We may still doubt,
We may still fear.
Still full of pain,
And held-back tears.

But on we go.
On we go.

She closed her mouth and resumed humming.

Mohawk turned his face to her, closed his eyes nearly all the way, leaving the smallest slit of vision.

Abe had no idea what it meant, but it was the greatest physical reaction he'd seen a Singer make. And that seemed significant to Abe.

Winona's humming slowed, quieted and then stopped.

Mohawk turned to face the fire and looked back at his book.

Everyone followed suit and formed a circle around the burning leaves.

Abe sat with his legs crossed.

Winona lay down on her side and rested her head in Abe's lap.

"I think I've heard that before," Abe said as he stared into the green flames. "But not those words."

"My mom...." She sighed. "My mom hummed that tune to me when I couldn't sleep. The words—those words—just came to me."

Abe looked down at her.

"You mean that was all just"—Abe paused—"made up on the spot?"

She shrugged and smiled, then closed her eyes. Abe shook his head and realized that, besides his parents, Winona was the one person he cared for the most.

My Family, I am sure, is lost to me
Or I to them. Lost and, I feel,
Willingly forgotten.
And I cannot, do not, blame them.
I turned against our pact, against our Family,
Against Mother.
But Mother has not left me.
I still hear her melody
In the air, in the clouds, in the rocks,
In these new Frames.
I am lost to my Family, but these new Frames.
These two, young Frames hear me.
The one, he fought exhaustion to be with me as I sang to Mother.
The other, she communicated with a melody
As pure as any I've heard from my Family.
Perhaps they are as grand as Mother foretold.

Chapter 38

"Music," Yeance said as Smith sat next to him.

They were in a corner of the main cave. Two Singers stood with them as both species worked to understand each other.

"Music?" Smith said.

"Music, song, melody. A main part of song is how it makes us *feel*."

"Yeah, agreed," Smith said.

He thought of Fritz the night they had crashed on Aethera. Those few minutes singing with him had strengthened their connection more than all their other interactions combined. What Yeance was saying made sense.

"Tree," Yeance said to the Singers.

The Singer with thin white hair sang two notes that Smith had learned meant "tree." But the notes were more than just the human equivalent. They made Smith feel calm and warm, and he knew the Singer specifically meant a tree in summertime. Next, Scar sang the same two notes. But, somehow, something was different. Smith felt nervous, chaotic and cold. A tree in the midst of a storm.

The feeling quickly passed, and Smith laughed. "Incredible," he said.

Yeance nodded, smiling.

Smith clicked his tongue and stretched his neck back, staring at the ceiling of the cave. He thought of both trees the Singers described, each time using the same sounds. He could not tell a difference between the two, but something had to be different.

He looked at Yeance. "Did they both make the exact same sound?"

"Exactly. I've had them do it over and over, and every time the notes for tree are identical."

"Then how?" Smith asked.

"No idea."

"Does Minow know about this?"

"She's the one who figured it out," Yeance answered.

"Right," Smith said. "Where is she?"

"Resting, I think. She was up all night with the Singers. She said they do the same with every note— or word, I guess we could say. A soft rain, a downpour, hail, snow. All the same word, each time evoking a feeling that denotes the specific meaning."

Smith smiled again and shook his head. Saddened that Evalee wasn't here to share in the discovery. Hopeful, most of the time, that she at least had an eye on Abe. And the hope helped him enjoy the discovery as he imagined Evalee watching it all unfold from the Fourth.

"What other words of ours are you certain they understand?" he asked Yeance.

"Not sure." Yeance exhaled loudly. "Mostly, we've used words about the natural world. Tree, cloud, sky, dirt, rock."

"What about human or Singer? What do they call their species? Ours?"

"Yeah," Yeance nodded. "It's just that, uh...."

"What?"

"Listen," Yeance said, turning to the Singers. "Singer."

Thinning Hair placed a hand in the center of her stomach and let out three notes. Two short, one long. Those three notes filled Smith with a sense of pride and well-being. He felt strong, sure of his path. Knew with certainty that the choice of strict pacifism was the one true way.

The feeling passed.

"Not a very humble species," Smith noted.

"And humans are?" Yeance responded.

"That's fair," Smith said. "The Singers who left, though. I would think their view of their own species would impact the emotions connected to those notes."

"Yes, most likely. Their views of what a Singer is seem to differ significantly."

"Their way of communicating must make lying impossible," Smith said calmly.

Yeance nodded. "Yes, yes it would."

"Human," Smith said to the Singers.

Scar sang two quick notes. Smith immediately felt at once hopeful and terrified, confused yet certain. Full of kindness and rage, dark and light.

This time, the feelings lingered far longer than with the previous Singer notes. He remembered much of the good he'd done in his life. And most of the bad. He felt as though everything might come crashing down around him, but also knew that he couldn't simply stay still. But, most of all, he wondered whether he was on the right path. Whether or not he was good.

"Damn, Yeance," he said. "They're more unsure of us than we are of them."

"In some ways, I think they are. But why let us stay in their caves, then?"

Smith shrugged. "That's a good question."

"My guess is it has to do with their promise of pacifism," Yeance said. "Maybe that entails more than just pacifism. Maybe it includes active acts of kindness and not just passive pacifism."

"That makes sense."

The Singer made the note for 'goodbye' and walked out of the large room. Smith let out a breath of relief. He liked the Singers, and enjoyed being with them. But he was always worried he would do something around them that would immediately ruin their relationship. Another successful meeting with them done, though, and his worries lessened.

"What is everyone talking about lately?" he asked, looking at Yeance.

"Everything." Yeance laughed. "The Singers. These caves. Abe and the others. Ballas. Tashon and the Fourth, and his visions. The Crawlers."

"What are they saying about all of it? Are people hopeful? Scared?"

"Both." Yeance shrugged. "You know, in some ways, I think the Singer interpretation of humankind is accurate. Opposing emotions coexist in us all the time. Scared yet courageous. Sad but optimistic. I heard someone shout faith in Tashon and the path he was shown, only to question the existence of the Crawlers hours later."

It made sense to Smith. There was so much uncertainty, so many unanswered questions, that it was impossible to remain completely hopeful and faithful no matter what.

"What are people saying we should do?"

"Wait it out. At least for a while. It's the logical choice, but it's hard. People want to do something, take action. Especially our people. But fear is lingering everywhere. The doubt makes people nervous to make the wrong move."

"They're not wrong," Smith admitted. "Especially when the only guidance we have has been seen by just one person."

"One person in a dimension not our own," Yeance added. "It's difficult. And most of us trust the Singers now, but only to a point. The unknown of their emotionally-charged language is scary."

Smith sighed. "It is. But we won't know anything for sure until Abe and the others get back."

"If they get back." Yeance sucked air in through his lips. "Sorry, I—"

"It's okay, Yeance," Smith said. "I know I could lose Abe. From what Tashon says, we almost lost all of them already."

"You're a strong man to let him go."

Smith chuckled. "I don't know about that, but he needed to go. And he has some of the best people with him."

"And two Singers. With phenomenal nanotech."

"The smokies are amazing," Smith agreed.

"Have the engineers figured out how they work?" Yeance asked.

"Not yet. And it's driving them crazy." Smith laughed. "But I don't think we'll learn much until we can communicate effectively with the Singers."

"All right. That's still the main focus, then."

"That, and keeping our people safe," Smith said.

"They seem good to me," Yeance said. "Happy enough."

"Good to hear," Smith said.

He wondered what enough happiness meant, but didn't question it. Despite everything going on, there were no immediate concerns or dangers except for the possibility of Crawlers showing up. It was a waiting game, and Smith wasn't sure how long he'd be able to play.

Five were one,
Then four, and one.
Now three, and two.
Our Family is fracturing, tearing apart.
Mother, what is happening?
The new Frames were to wake us, to save us.
They are dividing us, Mother.
We have trusted in your foretelling, waited for them to come,
To free us from Neighbors, to wake our Family.
Each day, Mother, doubt dances around our Melodies.
Or, perhaps, we do not understand your Melody as we thought we did.
Mother, did we not hear you clearly?
Or did we hear something that was not there?

Chapter 39

Tashon and Braids covered the entirety of the fields in a single day without incident. Exactly what Tashon needed. He spent the entire day in his floating nanotech bowl, in and out of sleep, his head pounding and his stomach threatening to reject its contents.

At some point during the day, the Singer in the Fourth came back to him and gave him another dream. He was back on the Crawler beach with the others. This time, they decided to go into the next cave to the left. They walked deeper and deeper down a narrow tunnel.

After hours trudging through the dark, a sound from deeper in the tunnel crept toward them. Like thousands of dull knives scratching on stone. The group stopped in their tracks. The sounds grew louder as thousands of tiny lights rushed at them from the floors, the walls and the ceiling. Large biotech rodents circled them. Ran up their legs, pulled them to the ground.

Rosa was the first to scream. Then Abe. One of the creatures sank its teeth into Tashon's cheek. Heat spread from the rodent's mouth, covering his face in an invisible fire that ripped a scream from his throat. The shouts of those lost in pain echoed through the caverns for an eternity. And then, silence.

Tashon woke up, heart pounding, face soaked in sweat despite the cold air. Why couldn't the Singer just show him the right path to take? Why did he have to keep seeing his friends die?

He sat up and found he was no longer in his nanotech transport. A red rock towered above him, casting him in shadow. The sky was full of clouds, and he couldn't make out where the sun was, though it felt like morning to him. Braids was nowhere in sight, but he could hear her softly singing nearby. He focused in on the sound and tried to understand what she was saying or, at the very least, what she was feeling.

Her voice was soft and calm, but each note radiated with an intense fury that pierced Tashon. The rage built up inside him, and he had to force it away. He knew why Braids was angry. It even made sense to him. She was seething because her peers had refused to help Mohawk, all under the pretense of a pacifism pact.

Tashon knew he would be just as pissed if he were her. But he also knew he only understood her anger at a shallow level. There was no way for him to know all the nuances of their culture, the ins and outs of their own societal definition of pacifism. Letting her emotions fill him would do no good.

He stood, causing another wave of vertigo. He leaned against the rock and closed his eyes. It was over sooner than the last time, but that wasn't enough. He needed to be rid of the lingering effects of his journey into the Fourth before they made it across the water. Braids stopped her angry soliloquy and joined Tashon from the other side of the rock.

She spoke a few notes, and Tashon felt her concern. She was asking if he was okay. He shrugged and then nodded. Thought about telling her he was fine, but was almost certain she would sense his emotional state and not understand his words. So even if he told her that he was fine, all she would feel was that he obviously wasn't. But he was sure it didn't take an emotionally advanced species to figure that out.

"I think I'll be okay," he said.

It was mostly true.

Braids pulled out two new rods, sang a few notes, and soon they were back in the air. The cold breeze on Tashon's face awakened him, brought a sense of energy that he'd been longing. It didn't heal his vertigo or nausea, but he felt more alert. More hopeful, even.

"*Tashon,*" Laos called to him from the Fourth.

Tashon sighed, closed his eyes and asked Laos what he wanted.

"*Someone's coming.*"

A familiar figure appeared next to Laos, bringing a smile to Tashon's face.

"Evalee," he said aloud, in the Third. "How are you?"

"*Content,*" she responded silently. "*You look tired.*"

Tashon shrugged. "I've been better, but I've been worse too."

"*I don't think you have,*" Laos said.

"Shut up, Laos," Tashon said through half a smile. "I was worse just after I killed you," he added.

"*You did puke a lot then, too.*"

Silence. Tashon's mind, unaware to him, hung somewhere between the two dimensions, not completely belonging to either one.

"*Tashon, thank you for giving Smith and Abe some hope.*"

"Yeah," he said. "Just told them what I saw."

"I know, but it means more to them than you know. And to me."

"How is Abe?"

"Happy. He's seen so much. They've found the most beautiful place. You'll see it when you get to them."

He smiled. "I'm excited to get back to them."

Tashon's mind wandered, taking him to what he imagined that beautiful place might look like. Soft ground. Cool and breezy, with plants of every color scattered around.

"How's Smith?"

"Good, too. Worried about Abe. Worried about you."

"How can you tell?"

"I've known him for a long time." Her thoughts floated warmly into his.

In the breezy plains of his mind, creatures walked the ground, flew through the air. One walked up to him, nuzzled its head against his leg as he scratched it behind the ears.

"Really, Tash. Are you okay?"

The words swam through the wind of Tashon's landscape. Then the illusion slowly faded away. First the animals, then the plants, then the ground. He floated in cool breeze amidst absolute nothingness.

He opened his eyes. "No, not okay," he mumbled.

He was tightly curled in the fetal position, his body sunk as deep into the floating dish as possible, his head pounding, drool and vomit dripping from the corner of his mouth.

"*Laos*?" she asked.

"He's been coming into the Fourth. It's destroying him."

"I needed to," Tashon said as loud as he could.

"Not at the risk of dying, you didn't."

"I saved Ballas," he said matter of factly.

Evalee moved closer to that part of Tashon that ever remained in the Fourth. Her entire essence seemed to smile at him.

"I'm proud of you, Tashon."

That brought a small surge of energy and hope into Tashon, but not enough to speed his recovery. Or slow his death. "Evalee? Have you seen God? Or a creator?"

"I've asked. I've searched."

"And?"

"More... beings here have faith in a Creator. Nearly all do. There're more signs of God or gods or a Creator existing than there are down there."

"Signs?"

"It's different than down there. Here there are just places that... feel different, feel significant. As if made by something higher than even the Fourth. Something pure, benevolent, strong. Intelligent on a level that far surpasses any I've met here."

"The Higher Spheres?"

"Yes, that is one such place."

Tashon gently nodded, knowing that her answer raised countless more questions, but he couldn't find the words to ask them. He slowly fell out of consciousness, becoming blissfully unaware of anything in any dimension.

I have left three to follow one.
Doing is a Melody that I hear more than not doing.
Before these New Ones came, our Promise made sense.
We do not silence Melodies.
But the New Ones, I hear the good in their Melodies.
That good, hidden by fear and rage and hurt, but still there.
That good, though they have made no Promise.
They go to fight for us.
To silence for us.
And I go to fight with them.
Mother, what will silencing my Promise mean?
I do not know, truly,
If that answer matters to me.

Chapter 40

Abe, Winona and Johann walked west along the cliff edge in search of a way down. After three miles of nothing but snow and stunning ocean views, they came upon a dead sound bird. Its feathers were gone, presumably blown away in the wind or taken by some other creature, and open sores covered its flesh.

"Looks diseased," Winona said, looking away.

"Probably what it died from," Abe said.

"Too bad." Johann shook his head. "That's a lot of wasted meat."

Abe stepped closer, and slowly circled it. The rough, circular wounds vaguely resembled the hole the biotech beetle had bored into his own arm. But, if that was what happened to the sound bird, those beetles would have been much larger. That couldn't be what it was, he told himself. *But it could be*, he thought. Then, for the first time since setting out, the danger of their final destination fully settled on him. From everything he knew about the Crawlers, the most likely ending was that he would die when they reached the other side of the sea.

He looked out at the ocean, eyes scanning the horizon, but, of course, saw no land across that vast water. But something made him feel they would make it there. Maybe Rosa's faith was rubbing off on him. Or he simply didn't want to fail, didn't want the journey to end before the goal was met.

"Should we keep going?" Winona asked.

Abe pulled his eyes and attention to Winona.

"Still got plenty of daylight," Johann said. "Better than sitting still at camp, yeah?"

"It is," Abe agreed.

Sitting still would only give him more time to envision all the ways they could fail. Moving any way but backward helped dispel the doubt.

So they continued along the cliff, eyes ever searching for a way down to the trees and water below. Another mile, another three. They stepped into an expanse of deep black that blanketed the rock. Snow covered the ground around it, but not a single flake rested on its surface.

The three crouched down. It looked like moss or perhaps a form of lichen. Winona reached her hand toward it, stopping before her fingers touched it.

"It's hot," she said.

Abe held his hand out. Heat rose into his palm and spread to his fingertips.

"Odd," he whispered, peering intently at the substance. "It looks organic. Plant-like. But a plant radiating that kind of heat?"

"It could be another form of biotech," Winona said.

"Or a cluster of organic nanotech," Johann guessed.

Abe nodded. Both were possible, especially on Aethera. He slowly reached his hand down to touch it, thinking the texture would give him more information. He gently squeezed a piece between his finger and thumb. It was warm, almost hot, but not enough to burn him. He pushed his flat hand into it, and the black sunk under the pressure.

It was soft, flexible. Nothing broke or ripped. He could feel thin roots, or strings, crisscrossing underneath, and he was certain those were underneath the entire mass. The warmth of it filled his hand, travelled up his arm.

"Organic, I think," he said as he pulled his hand out.

"And filthy," Johann said.

Abe looked at his hand, turned it around. The palm side of his hand was ink black. He rubbed in the snow, but it did not come clean. A thought crossed his mind that made him feel utterly stupid. *What if it's poisonous?* He'd let curiosity take over. But his hand didn't itch or burn or tingle.

"Look," Winona said

Abe looked at her, followed her line of sight southward. Two airborne objects quickly flew toward them, growing bigger every second.

"Help?" Johann questioned. "Or something dangerous?"

Abe said nothing.

Winona remained silent.

The three watched as they objects grew closer. If it was help, they'd be easy to spot. If it was a threat, they wouldn't be able to outrun them at the speed they were traveling.

The shapes become clearer, like two bowls hovering through the air. A figure stood proudly in one. In the other, the figure sat, head down.

"Another Singer," Winona said happily.

"And I think that's Tashon," Johann said.

"Where's Ballas?" Abe asked.

The bowls landed in the snow a few feet in front of them. The Singer with uneven braids stepped gracefully onto the ground. Tashon stood, seemingly drunk, stumbled out and collapsed.

Chapter 41

Tashon lay on the ground near a single feather alight in green flame swishing in the soft, cold wind. His eyes half open, he tried to push back the dizziness. At times, he felt it was getting better; other times, he felt close to death. Thankfully, in that moment, he felt okay.

He looked at Rosa, who knelt beside him. Thought of her as a young woman, turning away from the religion her father held dear, only to become religiously devoted to Tashon.

Protestant Neo-Taoism. He remembered some Taoism, by itself, from his studies on the ship. They believed in finding an inner calm through various means that he couldn't remember. A balance.

"Rosa," he said. "Tell me about Taoism."

"What about it?" she asked with a smile.

He thought about it. There was a word for what he wanted to understand, what he wanted to accomplish. What he hoped would help him balance out the two dimensions of his mind. "Meditation," he whispered.

"I only did it a few times. Don't remember much."

He sat up and crossed his legs. "Tell me what you remember."

She rotated off her knees and crossed her legs. Placed her hands on her legs, palms cupping her knees.

Tashon rotated his hands in the same way.

"Close your eyes," she said calmly, soothingly.

He closed them.

"Inhale through your nose. Deep and slow."

He did so, as slow as his spinning head would allow.

"Now breathe out through your mouth."

He blew the air out.

"Keep doing that. Focus on that. Only that."

He inhaled, exhaled. Slow. Steady. Images of the pattern of breathing filled his mind in both dimensions. In the Third, the rise and fall of his lungs, the calming of his heartbeat. In the Fourth, a wave of colorful air that wooshed back and forth. The pounding in his head slowed, and then nearly subsided completely. The churning in his stomach calmed to a bubbling.

Better than he was, but not strong enough to return to the Fourth if he had to. He longed to return to the higher dimension. He opened his eyes and focused them on the trembling flames, then rose to his feet. His head twisted, his stomach leapt, but he stayed upright. Continued his steady breathing.

Balance. Connection and separation. To the Fourth, from the Fourth. Separation and connection. From the Third, to the Third.

He needed both, needed all.

With eyes open, his mind looked to his view from the Fourth. As always, he saw himself at the center and the area surrounding him. His body stood still, but he imagined solely the Fourth part of his brain moving to the left.

It did, if only inches, so that Tashon was no longer the center point. He moved it to the right with the same outcome. As he moved his view back and forth, he found it was less jarring, less disorienting when he was not the focal point.

Leaving himself off-centered in his Fourth sight, he pulled himself back to his physical mind. If he was able to pull his third-dimensional body into the Fourth, shouldn't he be able to pull that part of him in the Fourth back into his tangible form?

He paused, focused on his breathing. As he inhaled, he lifted both hands above his head. Held an invisible ball he imagined to be his Fourth mind. A warmth filled his hands. Real or imagined, he had no idea. But it felt as real as anything ever had.

He pinched his fingers together, stretched out the warmth until it burst. The warmth fell like fog around him, sunk into his body, but his Fourth mind remained in the Fourth. He lowered his hands to his sides.

Inhaled. Exhaled. Inhaled. Closed his eyes. Exhaled. From the Fourth, he was still not the focal point. He focused on that, on the idea that moving himself from the center of his vision made him feel more balanced. As he did, his form blurred while those around came into sharp focus.

He thought of how he had nearly killed himself taking Ballas through the Fourth. But he would do it over, he realized. Do it again if he had to. The thought calmed him, lessened the pain in his head, in his gut.

As the healing calm spread through his body, he looked at those who surrounded the fire. At some point, Rosa had walked away from him and joined the two Singers. The three sat together silently, staring at the flames. Though he knew they must have been watching him. Had they seen the warmth that he felt in his hands?

He took the few steps it took to get to them, seeing them from the Fourth at the center of his vision, his own body at the edge, barely visible. Rosa smiled at him. The Singers covered their mouths. Tashon sat down.

"Better?" Rosa asked.

Tashon nodded. He still had a soft, rhythmic tapping inside his skull. A thin, acidic feeling in his stomach. But the meditation and adjustments in the Fourth had done what he had hoped.

Without a word, he lay down, back to the flame, and closed his eyes.

Immediately, the higher Singer appeared. A scene flowed from her into his mind. They were all back on the Crawler beach.

"Wait," Tashon whispered. "I can't see them die again."

"What was that?" Rosa asked.

Tashon didn't hear her.

"Please, just show me the right way," he said.

"Tashon?" Rosa said.

Again, her voice passed by him, unheard.

In his mind, on the beach, the group walked into the narrow canyon, single file. The sandy-white cliffs rose high above them, the tops obscured by thick fog. Speckled across the rock faces were dark green markings. Each an ellipse, some as small as child's palm, others a few yards tall.

They walked through the serpentine canyon for hours, unmolested by Crawler or Crawler creation. Stomachs growling, they stopped to eat. Mentioned how odd that they had seen no Crawlers, and continued on.

As the sun rose, the fog burned away. A scratching, scurrying sounded from above them. One Crawler rushed down at them, jumped off the cliff face and landed on Johann, knocking him to the ground. Johann pulled out a knife and drove it into one of the creature's legs. It let out a vibrating screech. Johann kicked it off and onto its back. Rosa kneeled on its exoskeleton stomach and dug her knife into the flesh underneath its head. Purple blood drained out, and the Crawler was dead.

They walked on and soon found themselves at the edge of the Crawler city.

"Thank you," Tashon said aloud to the Singer in the Fourth.

He didn't hear Rosa ask what he was thanking her for. The Singer above left him, and he closed his eyes, thankful that he had regained control of both dimensions of his mind.

Chapter 42

Growing up on the Ship of Nations, Abe had never had the chance to swim, to be in any water deep enough to drown him. But that morning he hovered in his own nanotech dish, mere feet above dark green water deeper than he could fathom. The wind that whipped around them was cold, but when he sat, the walls of the nanotech vehicle were as tall as his shoulders. A soft warmth rose from them just as it had in the smokie dome.

It was cold, but he wouldn't freeze.

The Singers, Rosa and Johann kept their eyes forward. Abe and Winona stared at the dark shapes beneath the water's surface. Thick plants swished back and forth with the motion of the water. Aquatic creatures maneuvered in and out of the grassy maze. Some were snake-like in appearance and movement. Others resembled cubes that, at first sight, Abe thought were inanimate objects. But as he saw more of them, he noticed that each had six translucent fins, one for each surface. The fins worked independently of each other, giving the right-angled fish immense maneuverability. They turned on a dime while also spiraling sideways, shooting off in another direction without losing any momentum.

Soon, all signs of life disappeared completely. They sailed over an ocean that appeared to be completely empty. But, after all they'd seen on Aethera, Abe feared what might lurk at unseen depths.

"Does the Fourth show anything in the water we can't see?" Abe asked Tashon.

Tashon shook his head. "No."

Abe looked at Winona. She shrugged and smiled. They'd both seen the meditative trance Tashon had fallen into the night before. Noticed how he'd hardly said a single word since they set out over the ocean.

"Does anyone have a working memory of the Aetheran map?" Winona asked.

"How working?" Abe asked.

"Just wondering if we could estimate when we'll get there."

"Do you see land on the horizon?" Johann asked.

Abe and Winona looked ahead. Nothing in sight but sky and water.

"When we see it, we're close enough," Johann said.

"Close enough for what?" Abe asked.

Johann chuckled. "Close enough to see it."

Abe rolled his eyes and Winona let out a single courtesy laugh.

Johann sat, a smile on his face, running his fingers through his beard.

"What do we do once we get there?" Abe asked.

"Do whatever we can to seem nonthreatening and nonviolent," Johann said. "From the moment we step onto their land, even if we can't see them."

"How do we do that?" Winona asked.

"Make sure our hands are empty," Rosa said. "And visible at all times. Make every movement slow, no matter how peaceful of a movement you think it is."

Abe stretched a hand out to Winona. She grasped his hand, and the two pulled themselves together. The edges of their vehicles merged together and became one large dish. They slid together, and Winona put her head on Abe's shoulder. He rested his head on hers.

He glanced back into the water, expecting some large sea monster to break the still surface. No such creature appeared. They continued on, uneventfully, for hours.

The daylight faded, and moon and stars rose into the sky. Braids sang, and the nanotech plates converged into one large disc. Mohawk took over with another string of notes, and a dome covered the group's nanotech bowl as they floated over the deep, vast ocean.

"Kind of like we're back on the ship," Winona said.

"But out in space, we knew there wasn't anything living out there that could attack us."

"We didn't know that for sure," Winona retorted. "There could be creatures that exist without oxygen or gravity, waiting in the depths of space for some carbon-based life-form to stumble into its web for it to devour whole."

Abe sat up straight, looked her in the eyes and laughed.

She met his gaze, remaining completely serious.

Abe stopped laughing. "You think so?"

"Why the hell not?" Rosa asked. "Aleron's shadow exists. Alive and interactive in the Fourth. Yeah, maybe a creature like that existing is improbable. But with the knowledge we've gained recently, its existence is a little more probable now."

Abe shook his head. She wasn't wrong, but the idea of something worse than Aleron's shadow living out in the universe wasn't one he wanted to consider.

"Yeah, Abe," Johann said. "Sometimes not knowing is not fearing."

"And sometimes not knowing will get you killed," Rosa said.

Abe dropped onto his back and closed his eyes. He didn't know what was going to happen when they got to Crawler land, and was filled with fear because of that lack of knowledge. It seemed to him that Rosa might be right.

One of the Singers began a slow, lulling melody and Abe disappeared into a land of fear-fueled dreams.

Chapter 43

To keep the waiting from driving him crazy, Smith had gathered a group together to put their ideas of mercy, justice and the political future for humanity on Aethera to paper. After hours of discussion, Smith knew two things. First, everyone agreed that creating a society with a central focus on kindness and mercy would have a positive impact on the lives of future generations. Second, nearly every person drew the line between mercy and justice in different positions.

All agreed that first-time offenders of small crimes, such as petty theft, deserved the utmost mercy. Particularly if that person was poor and struggling to eat, which had sent them on a long tangent of discussion on how to avoid financial class differences so that no one would feel the need to steal in order to survive. They decided to put that discussion off until another day, though it was something Smith wanted to revisit. He thought of the young single mom he had helped on Earth, and wondered how much better her life might have been had she been provided with the same opportunity he had. Was that even possible?

"We need some sort of line," a man was saying. "That, if crossed, the mercy rule doesn't apply."

"But doesn't that defeat the purpose?" another responded.

"It might," Smith said. "Because the mercy rule, as you called it, essentially means that the offended person is given the opportunity to pass sentence on the offender. Are we agreed on that?"

Everyone agreed, and Theresa spoke into a cube she held in her palm. The definition of the Mercy Rule floated in the air.

"I'm still not sure how allowing the person that has been hurt to pass judgment encourages mercy," a woman said.

"I think it's about setting a system up that encourages us to always see each other as people," an older woman said. "When I was in my twenties on Earth, I was robbed on the street. Guy pulled a gun on me. Gave him everything I had. Told the police, they found him and arrested him. I was young and I was pissed, and told them to charge him with as high of a crime as possible. They did, and he ended up in prison for six years."

She paused, took a breath.

"I found out later it was a fake gun, and that he had a wife and five kids. Two of them had cancer. One died while he was in jail. He was just trying to pay the medical bills.

"He committed a crime, and deserved punishment. But not that. If I had met him, had known why he did it, I would've offered mercy."

No one spoke for a few minutes.

"And do you think," Smith said quietly, "if he met you, saw you humanized, it might've kept him from doing it again?"

"Maybe." She shrugged. "I would've been willing to. But I don't think every victim would be like victims of rape or violent assault."

"Yeah, and those people would be less likely to offer mercy."

"Which is more than reasonable. The more severe the crime, the less opportunity for mercy."

"But how do we decide?"

"A meditator," Smith said. "A judge."

The group voiced their agreement.

"I think that's two more items to put down, Theresa," Smith said.

"The offended and offender will meet, and learn about the other's lives," she said. "And a mediator must be present."

"Everyone?" Smith said.

"Yes, but what if they don't want to meet?" a voice asked. "We can't force a wife to sit down with her husband's murderer."

"Okay." Theresa nodded. "Let's add that if the offended party is willing, they will meet."

"And the offended will choose a punishment for the offender," a man said as he stood and stretched. "With the guidance of the mediator."

"Right," Smith nodded.

Theresa spoke the words into the cube. Smith looked around the room and smiled. It felt good to plan for the future, to feel that humans had a future on Aethera.

"Now, my other concern," he said. "Is how do we let this system of law soak into our culture? Let mercy be the guiding factor in how people treat each other?"

"What do you mean?"

"When it comes to things that aren't crimes," he said. "A man yells at another man, shouts profanities, calls his manhood into question. If mercy is a part of our culture, the offended man won't react violently. It won't even turn into a situation where the law needs to get involved."

"But now we're talking an ideal society," someone said.

"Just more ideal than Earth," another responded. "Wasn't that the point of leaving?"

"We can cultivate that within our culture," Theresa said, setting the cube down. "But it would have to start with us. We set the example. The first generation on Aethera. And then educators teach it from an early age. Parents, too."

"It starts with us," Smith said.

The group agreed, but none left. They talked into the night. About mercy, about justice. How those ideals would hold up when it came to interactions between the three species that called Aethera home. Which brought up questions of foreign policy, of patriotism, of whether nations and nationality would be determined by species or location.

And on they went, the conversation taking them where it may. Eventually, exhaustion took over the group. Smith made his way to one of the white benches, and dropped onto his side.

Just before his eyes closed, something skittered across the floor. He jumped to his feet.

"Stop moving," he called.

Everyone stood still, staring at him. He moved quickly to another white bench, got down on his hands and knee, and stared at something he hoped to never see again: a biotech beetle.

"Does anyone else see that?" he asked frantically.

He needed to know if it was real or if, somehow, a new beetle had bored into his brain. Minow jogged quickly to his side and peered under the bench.

"Is that one of the biotech beetles?" she asked.

"It's real." He sighed, but then his mind caught up with his words. "No, no. Damn it. Not good. Where are the Singers? A Singer?"

"Singers!" Yeance's voice called.

A side door swung open, the three remaining Singers sped into the room and encircled the bench. They dropped onto their stomachs, bodies prone, eyes emotionless as they faced one of the creatures that nearly destroyed their entire species.

Each let out a different strand of notes. One lamenting, one fearful, one a mixture of anger and confusion.

For the first time, it seemed, Crawler tech had made it into the caves. Smith caught the beetle in his hand, threw it as hard as he could into the ground, and stomped on it. The humans stood by silently, the Singers continuing their chorus.

Was the waiting game over? Was this the start of a Crawler invasion?

Chapter 44

Sleep evaded Tashon. He sat, legs crossed, back straight, focusing on his breathing. Focused on keeping himself off-center, on noticing the differences between his view from the Third and his view from the Fourth.

In the Third, his friends surrounded him, sleeping in the soft-blue light of the flying smokie dome. In the Fourth, he saw himself and his friends all sitting within the dome. But he could also see outside the dome, knew that they were all small creatures in a much wider universe. Knew that, even though the journey they took was of great significance to their short lives, they were all merely atoms within the infinite span of existence.

"But nothing exists without atoms," he whispered to himself. "We are all minuscule yet crucial. At once significant and insignificant."

He smiled, breathed in, breathed out. He didn't matter, yet he did. A dichotomy that, Tashon felt, must have always existed. Was a key part of being alive within the universe. That understanding calmed him, centered him in way he had never known, never dreamed of. He spent the remaining hours of the night floating between dimensions, hovering between his nothingness and his importance.

The smokie dome parted as the sun began its climb into the sky. And on the horizon was the land of the Crawlers. Tashon stretched and looked at the others.

"Think we'll be there before nightfall," Johann said.

"Yeah," Rosa agreed. "We all ready for that?"

Abe laughed nervously. "Sure."

"I am," Tashon said. "But I wish Ballas was with us."

"He'd be a big help with first contact," Winona responded. "But I think we'll be okay."

"I think so too," Abe said, in a less convincing tone.

Tashon looked at the Crawler pillars reaching out of the water, grasping for the sky. The visions of his friends being ripped apart in the tunnels flashed through his mind.

"Tash, you seen anything that will help us when we get there?" Rosa asked.

Tashon turned to face her, and paused to consider all he'd seen.

"Nothing you don't already know," he said.

"Are you sure?" Abe asked.

"Yes, Abe. Positive."

Minute by minute, hour by hour, they closed in on their destination. Neared the end of their journey. The group, even the Singers, were quiet for most of the day. There was an occasional attempt at humor to lighten the mood. A note or two of encouragement from one of the Singers. None of it seemed to calm anyone's nerves.

Hours passed. Clouds darkened the sky. The wind picked up speed, the soft bumps in the ocean turning to waves that splashed Tashon's face. Lightning flashed across the sky, immediately followed by rumbling thunder. Icy rain fell from the sky. The dome closed over the bowl yet again, leaving everyone but Tashon blind to what was going on outside.

The dome jerked left, right, down. A wave slammed into it and the whole vessel turned upright, crumpling everyone to the same side. Braids sang, and the vessel angled downward.

"Tashon, what the hell is going on out there?" Johann said.

Tashon closed his eyes, pulling himself higher. Their vessel dodged waves, swerving up and down, side to side. Its passengers tossed back and forth, their bodies slamming into each other.

The wind grew stronger still, shaking their nanotech container. A wave slammed into it, and it flipped into a barrel roll.

"We need to go higher," Rosa yelled.

"No," Johann shouted back. "Too high and the Crawlers will see us. Need to go in low."

Braids sang a few succinct notes, and the smokie dome leaned forward.

"Tashon, what's happening?" Abe asked.

Tashon watched calmly from above as they shot over the ocean.

"We're going into the water," he nodded.

He felt the group tense as he said it, but the calm from meditating was still with him. No fear about submerging beneath the volatile waters. No concern for his life, or for the life of those around him. He didn't know if that peace was a premonition of their safety or not.

"Don't worry," he said quietly. "We'll make it."

They slowed, their transport shuddering as it pierced the water's surface. For a few moments they bobbed up and down, then all went still.

"Can you see us?" Rosa looked to Tashon.

"No. I can't see beneath the surface."

"It's so quiet," Winona said.

"We must be deep for the water to be so calm," Johann said.

"How deep?" Abe asked.

Johann shrugged.

"Must be a lot of water pressure on top of us," Winona said.

Abe shot her a firm look, and then smiled. "Thanks for that thought."

But Tashon could tell they were all still nervous.

"We'll be okay," he reaffirmed. "I'm not worried about it."

And he was telling the truth. He wasn't, in any way, worried for their lives. The group nodded or said okay, then went silent. Another hour of silence, then both Singers let out an identical, elongated note. Their meaning resonated through the air, and it was unmistakable: get ready.

Tashon focused again on his view from the Fourth. Above them, the storm still raged. They neared a beach, and the smokie dome tilted up, gaining speed to break out of the water. But as soon as it met air, a mountain of a wave crashed into it. Everyone inside flipped, rolled and screamed.

Tashon's head cracked against a corner of Braids' metal pack. A warm trickle of blood slid down his cheek, and everything went black.

***

He awoke on cool sand, warm sun shining on his face. He smiled and sat up, opening his eyes.

The beach that he had seen in vision spread out before him, the three caves and single canyon identical to how he remembered them. He looked around, and saw no one else on the beach with him. A group of footprints trailed through the wet sand into one of the caves.

"No," he whispered, a bit of the calm he'd felt fleeing his mind.

"Hello," he called. "Rosa? Abe?"

"Tashon." Rosa's voice came from behind.

He turned. "Rosa. Where is everyone?"

"Wait." She knelt down next to him. "How's your head?"

"It feels fine. Where're the others?"

"Johann thought they should get going as quickly as possible. They left just before sunrise."

Tashon looked again at the footprints leading into the cave.

"Are those their footprints?" he asked, pointing.

"Yeah," she nodded. "We can—"

"Shit," he whispered, then got louder. "Shit, shit. Why did they go through a cave?" His heart rate increased, and all of the peace that had been with him fled his body.

"More cover," she said, confused by his question.

"No." He shook his head. "You all knew the canyon is the safest route! Why the hell?"

"What? That doesn't make sense."

"But she showed us," he shouted. "There are biotech creatures in the caves that will kill us."

Rosa's eyebrows shot up.

Tashon stood, and realization dawned. He'd made the same mistake he had before. The others didn't know the canyon was the safest route.

"Shit!" He kicked at the sand. "Damn it!"

"You saw that in a vision, Tash?"

He nodded, expecting her to ask why he didn't tell them, but it seemed she understood. Would this affect her faith in him?

"How long ago did they leave?"

"An hour, maybe a little longer."

"Let's go. Maybe we can catch up with them."

He ran to the cave, Rosa right behind him. Soon, they were swallowed in darkness. Rosa flicked on a flashlight. They move as fast as they could, doing their best to avoid injury.

"Do you think you could get there quicker through the Fourth?"

Tashon considered the idea, looked at the view from above. The higher vision showed the mountains through which they walked. The rocks were vaguely transparent, giving him a blurry view of Rosa and himself walking through the tunnels. His head spun at the thought of returning to the Fourth, but he didn't think it would help, anyway.

He shook his head. "No. When I come back out, I think it would drop me on top of the mountain."

"Right. Faster, then."

They sped up as much as they dared and wound back and forth silently, deeper into the mountain.

Chapter 45

Abe jumped every time a shadow moved, his mind convinced that Aleron's shadow had found sanctuary within the darkness of the caves. He knew it was more likely they would come across a Crawler or one of their biotech monsters, but his mind refused to separate the darkness from his memories of Aleron. With a deep breath, he reached out and squeezed Winona's hand.

The two walked side by side behind Mohawk, his hands aglow with blue light. Next to the Singer was Johann, a knife in each hand. Braids brought up the rear, her hand lights casting shadows at every step.

If they spoke, it was in whispers. Anything louder echoed off the tunnel walls, and they wanted their presence hidden for as long as possible.

Abe had grown so used to keeping track of time by the movement of the sun that he had no idea how long they traversed the tunnels. He tried counting their steps, but kept losing track. Then he tried numbering each turn they made. Even that number grew too high to manage.

They arrived at a split in the tunnel. To the right, the path curved gently away from them. On the left, it went straight for as far as they could see.

Johann pointed to each tunnel, then shrugged at Abe and Winona.

Abe walked to Johann's side. "The straight one?" he whispered.

They looked at the Singers. Abe wondered if they could feel the meaning behind his words when they didn't understand the words spoken. Braids and Mohawk stared at one another, no audible or visible communication passing between them.

Mohawk turned to the straight tunnel and stepped beneath its arch. The rest fell in line behind him, walking single file down the narrower path. They walked for what felt to Abe like another thirty minutes. An ear-piercing scratch bounced off the walls from farther down.

Startled, Abe jumped, heart pounding. Winona and Johann swore. Mohawk squeaked one high note while Braids let out a deep moan. The scratching got closer, louder and faster. Tiny dots appeared in the dark distance. Simultaneously, Braids and Mohawk sang a note Abe knew well.

"Run," he said.

The group stopped, turned and sprinted back up the tunnel. The skittering, scraping sound was close, and almost deafening. Abe whipped his head back to get a picture of what was chasing them. Centipede-like creatures scurried on hundreds of pinpoint legs along the walls, the ceiling and the floor. Most were the length of his forearm while others were over six feet long.

As he turned back, his foot caught on a stone and he smacked flat onto the ground. The air burst from his lungs. A centipede clawed up his arm, onto his back, each leg a needle pricking his skin. Mohawk ripped the creature off, wrapped an arm around Abe's waist, picked him up and dropped him onto his feet. On they ran.

The centipede creatures surrounded them as they burst into the cavern where the path had forked. Hundreds of the writhing creatures blocked each of the three tunnels, and they were closing in on them, crawling up their legs and falling from the ceiling onto their heads and shoulders. They shouted as they ripped piercing legs off their bodies and threw them into the walls.

Johann grabbed a five-foot creature and whipped it around, its thick body cracking the smaller creatures' mechanical shells, rendering them motionless. But there were too many of them, and soon Abe's body was covered with the slithering things. His skin was on fire with the hundreds of pin-sized holes from their legs. As he fell to his knees, he looked around and saw the others collapsing. Saw Winona, a creature covering her mouth, tears falling from her terrified eyes.

The stone wall behind her exploded in smoke, dust and rubble. Centipedes jumped off their bodies, dispersing to the edges of the cavern, but did not leave completely. Large forms emerged from the dust.

Crawlers. Five of them. Up close, they were more terrifying and more beautiful than they had seemed onscreen. Just under the skin of their pale, ovoid legs were thin pink veins in symmetrical patterns. Each crawler had a different design, and Abe thought if he was given time with the Crawlers, he'd be able to tell them apart by the layout of their veins. Their egg-like heads were identical, as were the wiry arms that reached out from under their chins.

The one in the front made a clicking, coughing sound and the biotech creatures crawled into the shadows. Abe slowly rose to his feet, sweat soaking through his clothes, heart in his throat. When the Crawlers didn't respond to his movement, the others stood. Abe looked to Winona, tears still rolling gently down her cheeks.

The Crawler whose veins spread out in concentric symmetry walked carefully toward Winona. It stopped a few steps in front of her and clicked softly. It lifted one of its thin arms. The appendage elongated, the fingers stretching out until they reached Winona's face. One finger uncurled, caught a tear, and wiped it from her cheek.

Braids sang a long line of confused notes, and uncertainty settled over the group. Where was the violence? Abe had hoped for a calm first interaction, but was expecting a fight.

The Crawler in front of Winona gingerly grabbed her hand. The other Crawlers followed, one grabbing Abe's hand, another taking hold of Johann's. Another reached out for Braids's hand, but she quickly stepped back and screeched four notes. The Crawler stopped, clicked at its companions and stepped back. The last Crawler didn't attempt to hold Mohawk's hand.

Slowly, as if not wanting to alarm anyone, the Crawlers turned, gently guiding the humans and Singers into the newly opened tunnel.

"Should we really go with them?" Abe whispered.

Winona sniffed, nodded. "I think they came to save us from the biotech creatures," she said.

"Okay," Abe said.

They stepped into the tunnel, the Crawlers leading the way. The Singers followed at a distance, Braids singing a melody of warning: if the Crawlers attempted violence, she would retaliate.

Chapter 46

Smith walked into a Singer cavern he'd never seen, searching for holes or cracks in the rock. Anything the beetle could have used to get into the caves. So far, they'd found nothing. Most likely it had gotten in on one of the humans, or in their supplies.

Which meant it was possible one or more had already lodged into the brains of Smith's fellow humans. He returned to the main cavern.

Possible weapons were laid out. Some were obvious, like knives and Security guns. But the guns were designed to fire low velocity bullets, powerful enough to harm a human but soft enough to not damage the hull of the ship. It was likely they would be ineffective against the Crawlers and their biotech. Near those were the less obvious weapons: shovels, pipes and electrical wire braided into whips.

All primitive forms of weapons compared to the high tech arsenal controlled by the Crawlers. They had the smokies, too. But Smith was convinced that tech created by a pacifist species wouldn't have a chance against that made by the Crawlers.

"How does this work into our culture of mercy?" Theresa asked as she joined Smith.

"We can be merciful but still take care of our own," Smith said. "And I've been thinking. The Singers aren't a united front. They're not all on the same page."

"You think it's the same with the Crawlers?" Theresa asked, raising her eyebrows.

"Why not?" Smith answered. "It makes sense to me that an intelligent species would have individuality."

"What about a hive mind?"

Smith shrugged. "It's possible."

"Ballas should have a better idea if that's likely with the Crawlers," she said.

"Yeah. He's still not awake though." Smith looked down at their meager items of defense.

Minow walked into the room, the three Singers directly behind her.

Smith inhaled nervously. No one was sure how the Singers would react to the weapons.

The Singers stopped a few feet short of them as Minow joined Smith and Theresa. Scar inhaled audibly and slowly sang a sentence or phrase, pausing between each note as if ensuring the humans understood.

Smith felt nervous, then grateful, but also wary, a bit frightened and antisocial. And, lastly, he felt an extreme sense of blessedness and gratitude. He understood Scar's meaning, and he translated it as, "We don't like seeing weapons here. We are indebted and grateful for your help. But please remember we will have no part in the violence. Your presence and aid is a blessing, and we thank you again for your aid."

All three Singers walked away, and Smith felt they might not show themselves again until the ordeal was over.

"I still hate that they're doing nothing," Theresa said.

"Yeah." Smith nodded, finding it hard not to feel taken advantage of.

"But they're not doing nothing," Minow said, her voice straining to stay calm. "They're letting all of us, an alien species with weapons, stay in their home. They might not be actively prepping for a fight, but they're not doing nothing."

"That's a good point," Smith said.

"We could lose our lives," Theresa said.

"So could they," Minow shot back. "Besides, we're not attacking the Crawlers. We're just prepping in case they attack us."

"We'll be in the front lines, and they'll be hiding." Theresa shook her head. "I know. We'd fight the Crawlers either way if they attack, with or without the Singers. It's just... I don't know."

"You still don't trust them?" Smith asked.

"I'm... unsure of them. I'm trying to understand their strict pacifism, but it makes no sense to me." She shook her head.

"At least you're trying to understand," Minow said, and walked away with a smile.

"I wish I were still on the ship," Theresa whispered.

Smith looked at her, not surprised she had said it, but still not understanding why. They were on a new trail of human experience, facing the unprecedented on a virtually daily basis. Yes, they'd lost far more than Smith could count. But with everything around them, how could she want to be back in space, stuck inside the ship?

Theresa laughed. "You're looking at me like I'm crazy."

Smith shrugged and wiggled his head back and forth.

"I know we're seeing and doing things that no one else has done. I get that." She inhaled deeply, and then exhaled loudly. "But of all my years on the ship, I never once felt unsafe. I never didn't understand what was happening. It was my home, and I was comfortable there. I was going to live the rest of my life there. The idea that I wouldn't never even crossed my mind."

Smith smiled softly and nodded. He hadn't thought of it that way. He had made the choice to leave the ship, to make Aethera his new home. But Theresa, and all the others who had been on the ship, were forced onto the planet. They lost their home. Maybe, when it came down to it, that's what had been bothering Theresa all along.

"Maybe this can feel like home," Smith said. "One day."

"Let's survive whatever's coming, first." She forced a smile. "Before we start laying roots."

"We started laying roots the moment we got here. Just don't know what those roots will grow into."

Yeance, an engineer by his side, ran into the room. The engineer smiled and said he had good news.

"What is it?" Smith asked, trying not to get too excited. Good news was always subjective.

"Here." The engineer pulled a Security gun from his belt. "We've enhanced them."

"Wait," Yeance said. "Don't test it in here."

They walked quickly through the halls and stepped out to find snow covering the yellow forest. It had only been a few days since any of them had ventured outside, but the difference was jarring. Clouds escaped their mouths as they breathed, and Smith relished the serene beauty of untouched snow amid towering trees. He knew all too well that the serenity could soon be torn apart by battle. The engineer lifted the small pistol with one hand and pointed it at a boulder thirty yards away.

He pulled the trigger. The gun clicked, puffed and a red pebble shot toward the boulder. It made contact with a loud crack and a small puff of dust, leaving a hole in the boulder's surface. Yeance and the engineer smiled at Smith and Theresa.

"Check it out." The engineer nodded to the boulder.

Smith walked to the boulder. The hole was as wide as his thumb and at least three inches deep.

"How?" Smith asked.

"I adjusted the power settings," the engineer said. "And one of the Singers showed us boxes of polished red pebbles that are a bit smaller than our bullets."

"A Singer showed you?" Theresa asked with skepticism in her voice.

Yeance nodded. "Yes. Either they didn't feel it broke their pact, or they didn't care."

Smith held his hand out for the gun and the engineer handed it over.

"How did you increase the power?" Smith asked, examining the weapon. "They were specifically designed to prevent tampering. A shot like that would have put a hole in the ship's exterior."

"I narrowed the barrel, which increases the PSI when it's fired. I was actually just trying to narrow it to fit the pebbles. I wasn't thinking about the increased pressure."

Smith nodded and returned the gun to the engineer.

"How many have you upgraded?" Theresa asked.

"Just this one," Yeance said. "We wanted to run it by you two first."

Smith and Theresa looked at each other and nodded.

"How soon can all of them be done?" Smith asked.

"Once we teach others how to do it"—the engineer clicked his tongue—"within a day."

Smith nodded. "Good."

The engineer turned to walk away, but Theresa put a hand in his shoulder.

"Will these stop the Crawlers or their biotech?" she asked, her voice tinged with fear.

"No way to know for sure," the engineer replied with a slight smile. "But our chances are better now than they were this morning."

He jogged off, leaving Smith, Theresa and Yeance to consider what the small victory might mean for the upcoming struggle.

Chapter 47

Tashon and Rosa stood in a cavern, deciding which of the three tunnels ahead of them to follow. One looked as if it had been carved out far more recently than the other two. Freshly crumbled stones were scattered at its entrance and footprints were pressed into a thin layer of dust. Human, Singer and Crawler feet. Without speaking, the two sped quickly down the jagged stone hallway.

The deeper they got, the clearer it became that the tunnel was recently carved from the rock. Dust and debris were scattered amid tools unfamiliar to Tashon. Everything about the tunnel made it feel like a rushed project. The uneven walls, the varying width and height of the walkway, the uneven floor.

Rosa broke the silence. "The footprints don't show any sign of struggle."

Tashon looked at the ground. The footprints were evenly spaced, always facing the same direction. No indication that human or Singer had felt the need to run or fight or escape. Based on everything they could see in the Third, the rest of their group had gone with the Crawlers willingly.

"Hold on," Tashon said to Rosa.

They stopped, and Tashon closed his eyes. He moved his higher vision farther down the tunnel, stretching as far as he could. With a sigh, he opened his eyes and shook his head at Rosa.

"Can't see them," he said, and they moved on.

Soon, the tunnel turned to the right and dropped down in a roughly carved staircase. Rosa shone her light down into the abyss. They could not see the bottom, and the footprints continued past the reach of the light. There was no choice but down.

Twenty steps down, and Tashon had already fallen twice, and Rosa once. The stairs were painfully uneven, some pointed up and others angled down so steeply that it was impossible to step on them without a foot slipping off.

After some more trial and error, they fell into a slow and steady pace of getting two feet on a single step before stretching down to the next one.

"They rushed this tunnel," Tashon reiterated the thought aloud.

Rosa nodded softly. "Just be careful."

Still, Tashon could not see anyone from the Fourth other than Rosa and himself. Frustration and anxiety settled over him, and the slightest headache entered his skull. He placed a hand on the wall to help keep his balance, and soon they found the bottom of the staircase.

They stood in a small cavern, a brass colored door in front of them. It was open a few inches, the sounds of voices coming through the gap.

A gravelly, unfamiliar voice spoke in clipped phrases. "We fight. With you," it said. "Fix future. Our future."

The words seemed positive to Tashon. He pushed the door open and walked into a square, brass room. The two Singers, Abe and Winona stood against a wall, each accompanied by a Crawler. Johann stood in the center, arms limp at his sides, knees bent, mouth slightly open. Inserted into the back of his head was a spiraled cord that stretched from him to the forehead of a Crawler.

Tashon tensed, clenched his fists, and moved to pounce on the creature.

"Stop!" Winona screamed, as Mohawk said the same with a quick note.

Confused yet obedient, Tashon held still but remained ready to attack if needed.

"It's learning our language," Abe said. "Watch."

Johann's mouth moved, but it wasn't his voice that came out.

"Sorry," the gravelly voice said. "Fear. I know. Pro-proc-processing words. Human. Human words. Hold."

Tashon and Rosa glanced at each other, and then back at Johann. It wasn't anything close to what Tashon had expected. Murder. Capture. Death by terrifying biotech. Definitely not an attempt at communication and understanding. And the fact that they hadn't been ripped to shreds in the tunnels made him question everything the Singers in the Fourth had shown him. Had their entire journey been for nothing? Had Ballas lost a leg for no reason?

He pushed the thoughts aside for the moment, focusing on Johann and the Crawler connected to him. With a click and a puff of air, the cable detached from Johann's head, retracting back into the Crawler's skull.

Johann straightened his posture, blinked his eyes vigorously, and looked at the Crawler.

"Can you understand me?" he asked.

The Crawler clicked its tongue and twitched its head side to side. "Hear you. I explain now."

The Crawler paused, and Tashon couldn't tell whether it was looking for the words to say or waiting for a response.

"Explain what?" Johann asked.

"All," the Crawler responded. "Why here. Why we save you. All. Explain all."

Through chopped phrases and sentences, the Crawler explained what had been going on in its nation. After many questions and answers, misunderstandings and clarifications, the recent history of the Crawler species became clear.

They were a nation torn by civil war, the roots of which were laid the day the Crawler leaders ordered the Singer genocide. Protests and riots rocked the society when the civilians learned what their biotech had been used for. Yet others praised the preemptive actions, claiming it was better to kill the Singers upfront than allow the Singers to mount a greater attack.

For a time, fights were fought, battles won and lost as different parties vied for power. And when no Singers emerged from the mountains, the Crawlers were convinced that the genocide had been successful. Which led to more outrage and riots until the leaders promised to stay their hands in the future.

"And the citizens believed the promise of the leaders?" Johann asked skeptically.

"Promises important," the Crawler said. "Then humans come."

More parsed sentences. As soon as the Crawlers knew of the human presence, their leaders showed they had no intention of keeping their promise. With fear-inducing rhetoric, they convinced many that the humans were a threat that needed to be dealt with. They rallied together a large portion of the population to prepare for an attack.

But not all were convinced. The Crawlers in front of them, along with roughly forty percent of the species, had been fighting those in power to keep them from killing yet another species. They destroyed biotech factories and sent in spies to alter the internal compasses of the engineered creatures so that they would end up somewhere far from the humans.

Crawlers had died to protect human life.

Tashon shook his head. He was glad they had the support of so many Crawlers, but was still confused that what the higher Singer had shown him proved to be false. He had assumed that because she was a being of the fourth dimension, of that Heaven-like plane, that she was something akin to a guardian angel. And maybe, in a way, she was. She was right that the Crawlers were mounting an attack. But not all of the Crawlers were. The danger was real, but it was not the threat of an entire species seeking to destroy all human and Singer life. The Crawlers were individuals. *Maybe his guardian Singer still held biases from her life in the Third,* Tashon thought. *Biases that would not let her see the good in the Crawlers. Perhaps being in the Fourth did not make one perfect or infallible.*

Braids stepped forward and let out a string of confused yet thankful notes. Tashon felt the same way. He still didn't completely understand the Crawlers defending human and Singer life so intensely. But he was grateful for it nonetheless.

In response to the Singer's confusion, the Crawler next to her walked forward and turned so that the two were face-to-face. The Crawler bent one of its skinny arms backward and reached into a small pouch between its neck and back legs. Carefully, it produced a small rectangular object. It looked old and faded. As the Crawler held it out to Braids, Tashon recognized what it was: a book.

Chapter 48

Abe stared in disbelief. In its small, spindly hands, the Crawler held the same book Mohawk had sang from that night on top of the rock. Mohawk and Braids both made a sound like a melodious gasp. They were just as shocked as Abe was.

"Holy shit," Rosa whispered.

"We found Singer words," the Crawler with the book said. "Beautiful words. Peaceful people Singers. Not danger. Not scary. Protect Singer. Protect human."

Braids sang the most uneven notes Abe had heard come from any Singer. But despite its wavering tone, it was also the most piercing. It filled Abe with a deep sense of relief and happiness. Emotions he would have felt on his own because of the unexpected aid of the Crawlers. But the addition of Braids's musical emoting nearly brought him to tears. Braids, Mohawk, even Abe. They had all been so wrong about the Crawlers, and hadn't even considered that some of them would be willing to sacrifice themselves to protect the other two species. Had thought of them more as wild, violent animals than as an intelligent species with the ability to see wrong among themselves and then act to right it.

"Thank you," Abe said, and his companions echoed the sentiment.

After a minute of silence, a chirping click echoed from above them.

"Come," the Crawler by Johann said.

It walked to the brass door, tapped it in what seemed like a random patter, and the entire room shook and trembled. When it went still, the Crawler pushed the door open to reveal that they were no longer at the bottom of the roughly carved stairs. Instead, they walked through the door into blinding sunlight.

Abe squinted and blinked against the brightness, his eyes slowly adjusting until he realized where he stood. He stopped and stared. They stood at the bottom of a massive crater. Its steep, sand-colored walls went thousands of feet above them, the concave surface a mile wide.

Hundreds of Crawlers bustled around, various unknown items held in their hands. Metal spheres surrounded by sharp red leaves. Wood shovels with shafts that moved like snakes. Flat discs with carved eggs on the top and bottom. Abe didn't know for sure, but something told him most of them were weapons.

Among the four-legged crowd were dozens of biotech animals, each its own unique creation. A thin, oval creature made of shining blue metal and pink flesh hovered a few feet off the ground, trailing a long tail of white mist. A hairless rabbit that looked like it was stuffed in a turtle shell scurried to a Crawler, climbed up its leg, and handed him a metal cylinder. Abe looked around and saw that each specimen of biotech was actively performing a specific function. Various creatures scampered across the ground delivering tools and objects to Crawlers. Others sat on Crawlers' shoulders, sticking pieces of food in their mouths so that the Crawlers' hands were free to work. And the ones that flew around—flat discs to armadillos with butterfly wings—seemed to patrol the air, flying back and forth between the crater's top edge and the surface.

The Crawler that led them walked forward, the crowd parting to let the humans and Singers through. Not one of the Crawlers seemed angry or violent toward them. Abe and the others followed, each still with a Crawler by their side. They stopped at a wide, metal cylinder sunk into the ground.

To the left was a large cylinder, the bottom half sunk into a hole and surrounded by muddy water. It was made from two distinctly different materials, alternating in a pattern not unlike a pie. Dull metal was split apart by a dark brown substance that had constant ripples running along it. The Crawler that had been connected to Johann walked to the edge of the hole, crouched, and dipped a single finger in the water. It stood again, closed its eyes, and the braided cable extended out of its forehead, connecting to a divot in the top of the cylinder.

The brown sections expanded, producing thick vines that twisted out then down into the water. A soft vibration spread outward, with the cylinder the epicenter. Abe turned to see the crowd of Crawlers stop and look at the ground. Each extended the same cable from their foreheads as thick vines pushed out of the ground. Vines connected to cables, and every Crawler went slack, as if deep in relaxed meditation.

Abe looked at his companions, dumbfounded. He was still wrapping his mind around the idea that these Crawlers were fighting to save them. And he wasn't sure he completely believed it, either. But what else could he have done? At least he was still alive, still seeing new parts of Aethera. With a smile, he looked at Winona, who stood a few feet away from him. He wanted to walk to her side, grab hold of her hand, but felt he shouldn't disturb the silence and stillness of the Crawlers.

He looked at the two Singers, trying to discern if they felt any fear among so many of the Crawlers. The Singers had spent years living in terror of the Crawlers that it would make sense for them to be afraid. Yet, as always, they stood still, giving no physical indication of their emotional state. No trembling hands or quivering legs.

The Crawler at the cylinder made a clicking sound and retracted its cable. Across the crater, vines and cables disconnected, and each Crawler looked up, turning their gaze toward the humans. All at once, they erupted in a chorus of various human greetings, called out in grainy voices.

"Welcome."

"Hi."

"Howdy."

"What's up?"

Abe waved a hand and, trying to sound strong, loudly shouting, "Thank you."

Rosa and Johann did the same.

Winona simply gave a smile in return.

Tashon waved silently, a mixed look of confusion and happiness on his face.

"Come, please," their Crawler guide said, his sentence flow sounding more like a human's. "Show you plans."

The crowd of Crawlers parted, continuing to call out greetings, as humans and Singer were led across the crater. Abe tried to respond to every Crawler that greeted him, but it was impossible. There were at least hundreds of the four-legged species filling the massive hole in the ground. It was overwhelming, almost suffocating, but then he thought of the excitement they must be feeling. Here were representatives from the two species they were fighting to protect. Species that most of the Crawlers had never seen in person.

Abe grabbed Winona's hand as they all followed the Crawler through a silver door pressed into the side of the crater. Rather than rough tunnels of rock, the door led into one domed, circular room ten yards across, an elliptical table at its center. The silver walls were ribbed with soft yellow lights that dimly lit the room. The Crawler walked to the table and looked at the group.

"See," it said, eyes at the table.

Johann and Tashon stood on either side of the Crawler, with Rosa next to Tashon. Abe and Winona stood opposite them, and the two Singers stood at each end.

The table was a topographical map of Aethera, with raised areas indicating elevation and indented areas indicating craters and valleys. It looked like the map was updated regularly, as the continent with the red mountains had a model of the downed Ship of Nations in the middle of the yellow forest. Across the water was the Crawler continent, along with the crater in which they stood. Northwest of that, a large city of towering pillars of rock and large metallic domes. All around it, hundreds of small-scale versions of terrifying biotech beasts.

"Here is us," the Crawler said.

Abe did not see it press any buttons, but the crater on the map lit up with a soft green glow.

"Human and Singer. Most."

The red mountains and the yellow forest glowed a gentle orange.

"Enemy," the Crawler said, voice harsher than normal. The city of domes and pillars shone a vibrant blue.

Abe looked at the map, realizing that they were closer to those the Crawlers called their enemies than they were to the ocean.

"What's the plan?" Johann asked, leaning on the table with one hand, scratching his beard and scrutinizing the map.

"Seen enemy ready weapons." Each biotech creature lit up in various colors. "Enemy attack soon."

"Attack here, or attack there?" Tashon asked, pointing at the red mountains.

The Crawler stood silently, staring at the map.

Abe took a deep breath, unsure of what answer he would prefer. His stomach churned and his heart thumped. A few hours before, he'd been prepared for a fight. Then the Crawlers welcomed them, and he had slowly calmed down, enjoying discovering the new species. But now? Now they were in the middle of a war.

"Not know," the Crawler said. "Plan, we hit first."

Abe felt Winona tense and she dug her nails into his hand. He returned the squeeze and gave her a reassuring nod.

"How?" Abe asked, a part of him worried that they would rush the enemy with no forethought.

"Follow." The Crawler turned and a section of the back wall slid up, revealing a large metal hangar, the floor stone and dirt.

A biotech sphere, over ten feet tall, covered in dirt, hung from the ceiling.

Abe looked at Winona and the two shrugged at each other.

"What is it?" she asked.

"It dig," the Crawler said.

It stopped directly under the sphere, clicked and popped its tongue and the sphere spun. Slowly at first, and as the speed increased, spikes and scoops popped out, covering it entirely.

"We're tunneling in?" Rosa said.

"Tunnel-ig?" the Crawler said.

"Go under," Abe said, pointing at the ground.

"Will the enemy hear it?" Johann asked.

"Not all under. Some over," the Crawler clicked out another rhythm and another section of the hangar lit up.

More biotech hung from the ceiling, these ones long and round, with half a dozen thin wings along each side.

"Enemy see above first. Not looking below."

Johann smiled. "A distraction."

"When?" Rosa asked.

"First dark, next light, next go." The Crawler turned and walked back toward the crater. "Come. Rest."

Chapter 49

It didn't take long for most of the Crawlers to drop to the ground and fall asleep. Tashon sat at the outskirts of the crater with the only other bipeds around. He tried to focus on the conversation, but his attention kept drifting to the Fourth, looking for the Singer who had guided them to the Crawlers. She was nowhere to be seen.

"Laos, I don't get it. It's not what she showed me."

A pause. *"Remember, she only showed you. Not me."*

Tashon nodded. Why were visions never shown to more the one person? He looked at the ground.

"Are they expecting us to fight?" Winona asked.

"I will be," Johann said.

"You have experience in war," Tashon said. "We don't."

"You fought on the ship," Rosa pointed out.

Tashon nodded and looked away, turning his mind back to Laos.

"Have you seen her?"

"No, Tashon."

"Are the beings there...." Tashon paused. *"Perfect? Like the old idea of angels?"*

"I'm not. Though I think I'm better than I was."

"Could you lie to me if you wanted to?"

"I could, yes. But I haven't."

Tashon closed his eyes and took a deep breath. The Singer could have lied to him, or could have been confused. But the core meaning of her message was accurate: the Crawlers were a threat. Just not all of them, and not in the way they had expected.

"Laos, have you changed since you've been there?"

"Yes."

"For the better?"

"I believe so."

Tashon shook his head, wondering at the structure of the Fourth. The afterlife was not the end of growth, nor the halting of progression. Did that mean that pain and trials still exist after life in the Third ended? He thought of asking Laos, but wasn't sure he wanted the answer.

"Winona, you don't have to," Johann's firm voice snatched Tashon's focus.

"I do." Winona met Johann's firm gaze. "The Crawlers are risking their lives for us. For me. And the fight could end up here, too. Safer to be with the Crawlers that are helping us."

Everyone eyed each other silently. Tashon felt the same way as Winona, though willingly going into another fight terrified him. He didn't want to face the guilt of taking another life.

Then Braids echoed Winona's desire to fight, her firm and short notes filling Tashon with the fire to enter battle and defend those who sought to protect him. Braids was planning to fight, to break her people's promise of pacifism. Mohawk remained silent. Tashon wondered why Braids was so willing to end her pact when it seemed like the others, even Mohawk, were terrified to break that promise. *Every living creature is an individual*, he thought.

"We need to make sure we get weapons from the Crawlers," Abe said. "All we have are Johann's knives and Rosa's bomb."

"I think their weapons are the biotech animals," Rosa said.

"Yeah," Abe replied. "But what about all those... things the Crawlers were holding?"

"Probably close-range weapons," Johann said. "But I think we'd all rather not be forced to use those."

As if listening to their conversation, and only pretending to be asleep, the two nearest Crawlers rose and joined them.

One of the Crawlers looked at Braids. "You don't end your peace."

Mohawk melodized the same sentiment, obviously not wanting his peer to break her pact.

She began to protest, but was cut off by the Crawler.

"We protect you. And Singer ways," it said.

The second crawler turned to Johann and Tashon.

"Humans, come," it said and turned, quickly walking away.

The humans followed, Tashon listening to the Crawler and Mohawk try to convince Braids not to fight. He hoped they succeeded. There was something beautiful about the Singers' peaceful nature, and he didn't want to see that ruined. Even if it were a single Singer.

They walked down and into a dirt pit lined with metal shelves. Objects that Tashon presumed to be weapons were haphazardly scattered everywhere. Not one of them looked like a gun or knife or any other weapon Tashon knew. *Though some of them,* he thought, *would work perfectly well to beat a Crawler to death.*

Johann and Rosa didn't hesitate, quickly digging through the shelves to find a weapon that suited them. Tashon, Abe and Winona held back. Abe and Winona seemed uncertain, but Tashon paused because he hadn't held a weapon since the fight against Aleron and his followers back on the ship. He wanted to fight with the Crawlers, but felt nauseous at the thought of carrying a weapon again.

"Want weapon?" the Crawler asked.

"I don't know where to start," Abe said.

Winona nodded.

"A simple weapon," the Crawler walked to the farthest edge of the pit and returned holding three different objects.

He held the first out with one hand. It resembled a cup, completely smooth, with a silvery stone. The Crawler pointed to the opening at the ground and tapped the bottom. A jumbled mass of sharp light shot a few feet into the ground and dissipated. He handed the weapon to Winona, who looked inside the weaponized dish.

"Looks empty," she whispered in amazement.

The next was a square plate, half metal, half plant-based, a handle on one side. Vines slithered within silver stripes. The Crawler held it up.

"Squeeze," he said, and a wave of inch-long thorns shot into the crater wall, exploding on impact.

Tashon's breathing quickened as the Crawler looked at him. He was excited to handle a piece of tech created by another species, but still feared the outcome. If only the tech wasn't meant to kill. The Crawler handed him a rectangle that was heavy in his hand and cool to the touch. It felt like some type of hardened soil, perhaps clay. He squeezed it. The front section broke off, split into hundreds of glowing specs. The bright cloud flew and spun around the nearest shelf. The entire structure collapsed, the weapons clattering to the dirt. The cloud returned to the block in Tashon's hand, rendering it whole again.

"Damn," Abe said.

Tashon nodded his agreement, amazed at the stark differences between each weapon. Humans had created lots of weapons, but they were essentially the same. Clubs. Knives. Guns. Bombs. The Crawler weapons, though, seemed as though each one was made with different logic and tech than the others. He was fascinated by the new weapons, but promised himself not to let that amazement lead him to killing.

Excited to try out the new tech, but not about the prospect of killing again. He would only kill if he absolutely needed to. And, unfortunately, he knew that the need would likely arise in the coming days.

"Go rest," the Crawler said. "Leave when light returns."

They tell me to keep the Promise
Brother and Neighbors tell me.
Did you perceive that, Mother?
Neighbors dividing, fighting to save us,
To preserve our ways?
If you did and told us,
We would have called you mad.
Sung liar.
So, Mother, perhaps you did perceive and kept it from us,
Knowing we would not believe
such a change to befall Neighbors.
I left, willing and wanting to break the Promise.
But will I? Should I?
Does it matter? That, I don't know.
Mother, your words matter, it seems.
Your words that changed these Neighbors.
Your words that, perhaps, will save us all.
But will words always hold such sway?
That, Mother, I greatly doubt.

Chapter 50

Screams of terror echoed off the walls of the red caverns, pulling Smith from his dreams. He stumbled to his feet, following the sound as quickly as he could, wiping the sleep from his eyes. Down a narrow tunnel, through a door. The screaming intensified. The grogginess wore off as Smith quickened his pace, realizing the sound was coming from the main cavern. One more tunnel and another door to go.

He hoped it wasn't a full-scale Crawler invasion.

No, it wasn't, he was sure. It was only one voice screaming. A woman. He burst into the main cavern to find Theresa on her knees, one hand on a white bench. Her head hung forward, the screams quieting down, turning into heaving sobs. Minow stood at her side, a supportive hand on Theresa's shoulder. A few others stood farther away, concern and confusion on their faces.

Smith walked slowly to the two women and knelt next to Theresa. She lifted her eyes and attempted a smile, her face wet with tears and snot. With a deep breath, Smith smiled back, and waited for her to tell him what was going on.

He waited patiently, hoping it was nothing serious. The two may have had their disagreements, but he hated seeing her that way. Would hate seeing any of them that way. Then she turned her head, and Smith noticed the thin line of dried blood running from her ear down to her neck.

After a few minutes, her tears were done and she moved to the bench. Smith sat by her side.

"There were hundreds," she said quietly. "Big, small. Everywhere."

Smith shook his head, trying to process what this all meant.

"Hundreds of what?" Minow asked, sitting on Theresa's other side.

Smith knew the answer, but remained silent, hoping he was wrong.

"Biotech beetles," she said.

Smith's stomach churned, and his heart sank.

"Does that mean...?" Theresa trailed off as if she didn't want to ask.

"Let me see," Smith said as kindly as he could.

He gently placed a hand on the top of her head and turned it so he could see the back. And right where he feared it would be, under her skin at the crown of her head, a lump moved back and forth.

He turned her eyes to face his.

"There's one in there," he said. "But we can get it out. Come on."

She choked on a fresh sob, but nodded and shakily rose to her feet. Minow wrapped an arm around Theresa and the three walked slowly to the exit that led out to the yellow forest. Smith thought back to when the beetle was in his head, when the hallucinations and the moving of an insect inside his mind nearly drove him insane. How the tree had pulled him into a dream, into a nightmare. He'd thought often about that day. The tree and the smokie both played rolls in setting his mind free, but if he hadn't seen through the lie of the dream, he could have been lost in it for days or months or years.

He turned to explain it to Theresa. Before he could, she gasped and jumped back, staring at the ground. In reality, there was nothing there, though Smith knew that to Theresa's eyes, the way must be blocked.

"Theresa," he said, placing a hand on her shoulder, "it's not real, okay?"

She nodded but remained frozen.

"What is it?" Minow asked.

"A beetle," Theresa said, her face pale and sweating. "Big. Eating another one."

Minow stepped in front of Theresa.

"Here?" she asked, pointing at the ground.

Theresa nodded.

Minow stepped back, pulled her foot back, and kicked the empty space as hard as she could.

"Now?"

"Still there."

"Damn it," Minow said.

"I know it's not there," Theresa said, taking a cautious step forward.

Her foot found purchase on solid ground and she let out a relieved sigh.

"Keep going," she told herself, walking slowly forward.

Smith and Winona exchanged worries looks and continued toward the door. Theresa made it the rest of the way without stopping or speaking. Either she didn't see any more beetles or she was hiding her hallucinations well.

They reached the door, opened it and stepped into a cloudless twilight sky. Their feet crunched on icy snow as they walked to the nearest tree. Theresa stopped and looked at Smith.

"Are you sure this will work?"

"It did for me." Smith smiled thinly. "But I'm the only one who's had to try it."

Theresa nodded and sat down with her back against the tree. A smokie emerged from the trees and sat next to her.

"Okay, it's going to feel like a dream." Smith paused. "Or, for me, it did. The tree will help pull you into it, and the smokie will help get the beetle out. But you need to know that it's a dream. The tree, the smokie won't do it all for you."

Theresa nodded and leaned her head back. It sunk a few inches into the tree. She closed her eyes and was soon asleep.

"Is this really how you got yours out?" Minow asked.

Smith nodded. "You stay with her," he said. "I need to check on something else."

She nodded. "Okay. Bring a coat when you come back."

"Sure," Smith said as he ran back into the caves and down the hall.

He didn't tell Minow what he was checking on because he didn't want to scare her without need. There were now two confirmed Crawler beetles in the caves. The one Smith had killed, and now the one in Theresa's skull. Smith was afraid there were more, hiding in dark corners and human heads.

His heart pounded as he took gasping breaths. The last time he had run this fast was when they faced Aleron's monster.

Shouts rang from the cavern and into the hall. Smith moved his legs as fast as he could, which wasn't much faster than he was already going. He slid to a stop in the cavern.

Six bodies lay motionless on the floor. Each had a line of blood running out of one ear.

Chapter 51

Despite the Crawler's suggestion that they rest, Abe and Winona sat at the edge of the crater by themselves. Abe—more than ever—was facing crushing doubt.

"Nothing makes sense," he told Winona, staring at the ground. "I came because I wanted to help the Singers. I kept going because of what Tashon saw in the Fourth. But what he saw... it—"

"It's not what we found," Winona said, finishing his thought. "I know."

"And now, we're rushing into a civil war that we know nothing about. What if it has nothing to do with us or the Singers?"

"You don't trust these Crawlers?"

"Have they given us reason to?"

"They did save our lives," she said with a smile.

Abe shrugged. If anything was a sign of trustworthiness, that would be a big one. He just felt so uncertain. He had just barely come to a sense of belief in what Tashon had been saying, only for it to turn out different than they expected.

"I know it's different than what Tashon saw." She shook her head. "But it's similar. The Crawlers are a threat. But none of us thought some of the Crawlers would be on our side."

"Yeah." Abe nodded, understanding her point.

He had the same thought himself, but the fact that they knew so little of what was happening on Aethera worried him.

Humans, always assuming they know everything, Abe thought and shook his head. If he'd learned anything since landing on Aethera, it was how little he actually knew. How little any of them did.

"So we're just jumping onto whatever path looks right, and following it without question?" he asked, the frustration obvious in his voice.

"You're questioning it right now," she answered. "And I'm sure the others have had their doubts too. Except maybe Rosa," she added with a grin.

"Yeah." A small smile split his lips. "Everything made so much more sense on the ship."

"Can't argue with that. But are you saying you'd really rather be there than here?"

Abe looked at her, then looked at the sky, the stars. His gaze went to the sleeping Crawlers. Thought of the battle he was rushing into at first light.

He shook his head. "No."

She agreed with a nod. Neither spoke, and the next few minutes were spent in a peaceful silence.

Abe thought about the fight itself. Wondered if he would live or die. Wondered if, in the moment, he would freeze or act. Yet, for some reason, none of those details worried him. What concerned him the most was whether or not they were doing the right thing.

"Do you think we're on the right path?" Abe asked quietly.

Winona ran a hand over her bald head.

"Right for who?" she asked. "For you? For me? For humans or Singers or Crawlers?"

Abe said nothing, knowing that what was good or right for the humans might not, in fact, be for the other species on Aethera.

"It's impossible, I think, to know with certainty if what you're doing is the right thing."

"I asked if you *think* we're doing the right thing."

She shrugged. "Do you?"

Abe considered everything that had happened since they discovered the five living Singers. What the Singers said about the Crawlers. What Tashon was shown in the Fourth about the Crawlers. And the fact that there had never been an attack on the humans or Singers, other than the beetles. None of the large Crawler biotech ever made it to the yellow forest.

"What we're doing does make the most sense."

She smiled. "And I think that's the best answer we're ever going to come up with."

Abe nervously placed a hand on her cheek. Heart thumping, he leaned in and gently pressed his lips to hers. She pulled back, and they held each other for a moment. Abe pulled back and gave her another smile. She smiled back, and the two lay down to sleep through what little of the night they had left.

They jumped awake at the sound of a Crawler shouting in its native tongue. The loud clicks and pops echoed off the crater walls. Something about the unknown words, with the Crawler's hand and leg movements, convinced Abe that it was a rallying speech. Words to get the fire of battle into their hearts.

The rest of the Crawlers stared silently at the speaker. Bodies tensed, leg muscles bulged. The speech stopped, the Crawler pounded its four feet into the ground and then the crater exploded in clicks and clacks and stomps.

Rosa, Mohawk and a Crawler ran to their sides. Abe greeted them with a nod and quickly looked at the vein pattern on the Crawler's legs. Horizontal waves of varying thickness but a consistent wavelength. The Singer that had first spoken to them.

The lead Crawler made one more booming click. The mass of Crawlers broke into a jog, each heading to one of four wide doors that had opened along the Crater edge.

"Humans, Singers, follow," the Crawler said.

They fell in line behind a group heading to the nearest door.

"Where're the others?" Abe asked Rosa.

"Went with another Crawler," Rosa said, her eyes firmly focusing on the open door. "Tashon's vision from the Fourth gets messed up when we're underground."

"He's going in from the air?" Winona asked.

"Which means we're tunneling in," Abe said, trying to keep his nerves calm.

Rosa smiled. "Yes, we are."

They walked into the shadow of the hangar. The sphere from the day before rested on the ground, its digging instruments out and ready to tunnel. Scattered behind the sphere were what looked like personal vehicles, some already occupied by a Crawler.

Abe inspected one, trying to figure out how a human would sit in it. Everything about it was designed to accommodate a four-legged Crawler, not a biped. The waist high single cylinder had a seat directly on top designed for the Crawler to rest its underbelly. Stretching from underneath the seat were four leg supports that partially encased the single wheel. Those supports ended in round stirrups that locked in the Crawler's feet.

But if Abe, or any biped, tried to sit in one, they would fall off as soon things got rough. Which, undoubtedly, things would.

"For you, this way," the Crawler said.

It led them around the cluster of Crawler vehicles to the far side of the hangar. Four cylinders stood in a row, these reconfigured to accommodate those with only two legs. The Crawlers had attached a backrest to the stool, removed two leg rests, and repositioned the remaining two to allow biped riders to sit safely and comfortably on top of the cylinder.

Abe looked at the Crawler, a pang of guilt tightening his chest. With no real knowledge of the species, he had judged all off them to be violent and merciless, determined to exterminate all human and Singer life. But the Crawlers that surrounded him had determined the humans were worth protecting, with no real knowledge of who or what humans were. They had taken the time to ensure they had effective vehicles heading into battle. The Crawlers, at least the ones at the crater, were intelligent and understanding. They cared about the humans and the Singers. More than anything, that realization convinced Abe he was indeed on the right path.

"Thank you," he said to the Crawler.

"Yes," the Crawler responded. "Soon leave."

Abe got on a cylinder and it leaned with his weight. Left for left, right for right. He leaned forward, the cylinder buzzed and launched toward Winona. He tossed himself at the back of the seat and slammed to a stop. He shrugged as Winona laughed.

Then a loud whirring hummed from the digging sphere, and every being mounted a vehicle. The sphere spun forward and the crowd followed. Soon, it was digging down at a faster pace than Abe had expected, leading them into the earth and toward battle. They were on their way to take out a Crawler city.

Chapter 52

Tashon stood in a trench atop the airborne Crawler tech. The walkway's walls were about shoulder height, leaving his head exposed to the crisp wind. Johann and Braids stood next to him, both silently staring at the diminishing crater below. Dozens more soared with them, all rising steeply toward dark gray clouds.

With his eyes closed and a chill on his face, Tashon stretched his sight as far as he could, but could not glimpse their destination. He hoped there was a plan more than just distraction, because Tashon was certain that their enemy would have tech that could take them out of the sky.

They entered the dark clouds and the vessels leveled out. The density of the fog around them made it impossible to see any of the other ships, but Tashon had a feeling that the Crawler tech had some type of radar to account for the lack of visibility. And he hoped the clouds held all the way to the Crawler city to allow them the element of surprise.

Braids whispered a note that Tashon barely heard, but for a moment it filled him with confusion and guilt. He looked at her, wondering what must be going through her mind. It reminded him of the hours and days after he had killed Laos, wandering in the gut-wrenching pain of having taken another life. Braids, though, seemed to be facing the same pains before taking any action. The very prospect of breaking her promise, however justified she might feel about it weighed on her.

Tashon stepped closer to her. "You don't have to kill," he said, confident that she would understand.

She responded with a low, rumbling string of notes. Instantly, Tashon was filled with a sense of resolve: he would do what had to be done. The feeling quickly passed, leaving Tashon with the knowledge that Braids felt she had to fight. That her only option was to break her pact, to kill.

Tashon was about to tell her otherwise when a Crawler approached them. It tapped on the metal wall behind Johann. A flat surface slid out, a three-dimensional map of the city they would soon attack on display.

It detailed every stone tower, every dome, every path the other Crawlers frequented.

"Us," the Crawler said, placing a miniature replica of their airborne tech on the map.

"Thirty-five more." The Crawler circled the map with a finger. "Surround."

Tashon nodded and looked to Johann, relying on the older man's military experience to ask the right questions.

"And then what?" Johann asked, rubbing his beard. "Bombs? Are we landing? Dropping soldiers?"

"First, bombs. Here." The Crawler indicated a third of the city, one populated mostly by the towering rock pillars.

"Next, some land here." The Crawler indicated nearly half the city. "Young ones live here. And civilians. Not their fight. We bring them in. Protect them, leave."

Tashon smiled at that, shaking his head. He hadn't even considered Crawler children, or the innocent lives in the city. But now that he had, he was glad to know the Crawlers had a plan to keep them safe.

The Crawler pointed to the remaining section of the city. "Leaders here. We and fighters go, talk with leaders one time more. Listen, we leave. Don't listen, ground falls in."

Tashon inhaled sharply. The Crawlers were taking them to Crawler central in an attempt to convince their violent counterparts not to kill the humans and Singers.

"How long until we get there?" Johann asked, seemingly unconcerned with the role they would be playing.

"Some time, not much," the Crawler replied.

Loud clattering and clicking rang from the opposite end of the vessel, and the Crawler left the three to examine the map by themselves. Johann stared at it intently, tracing lines with his finger, occasionally sharing tips or concerns with Tashon. The longer they moved across the sky, though, the more Tashon's head spun.

The vertigo he had suffered from his last trip to the Fourth slowly returned. His heart pounded. He leaned against the metal hull and closed his eyes, then slowed his breaths. Tried to meditate the way he had before they crossed the ocean, but the frozen wind and the turbulent flight made it difficult. He bounced unwillingly between the Third and the Fourth as he tried to calm his body, center his mind.

He dragged his Fourth sight from himself, trying to focus in on where the Crawler had sped off. A group of Crawlers stood, loudly clicking and clacking at one another. Tashon wondered whether the volume was due to anger or excitement, or if it was simply how they communicated. He did all he could to zone in on the scene, pushing away the vertigo and hints of nausea. Perhaps the Crawlers were fighting over battle plans or assigned rules. Maybe they were getting psyched up for the battle—Tashon liked that thought. He watched them from the Fourth for a few minutes, his body resting limply against the wall.

The beat in his head calmed slightly, then a voice from the Fourth rang loudly in his mind.

"Tashon."

"Laos?" Tashon rubbed his temples. *"Not helping the headache."*

"I've been trying to get your attention."

"How long?"

"Too long. And time works differently here, anyway."

"Oh," Tashon said aloud.

"Listen. The Singer up here came and talked to me."

"Really?" Tashon stood up and turned all his attention to Laos. He felt as if fluid sloshed in his skull but he stayed steady.

"She was upset. Frantic."

"Yeah?" Tashon said in the Third, realizing his mistake when Johann gave him a confused look. *"What did she say?"*

"She apologized. But, mostly, she shot thoughts at me. Terrified that one of her descendants might break the pact. Confused that some of the Crawlers are looking out for you."

"I'm still surprised by that too." Tashon shifted his weight, vaguely noticing that the clouds in the Third were thinning. *"Did she say anything else?"*

"No."

Tashon nodded, a blank stare on his physical face.

Johann asked if he was all right, but Tashon didn't hear the question.

"She was upset? Confused?"

"Yes."

"Doubt still exists there?" Tashon whispered.

Johann squeezed Tashon's shoulder, and Tashon shifted his attention to him. The older man stood in front of him. Tashon's vision blurred as he tried to focus on Johann's face. Johann's lips moved as Laos said something to Tashon's mind. Tashon made no sense of either one.

A loud boom and the bright orange of flames shocked Tashon back to the third-dimensional present. The clouds had parted completely. The airborne snake-like machine to their left was on fire, its front end tipped steeply at the ground. Each of the dozens of wings along its sides disconnected, flew to the top of the snake-like machine, and pulled out a Crawler. As the vessel sank in flames, its passengers flew down to their target on tiny wings.

Screeching clicks rang all around and Crawler feet stomped. Their Crawler guide returned and harshly pushed Tashon against the wall. It pushed something on the metal surface, releasing a strap that wrapped around Tashon and pinned him in place. It quickly did the same to Johann, Braids and then itself.

"Hold tight," it said. "Faster."

Tashon braced himself and waited. They gently vibrated, and the vessel shot forward, whipping Tashon's head to the side, forcing a pop from his neck. The pounding dizziness he'd been trying to avoid flooded over him.

Words echoed into his mind from the Fourth. Clicks, screeches and whistling wind flooded his ears in the Third. The moths appeared. Tashon tried to focus both sights on them as they flew around in the Fourth, twisting in the colorful winds. Twirled and danced between him, Johann and Braids in the Third. One landed on his shoulder. He looked at it, feeling as if it had locked gazes with him. Another explosion shook the air.

The moths disappeared in a fluttering of wings until they burst into dust, carried away by the wind.

Laos remained, and Tashon knew nothing of what was real or unreal. Images—ghastly and angelic, gut-wrenching and awe-inspiring—rushed in and out of his Fourth sight, or perhaps only his mind.

A future Aethera, Singers and Crawlers and humans in one society, living in peace.

A future Aethera, more deranged and desolate than Earth ever was, humans slaughtering Singers, slaughtering Crawlers, making a mockery of their lives and culture.

Abe and Winona, a baby in their arms.

Abe and Winona, dead and decaying, half crushed underneath the Crawler city.

The rest of the Singers awaking and emerging from the red caves to find two more species willing to share Aethera.

The rest of the Singers, burned in their stasis chambers without ever seeing the sun again.

Doubt spread through him like wildfire.

All only in my head.

"Only in my head." His eyes shot open.

"You with us, Tash?" Johann called against the wind.

"I...." Tashon inhaled deeply. "Yeah."

No, not in my head. Real.

"Focus," Johann said loudly, yet calmly. "What's happening?"

Tashon pulled his sight as high as possible, widening his view. The pillars to the west collapsed in dust and flames. Fifteen of the Crawler ships had been shot down, their hulls crumpled. Five others were engulfed in flame, pulled down by gravity. Hundreds of Crawlers on the small wings flew in spirals to the ground.

Ten machines had landed amid smaller domes, its occupants quickly pulling other Crawlers aboard. Massive, terrifying biotech ripped into any Crawler trying to escape, whether it was a rebel Crawler or not.

The vessel they rode tipped forward, quickly heading to the largest dome in the city. The remaining five trailed closely behind them.

Tashon relayed all of this to Johann.

"Okay," Johann said. "You going to disappear again?"

Tashon shook his head, but he knew it was possible.

The Singer appeared next to Laos, and the two silently observed the battle. Again, Tashon wondered if they were real. What if everything he'd been seeing were hallucinogenic side effects of Aleron's beast piercing his mind?

Was he insane?

No.

A lot of what he'd seen had been proven true. The threat of the Crawlers, if only some of them. The code that lead them to the five Singers. He'd even seen beforehand exactly what the Crawler beach and tunnels looked like.

He'd traveled through the Fourth, taken Ballas with him. Insanity couldn't manifest physical outcomes so vividly real.

Something pounded against the outside of the hull directly behind Tashon, followed by another smash on the side he faced.

A skinny creature with enormous wings crawled over the edge. Thin fangs stretched out of its mouth, each over a foot long. It moved its feet up and down, fluttered its wings, and leapt at Tashon.

Chapter 53

Smith stood at the entrance to the red caves, staring out at the forest. Twenty-three men and women. Each of them sitting on the frozen ground, the backs of their heads sunk into the softened flesh of trees. Snow fell gently from the sky. He watched as Minow walked past each one, carefully brushing snow off their shoulders and laps.

She walked to Smith, leaned against the stone, and pulled a crumpled piece of cloth from one ear.

Smith cleared out his ear and turned to Minow.

"Why now?" Theresa glanced at Smith, then turned her attention back to the unconscious.

Smith looked at her, a slight frown on his face. He'd asked himself the same question over and over since the first few victims were found. He'd gone through every possible scenario, any reason that would make sense. Only one did.

"This must be the first part of their attack. Incapacitate as many of us as possible before the next one."

"Damn it." Minow shook her head. "I had the same thought. Was hoping there was another explanation."

"Could be," Smith admitted. "But I can't figure out what it would be."

"If they are launching their attack, what does that mean...?" She trailed off, and Smith got the impression she didn't know if she should finish the thought.

"What does it mean about Abe and everyone else?"

She nodded.

"I don't know." He paused, letting a thought form in his mind before continuing. "Sending the beetles could be their Plan B. If Abe and the others found a way to stop them, or even slow them, maybe this was the Crawlers' only option."

"Huh."

They went silent. Smith pushed the piece of cloth back into his ear and watched the snow fall. *It was possible,* he thought, *that Abe and the rest had successfully hindered the Crawlers' plans*. Yet something told him the struggle was far from over.

The sky darkened and the snow fell harder. Minow mumbled a goodbye and went into the caves.

Smith walked to Theresa and wiped the snow off her shoulders. He looked closely at her face, hoping to see some sign of conscious awareness. He saw none, and the only sign she was even alive was the misty cloud of air that escaped her nose each time she exhaled. One after the other, he brushed off snow, examined faces. Each the same as Theresa.

Yeance walked out of the caves and solemnly waved at Smith. With a nod and wave, Smith joined him at the entrance.

"I needed some fresh air," Yeance said. "And you need some rest."

Smith huffed a laugh.

"Don't think any of us will sleep for a while," he said. "It'd be nice to warm up though."

The two men exchanged half smiles, and Smith went through the doorway, quickly making his way to the main cavern. It was packed when he arrived. People talked or whispered in groups. Some held sleeping children tight against there chests, covering ears with blankets or hat or clothing. Others paced the floor, their eyes red with exhaustion. A few tried to lighten the mood with jokes and lighthearted stories, but they fell flat.

As Smith walked farther into the room, the voices quieted and the pacing stopped. They all looked at him expectantly, the fear and confusion clear in their eyes. For a moment, he wondered what they expected of him. Then he realized he was the only one of the three leaders present. They were looking for answers. For hope.

He wasn't sure he could give them either. Standing as tall as he could, he walked to the center of the room, all eyes following him as he took the only open seat on a white bench.

"I...." He paused, breathing deeply. "Damn it, I don't have all the answers. I can't tell you that everything is going to work out."

Saying those simple and honest words seemed to ease the crowd, though as Smith spoke them, they came out heavy. They didn't feel quite right.

"I don't know if it will," he continued. "But I do believe they will. Those we sent to the Crawlers are some of the people I trust most. If anyone can change how the Crawlers view us, it's them."

"What if they can't?" a woman asked.

"I've considered that, too." Smith ran a hand through his hair, looking at the ground then back at the crowd. "And I honestly don't know. But I know the ones hooked to the trees out there will recover. I did, and there's no reason to think they won't."

The crowd went silent. Smith knew they wanted more. More reason to believe it would all work. Or even a plan, something to do other than waiting for a potential massacre. But there was nowhere to go. Nothing to do but think of what might happen at the caves. What might be happening to Abe and the others.

"But as for everything else?" Smith leaned back and looked at the ceiling. "I can't say for sure that we'll be okay. This is new for all of us. But I can't say with certainty that it's the end for us, either."

Some in the crowd nodded at that, a few whispering among themselves.

"I don't think it's the end," a boy in his early teens said. "It just—I don't know—feels like humanity should have a life here."

Smith smiled. "I think we will," he said. "But we can't just keep sitting here in fear. So the question I have is this: what do we do now?"

"That depends," the same boy said.

"On what?" Smith asked.

"Do we want to be productive or distracted?" He shrugged.

Smith and many in the crowd chuckled. It was a valid point, though, and Smith acknowledged it with a nod. If there was nothing productive to be done, distraction could at least lighten their hearts and minds.

"Well?" Smith stood and looked around the room. "Distraction or productivity?"

A few in the crowd tossed out suggestions. They could play games or practice with the adjusted guns. No one had the heart for games, and wasting ammunition didn't seem like a smart decision.

The Singer, Scar, walked into the cavern and joined Smith.

"Hello," Smith said to the native with a smile.

The Singer sang a few strings of notes that filled Smith with a sense of being taken care of. He felt the way he and all the humans felt mattered. He pondered the emotion, realizing that the Singer was offering to help.

"Please." Smith nodded and sat down.

Scar kept his body perfectly still as he opened his mouth, letting a calm and soothing melody float from his lips. It filled the room, enveloped Smith, and sank into his bones. The last thought he had before succumbing mind, body and spirit to the melody was this: is giving into distraction really the best option right now?

Chapter 54

Just before the creature's fangs sunk into his shoulder, Tashon's mind leaped upward and pulled him into the Fourth. He twisted his head and vomited, leaving a puddle of digested Crawler vegetables on the translucent floor. Groaning and coughing, he rolled onto his side and tried to calm his mind. He hadn't intentionally jumped into the Fourth, yet there he was. When the fanged, butterfly-like creature attacked him, something in his subconscious mind had taken over. It was that part of his mind that was connected to the Fourth. In that moment, though, it had felt as though that specific section of his mind was active in a way it had never been before.

It was always there, of course. In the background, giving him a new viewpoint. There to access when he wanted. But in those few moments, that elevated part of his mind had taken complete control in order to preserve Tashon's life. He was grateful for it, but knew he wouldn't have been able to stop it if he wanted. And that scared him, made him feel momentarily like he was one of Aleron's puppets.

With a shake of his head to push aside the thought, he sat and stared at the battle taking place below him.

Crawler ships caught fire, crashed, exploded. Others landed safely only to be overrun by waves of enemy Crawlers and biotech monsters. The Crawlers that had escaped their sinking vessels on wings ran rampant across the city, rescuing the young and innocent or killing the enemy. A dozen winged, fanged creatures climbed along the hull of the ship he had just escaped.

Johann cut his safety straps with a knife and dove at the nearest one, severing its head in a single swipe. Another flew in behind the older man, mouth open, fangs ready to sink into his neck. Braids jumped in between the two and shoved her palm with exposed electrified wires into the creature's face. One of the wires sunk into her attacker's eye. It convulsed briefly and went limp. Braids freed her hand and left the partially organic corpse on the deck. Tashon wondered if killing an engineered being broke the pact.

"I need to be down there," he whispered, pressing his palm to his temple as another headache pounded in his ears.

He slowed his breathing as much as possible and closed his eyes, gathering an image in his mind of landing back on the ship on top of one of its attackers. Inhale, exhale. He stretched his hands toward the ground and pulled down, forcing himself to burst through the ground. The air rushed out of his lungs as his eyes went blurry and he suddenly felt weightless. For a moment, he floated—painless and free—between dimensions.

Then gravity grabbed hold of him and he slammed onto a hovering biotech creature, forcing it to the floor of the ship. Its spine crunched underneath him. He vomited again, but he forced himself to his feet and looked around.

The ship was covered in dead bioengineered butterflies and a handful of Crawler corpses. It slowed and leveled out as Johann walked to Tashon. The two nodded to each other, catching their breath as they examined the scene. A few feet away, Braids mumbled notes filled with rage. Whether it was directed at herself or the Crawlers, or something else entirely, Tashon had no idea.

Their Crawler guide sprinted down the walkway to join them.

"Where did you go?" He eyed Tashon carefully.

"Uh...." Tashon didn't know if there was time to explain it, or if the Crawler would even understand. "The fourth dimension."

"I...." the Crawler paused. "Don't understand the words."

Tashon tried to figure out the simplest way to explain it, but before he had a chance to speak, something crashed into the side of their flying snake. He fell forward, catching himself with his hands. Adrenaline fueling him, and he jumped back to his feet. Flames rose from one side, quickly growing. Everything trembled, and whatever mechanism was keeping them in the air failed.

Gravity was in control.

It felt as if his stomach rose into his throat. He floated above the metallic surface for a moment, and then crashed back into it. The screeching and clicking of Crawlers rose above the wind.

Another hit sent Tashon into the wall of the walkway, knocking the air out of his lungs. Two thin arms reached under his armpits and pulled him to his feet. A Crawler. It steadied Tashon with one hand while tapping the wall with the other. The wall slid open, revealing a narrow path that led to one of the many wings that lined the hull.

"Go." The Crawler gave him a soft push. "See you on ground."

Steering himself against his nerves, Tashon walked swiftly to the wing. Wind whipped around him as he stepped to the edge. Up close, the wing was larger than he had first thought, but it still didn't look like it would hold him.

"Button," the Crawler behind him yelled.

Tashon looked back to see the Crawler pointing at the floor. More bile threatened to come up, and he forced it back as he crouched down. A square button rested in the floor, directly above the metal stem that connected the wing to the hull.

After taking a moment to decide the best way to get onto the wing, he stood and stepped onto it before pressing the button. He sat , and with legs crossed, pushed the square down.

The wing shot away from the hull horizontally with a puff of air and glided downward in a spiral. It was designed that way, Tashon realized. Built to glide gently to the ground because it had no propulsion system.

Crawlers on wings spiraled down all around him. Flames quickly engulfed the ship they escaped and chunks of it broke off, flaming shrapnel falling to the ground below. Nervously, Tashon searched the air for his companions. A hundred feet above and to the left, Braids stood steady on a wing. Her lips moved, but there was no way for Tashon to hear her over the winds and explosions.

Johann was nowhere to be seen.

Tashon turned his attention to the ground. He, Braids and dozens of Crawlers spiraled down toward chaos. Crawlers hit, sliced and shot, leaving corpses scattered across the ground. Two Crawlers tumbled into a puddle of pale red blood, each wildly pounding the other with metal rods.

Tashon slid the weaponized brick from his pocket. They sank ever closer to the ground. From the Fourth, Tashon saw they were landing much farther from where they had planned. To make it to the Crawler leaders and plead their case one last time, they had to battle through two miles of enemy Crawlers and ravenous biotech.

Twenty feet from landing, Tashon rose to his feet, clutching his weapon.

Fifteen feet. A feline biotech charged into the battle, crushing Crawler heads with massive jaws.

Ten feet. The engineered tiger was right below Tashon.

Nine feet. Tashon committed himself to giving all he could in the fight.

Eight feet. Tashon bent his knees and jumped off the wing.

Seven feet.

Six feet.

Five feet. He aimed the brick at the ferocious feline and squeezed.

Four feet. The glowing cloud of destructive dust enveloped the beast's body.

Three feet. The body crumbled into a pile of dust.

Two feet. The head remained, its jaws chomping wildly.

One foot.

Tashon landed next to the severed head. The jaw clamped shut on his ankle, teeth sinking into his flesh. He shouted in pain and collapsed to his knees. He swung his free foot into the head over and over. Its grip loosened, and he ripped it off with his hands. He threw it as far as he could.

"Shit," he whispered, heaving oxygen in and out of his lungs.

Braids appeared at his side and reached out her hand. Tashon grabbed it and she pulled him to his feet. He winced as he put pressure on his injured foot, but he was confident he'd be able to walk. Explosions, shots, screeches and clicks echoed in the direction they needed to go. A group of Crawlers approached. Tashon recognized the vein patterns on two of them.

"Fight to our leaders," one said.

The group moved off in a brisk walk. Fifty yards away, a dozen Crawlers broke out from behind a pile of rubble and charged, weapons at the ready.

Chapter 55

The giant sphere easily dug through the rock and soil, quickly forming a jagged tunnel to their destination. Abe and Winona rolled side by side, surrounded by Crawlers that shared the same goals, the same vision.

Mohawk and Rosa rode in front of them, the two communicating with a Crawler. It was a scene Abe would have never pictured until the day before, and he couldn't help but smile.

After a few hours, the sphere stopped and everything went silent. Abe leaned forward and rolled to Rosa, Mohawk and their Crawler companion. He looked at Rosa, his expression asking why they stopped moving.

She shrugged, shaking her head. "No idea," she whispered.

Every Crawler remained still atop their wheels, as if moving would bring the entire tunnel down. Silent minutes went by.

Winona rolled to Abe's side and grabbed his hand. They exchanged smiles.

The top of the tunnel shook, sending down a soft flutter of dirt and pebbles. It turned to violent rumbling, and Abe jumped, his heart pounding in his throat. It rumbled, trembled, subsided. Rumbled, trembled, subsided.

Nothing more came down, but the pattern of trembling and stillness continued for hours. Abe wondered how Tashon, Johann and Braids were handling the fight above. He'd noticed Tashon's distraction, been concerned for the state of his friend's conscious mind. Had Braids broken her pact, or held true to her people's tradition of peace? What would it mean if she did break it?

"Too long," a Crawler's said, breaking into Abe's thoughts.

"What?" He turned to the Crawler next to Rosa.

"Fight too long." He looked up. "Should stopped."

Abe looked around the tunnel. As Crawlers slowly realized the same fact, the hushed clicks floating through the crowd eventually turned to loud, confused screeches. One Crawler rolled into the center of the impassioned soldiers, and the crowd quieted. It began speaking, an alternation of quiet clacks and piercing, hoarse scratches.

"What's he saying?" Rosa asked.

"Wait," the Crawler by them said. "For them up to get to right place."

"How long?" Winona said.

"No answer," it responded. "Went wrong up there."

Abe shook his head. Something had gone wrong, and the only thing they could do was wait.

"What happened?" he asked.

"No answer."

Chapter 56

A stone the size of a fist exploded from a tube held by a Crawler, whizzing past Tashon's head. He stumbled on his injured foot, squeezed the brick at the Crawler. The bright cloud surrounded its legs, turning them to dust, leaving the Crawler on the ground, a lone head screeching at Tashon.

An ally Crawler jabbed a spear into the head and swung it into another herd of charging Crawlers. It tripped up two of them, but the rest continued.

They'd traveled, at most, half a mile. Fighting for every foot. Tashon hadn't served the death blow on any of the Crawlers, but his actions already contributed to multiple deaths. He pushed the thought aside as a Crawler leaped into the air toward him. The destructive cloud had yet to return to his weapon, so he stumbled out of the way, barely getting clear of its massive legs crunching into the ground.

Something popped behind him. A hole formed in the Crawler's head, and it collapsed. A Crawler behind Tashon clicked loudly, drawing his attention to the five remaining enemy Crawlers. Corpses of the four-legged species littered the ground, but Tashon knew they had to keep moving. No time for grief, regret or doubts.

That would come later.

He let out a primal scream. Braids joined him with a deep, rumbling note. Resigning to the need to fight and kill in order to survive, Tashon hefted the tube that launched the stone and pointed it at the enemy. There was no trigger. He squeezed it the way he did the brick, but nothing happened.

"Damn it."

A Crawler was on top of him. He swung the tube, but his attacker dodged it easily, slamming a large foot into Tashon's chest. The force sent him into the air, and he landed hard, the wind escaping his lungs, the tube and brick leaving his grip. From the Fourth, he saw Crawlers fainting, collapsing and dying. Only a few remained, and he wasn't sure which ones were with him.

Braids fought a Crawler off, swinging what looked like an electrified stick. She landed a hit on its leg and it collapsed, body convulsing. Tashon hadn't seen her kill yet, but she was not opposed to the violence. Every movement she made was accompanied with determined, rage-fueled melodies.

A Crawler ran at Tashon. He jumped to his feet though there were no weapons within reach. It was almost on him. Braids jumped in front of him, facing the Crawler, electrified stick held high. At the perfect moment, she swung. It struck the Crawler across the eyes. Its head snapped back, something cracked, and it went still, slumping to the ground.

"Thanks." Tashon breathed heavily.

The two were quickly encircled by eight Crawlers.

Tashon looked around. His brick lay a dozen feet away, behind one of the Crawlers.

"Friends," one of the Crawlers said.

"All?" Tashon asked.

"Yes, all."

Tashon looked carefully at each and nodded.

"Now what?" Tashon walked past the Crawlers and picked up his weapon.

"Keep going," the Crawler replied simply. "Always right answer."

They walked on, through rubble and over corpses. Past ash and smoke and dying flames. Tashon's ankle throbbed, his head pounded. He barely noticed the pain. His attention was focused on the destruction.

Of course he'd learned of war when he studied Earth history, experienced it to some degree when the terrorists fought to take over the Ship of Nations. What surrounded him was something altogether worse. The city had been razed. Every dome they passed was nothing but shrapnel. Pillars lay prone, sunk into the dirt, shattered to pieces. Corpses everywhere. Some whole, some in pieces. Dying biotech twitched and sparked in the shadow of a boulder. Something like a dog, split into pieces, each section still moving. Behind them, the smoldering husk of their vessel. All around, more of the same.

Everything silent.

Nearly everything dead.

And Tashon had played a roll in silencing it. In killing it. More than ever, he understood the Singers' promise of non-violence. Perhaps it was not from some altruistic desire. Maybe it was simply to avoid feeling the guilt and despair that enveloped Tashon.

A harsh, cold wind whipped from the west. With it, dark clouds that sparked with lightning dumped heavy drops of rain. The dirt quickly turned to mud. Tashon was soaked through and shivering within minutes.

They walked on. After a hundred feet, perhaps two hundred, and Tashon stumbled to his knees. The wound in his ankle throbbed. He tried to stand up, but to no avail. On all fours, hands and knees sinking into the mud, tears streamed from his eyes.

Heavy.

Twisted. Everything spun.

Stomach pulsed. Throat clenched.

Everything. Everything heavy.

The Ship of Nations had left Earth to escape such useless destruction.

But had it been useless? If they hadn't done it, would the Crawlers have committed genocide of two species?

He didn't have the answers.

His wrists gave out. His face sunk into the mud, and he turned just enough for air to get into his mouth.

Heavy. Excruciatingly heavy.

He needed to be away from that place.

He closed his eyes. Pushed a hand against his chest. Voices and words sounded from all around. Laos. Braids. Evalee. Then voices he knew but could not name. The clicking tongues of all who died that day.

His body, his soul trembled in painful sorrow. Not what this was meant to be.

Where to go when everywhere brought suffering?

The answer: nowhere.

Arms lifted Tashon's limp body, carrying him.

No. Nowhere, please.

He pulled up with his mind. Felt himself stretching toward Laos's watchful perch. Letting that higher part of him pull upward, ready to stop it at just the right moment.

He lifted, gravity slowly losing its grasp on him. Colors faded away, all becoming whiter. And when he was encircled by no gravity, no color at all, he cut the connection.

No weight.

No color.

Nothing was everything that surrounded him.

Everything was nothing.

Nothing.

Before everything.

Nothing.

I am nothing

Yet—
I am everything.
Wait—
All are nothing
And—
All are everything.
Thus—
All are one
And—
One are all.
But—
No questions, all answers.
What—
All questions, no answers.
Contradiction.
True.
True.
True contradiction.
Everything opposite.
Nothing opposite.
Good—evil.
No good—no evil.
Rich—poor.
No rich—no poor.
Mercy—justice.
No mercy—no justice.
Law—crime.
No law—no crime.
Beauty—ugliness.
No beauty—no ugliness.
Joy—despair.
No joy—no despair.
Life—death
No life—no death.
This all is nothing.
Is everything.
Nothing is everything.
Everything is nothing.
Nothing.
Nothing.

Chapter 57

"Talk about meditation," Smith said as he stood and stretched, watching Scar leave the cavern.

As soon Smith gave into the Singer's melody, his mind had been whisked off to a place where only one thing existed: peace. His eyes saw the cavern he sat in, saw the people sitting and standing around. Was aware of the dangers and terrors that might come, but felt no fear at the thought.

All that mattered was that moment. Not the tragedies that came before, nor the challenges that may yet come. Just that moment, and the peace he felt.

And when Scar finished his melody, some of that peace lingered in Smith's mind. He looked at the people, watched as they too came out of the tranquil daze, contented smiles on their faces.

Surprisingly, there was no fear in the crowd. They all seemed to understand that the Singer provided them with a respite from their stress and worries. And Smith felt the same way, realizing that despite their aversion to violence, the Singers were still trying to show support.

And now he felt like he could take on whatever might come.

If it ever came.

Slowly, the room grew louder with voices. The peace Smith felt brought clarity to his mind, and he was able to discern that there were indeed things to be done. He made his way to the far side of the cavern, exchanging handshakes, greetings and nods along the way. He spotted Minow, and asked her to join him. The two went through the same door Scar had used, and entered a narrow hallway.

It was a hall Smith had been in once, when they were looking for how the beetle could have gotten in the caves. He followed it quickly yet calmly, knowing it ended in a single room.

"What are we doing?" Minow asked.

"We've begun to understand each other," Smith said. "Us and the Singers. Learned each other's history, made attempts to understand cultural differences."

Minow smiled. "We've made incredible advancements."

"But do you truly feel we have a solid relationship with them?"

"They're letting us live in their home. Offered us unprecedented guided meditation that probably saved many of complete mental breakdowns."

"I know," Smith said. "I know. But we're doing something for them. They're just returning the favor."

Minow stopped walking. "This might sound cynical, but isn't that what relationships are? Two sides swapping favors?"

Smith paused, thinking of his marriage with Evalee.

"Political relationships, usually," Smith agreed. "But let's say a century down the road, a human goes rogue and attacks a political icon of the Singer nation.

"Now, in a hundred years, let's assume not all Singers are followers of their pact of pacifism."

"Okay," Minow said, looking equally interested and confused.

"So, what did the Crawlers do when one Singer went rogue?"

"Genocide," Minow said. "We both know this."

Smith nodded. "I know, but think. What if it had been a strong relationship between the two nations, one that had been built on a solid foundation of respect and understanding?"

"More likely that the Crawlers would not have reacted so aggressively."

"Right," Smith said. "We should have that solid relationship with the Singers as soon as possible. It, hopefully, will help future generations."

"And you think humanity will be on Aethera long enough for that to matter?"

"I do," Smith said honestly.

"Where do you say we start?" Minow asked, leaning against the wall.

"Names."

"We've been referring to them by their physical attributes," Smith said. "But know nothing about them as individuals. Let's start with names."

"I like the idea," Minow said. "But how is it going to work? We can't physically say their exact names."

"But we can at least figure out the emotional state connected to their names, and come up with the best equivalent."

"Let's try it, then."

The two resumed walking, neither speaking until they reached the entryway of a small, dome-shaped cavern. The three remaining Singers sat silently on the floor, their backs to the door. Scar was perfectly still.

The one with long, thinning hair chewed on some type of meat while the one with short yellow hair drew with her finger in the sand that layered the floor.

When Smith and Minow walked in, the Singers did not react to their presence until both sat down, creating a circle of five.

Smith looked at Scar. "Thank you for... calming us. It helped."

Scar sang a phrase that let Smith feel that the Singer had been happy to help.

"Anytime I'm learning a new language," Minow said. "We start with words we already know."

"Humans," she said to the Singers, indicating Smith and herself.

Each of the Singers made their note for human, the same one Smith had heard earlier with Yeance.

Smith continued to watch silently, letting Minow take the lead. It may have been his idea, but Minow had been working harder than anyone to understand the Singers. If anyone had a strong relationship with them, it was her.

"Singers," she said, indicating the three in the circle.

Again, each Singer made the note for their own species.

Minow smiled and took a deep breath.

"Minow," she said, indicating herself.

The Singers, still and silent, seemed lost in thought. The one with thinning hair, that Smith assumed to be the eldest, adjusted her position and opened her mouth. She sang two smooth, soft notes. Smith recognized one of them immediately: the note for tall grass blowing in the breeze. The other he hadn't heard or felt before, but it reminded him of those times when Evalee looked at him and he just knew that she understood him on a level no one else did. Evidently, the Singers cared deeply for Minow.

Minow smiled and gently shook her head before indicating Smith and saying his name.

Nerves unexpectedly flooded his stomach and chest. Receiving a new name from an alien species would be significant under any circumstance. But a Singer name came with emotional power that would tell Smith how they viewed him.

The same Singer spoke. One note for a word Smith had heard multiple times: tree. And another note, the emotion resonating with it conjuring images of a massive tree being massacred by wind, rain, hail and lightning. Any and every natural disaster that could befall it.

Yet the tree remained.

Smith closed his wet eyes and breathed deep, steadying breaths. The way they viewed him was humbling, and a part of him thought that they had him all wrong. But he decided telling them that wouldn't help build the relationship.

He blinked away the tears and looked at Minow.

"You good?" she asked him.

He nodded. She looked at the three Singers and indicated the eldest, with thinning hair.

"Name?"

Without hesitation, the Singer let out a long, vibrating note. Smith didn't understand a physical definition from it, but he momentarily felt at one with... everything. Connected to the wind, the rocks, the soil.

The feeling passed. How to compact such a feeling into a single name? He looked to Minow with raised eyebrows and shrugged.

"Air touches everything?" Smith made the statement a question.

"True," Minow paused. "But air doesn't feel right."

Smith agreed, but no other ideas came to him.

"Atom," Minow said with a smile.

"Adam?"

"No, with a 't.' Atoms are part of everything, right?" Minow said happily.

"Right." Smith softly chuckled.

They repeated the process with the other two Singers. For the Singer with the cropped hair, they settled on the name 'Comet.' Bright and ever-moving, piercing through the darkness of the void.

Scar's new name: Wave. Not consistent in strength and fervor, but always there, ready to broil to towering heights when the need arose.

The five continued communicating, falling into a comfortable, yet unfamiliar, rhythm of hearing, translating and responding. Eventually, the conversation died out, and Smith left to check on everyone else.

As he walked down the hall, he felt lighter than he had in days. Outwardly, the situation they were in hadn't changed at all. The Crawlers could still attack at any minute. There were still people connected to the trees, fighting to rid their minds of the beetles. He had no idea if Abe was alive.

Yet, despite all of it, a sense of calm had settled over him. He believed everything would turn out okay. Whether it was a symptom of Wave's guided meditation or the result of connecting personally with the Singers, he had no idea. And in that moment, he didn't care.

Chapter 58

Underground, Abe nervously rolled back and forth. For over an hour, the ground above had trembled with explosions, and then stopped.

Two Crawlers pointed to a device above them, a wide array of lights spread across the ceiling. Symbols unrecognized by Abe were sporadically spaced amid the brightness. He had no idea what any of it meant, but each Crawler was transfixed by the display.

The Crawlers talked in their clicking tongue. Quiet at first, it quickly grew into a roar that echoed all around.

"What the hell's going on?" Rosa asked.

Abe and Winona locked eyes, both shaking their heads. Their Crawler guide rolled toward them, chattering loudly before coming to a stop.

"What's happening?" Abe asked.

"We waited for call from above," the Crawler said. "Did not come. Something wrong."

"What's wrong?" Winona asked.

"No answer. Get ready. Going up."

The Crawler turned to face the digging sphere. The chittering of the Crawlers grew louder, vibrating into the dirt and stone, into Abe's heart. The sphere resumed rotating, and then all went silent.

The spinning ball lifted off the ground, pushing through the packed earth of the ceiling. It rose higher and moved faster. The Crawlers nearest followed its path, rolling underneath it then lifting into the air. With no movement from Abe, his wheel rolled forward and fell into ranks with all the others. Winona gasped as hers did the same.

"Okay," the Crawler said. "Next too hard control. Trust it."

"Yeah, okay," Abe said.

He'd been doing everything the past days with a mix of trust and distrust, so why stop?

The sphere accelerated, crushing into the ground, moving ever higher. Abe's vehicle accelerated, in sync with Winona's and the others around them. He rose toward the now silenced explosions, heart pounding. Dirt and rocks cascaded around the ball, a wall of soil surrounding them.

They burst into open air, a fierce wind whipping freezing rain into Abe's face. He landed on muddy ground amidst the crowd of stunned Crawlers, surrounded by destruction. Crawler vessels, grounded, broken into chunks of shrapnel. Corpses slowly sinking into the softening soil. Nothing living in sight that wasn't on a wheel.

"There," a Crawler said, looking at a hazy shape in the distance.

Some type of building, Abe thought. The tallest structure around. Every wheel sped off toward their destination, the Crawlers seemingly unaffected by the cold and the wet. Abe let the wheel pull him with the others, his eyes and mind focused on the silence and the stillness. He had been ready to fight, possibly kill. Braced to emerge into a raging battle. Instead, he found himself surrounded by what felt like nothing.

The shapes of corpses, Crawler and biotech alike, seemed to him mere objects. Inanimate. Soulless. Like his mom had been. Like he would be when his time came.

"What's the point?" he wondered aloud.

"What?" Winona shouted over the weather.

Abe looked at her and shook his head. It wasn't the time for philosophy, though he couldn't help the question: if his life in the Third was not the only he would have, what was the point of killing others to survive? Which question brought another: was the Singer's pacifism based on some unknown insight into the afterlife? He sighed and wiped rain from his eyes. They were closing in on the building.

A dome nearly a mile wide and hundred feet tall stood atop a towering pyramid of stairs, its shape a shadow obscured by blowing sheets of water. A line of Crawlers and biotech beasts stood at the base of the steps. Small from that distance, but Abe felt the nervous fire of impending battle sink into his heart.

They moved on. Slower, cautiously, weapons raised. The rain and wind slowed, then stopped. Clouds continued to darken the sky as they came within one hundred yards of the enemy. A biotech creature stood at the side of each Crawler, an eclectic mix of deadly technology. An eight-legged behemoth a dozen feet long, its sides layered with glistening spikes. A reptilian creation, standing on two legs with elongated arms that ended in hammerhead cubes sparking with electricity. Then a form that appeared far less threatening: a biped with no apparent weaponized limbs.

Abe squinted as he rolled forward. It wasn't a Crawler, nor any form of biotech. A human, arms strapped tightly to his side by a Crawler cable, stood firmly though entrapped by a hostile enemy.

"Johann," Abe shouted.

"What?" Rosa said.

An enemy Crawler hissed loudly.

Rosa ignored the Crawler. "Shit! Braids? Tashon?"

"No," Abe said. "Winona?"

"Just Johann," she replied.

The gap closed to twenty feet, and the small line of combatants stopped, their numbers nearly equal to those in front of the dome. Not including the biotech.

Johann stumbled to his knees as his Crawler handler shoved him forward. The old man stood back up, his expression cold. Confident. The Crawler that held Johann's leash spoke loudly, its clicks a higher pitch than Abe had heard from other Crawlers.

"What's happening?" Abe asked.

"That's first leader," the closest Crawler said quietly.

"The main leader of the Crawlers?" Abe asked, surprised that such an important figure would be out on the battlefront.

"Yes."

"What's he saying?"

"He will not kill man if we stop."

"That's what we were hoping for, right?" Abe said.

Perhaps they would not have to fight after all.

"It what we want," the Crawler agreed. "But first leader not true."

"How do you know?"

"Wait."

An ally Crawler rolled a few feet forward, loudly clacking a response to the first leader. Abe asked what was being said, but received only silence.

First leader answered, and then the ally Crawler responded. Back and forth the conversation went until neither spoke.

And with no sign, no rallying call, both sides charged. Moments behind his allies, Abe leaned forward and hefted his explosive thorn shield. He rolled toward running Crawlers, speeding biotech. Something launched toward him, just missing the side of his face, striking Winona's shoulder. She faltered, wobbled and then fell off her wheel into a puddle of mud. An engineered beast descended on her from the sky as Abe whipped around to get her. He launched two thorns at its side. They burst into small balls of flame as they hit their targets, sending the creature spinning through the air, smacking against an enemy Crawler. The two lay motionless in the wet soil.

Winona rolled onto her knees. Abe grabbed her hand and pulled her onto the wheel behind him. She wrapped her arms tight around his waist and he turned back to find Johann. The old man was on his knees, the first leader pulling the cable taught, eyes staring blankly at the carnage of battle.

A Crawler behind him screamed in pain. A monstrosity with razor-like arms decapitated three Crawlers at once before it was taken down. Muddy water splashed against wheels, against Crawler feet, atop freshly created corpses. Mere minutes passed and there already seemed to be more dead than alive.

Abe hastened his rolling. A Crawler attacked from the side. He fired one thorn into its leg, the limb exploding on impact. The Crawler screeched as it rolled to a stop.

He was closer to Johann, but the Crawlers had recognized his plan. The path was blocked by one Crawler, flanked on each side by matching biotech. Resembling smokies standing on hind legs, both held glowing boomerangs in their hands. Abe slowed, assessing the risk. Most likely, he wouldn't make it to Johann. But that brought a reversal of his previous question: if life in the Third wasn't all he would have, then why fear risking his life to save a friend?

Rosa rolled to his side and nodded at him. Abe grabbed Winona's hands, pulling them off his waist. He knew she wouldn't want to get off, but she didn't protest. She jumped into the mud, pulled out her weapon, and ran to help a Crawler that was losing a fight against a winged centipede.

Abe glanced one more time at Rosa, and the two moved full speed at the enemies guarding Johann. A boomerang slid past Abe's face, slicing his cheek open. He fired a battery of thorns at the creature that had thrown it, but missed the target. Instead, they sunk into the head of the Crawler, which blew apart in chunks of flesh and brain matter. Its body collapsed.

Rosa heaved a long metal rod onto her shoulder. A thin line of blue light lasered out, hitting one of the creatures in the forehead. No visible damage, but it immediately collapsed, body convulsing. Abe caught a glimpse of Johann and the first leader behind the remaining biotech guard. He allowed the smallest smile to cross his face. *They might actually pull it off*, he thought.

The wound on his cheek burned, his vision blurred, his head spun, and he fell off his wheel.

Everything went dark.

Chapter 59

Noise seeped into the nothing of Tashon's conscious existence. Subtle and dense, it vibrated his mind more than penetrated his ears. He knew he could not remain in the nothing of everything. He let the noise guide him out and back to something.

The noise grew lighter as he reached out for his connection to the Fourth, the Third. It left his mind, turned into a gentle wind on his face. Knowing that he knew nothing of happenings in the Third, he pulled more firmly on the Fourth.

The wind on his face found a rhythm, a flapping. Colors returned. Gravity. A sense of physical form, which felt heavy and cumbersome after being off in nothing. He opened his eyes. The moths encircled him, beating their wings in matching rhythm. Registering his awareness, they twirled into a single line and fluttered off, and Tashon knew he was meant to follow.

He took a step, and another, feeling steadier than any other time in the Fourth. Not perfect, still out of place, but greatly improved. Ahead, the moths stopped in front of a figure Tashon knew well: the godlike being who offered advice, aid and warnings.

Tashon felt no fear at the sight and followed the moths to the form.

"You have returned."

"Yes."

"You would have died had you not pulled away into nothing."

"I believe so."

"Eternities I have been here. I have seen none like you."

"What am I like?"

"One who has survived the touch of a shadow. Been given this connection to things above his physical existence."

"Given?"

"Given. Blessed with. Cursed with. Is there a difference?"

Tashon shook his head.

"I see that you've done well enough with what you've been given."

Tashon nodded. "Are you God? A god?"

The being shook with a gentle laughter. *"I have been called that. I was once alive on a world in what you call the third dimension."*

"What do you call it?"

"Not important, my friend. I was a being in a place like yours. Lived a life like yours. Died a death like you will. Found myself here. Searched for meaning. For answers. Decades. Centuries. Millenia. Found knowledge."

"What knowledge?"

"Nothing more important that what you learned of nothing. More interesting to some, perhaps."

"Will you share?"

"All things in their time. Now you need to be in the Third."

Tashon inhaled deeply as the memory of devastating battle flooded into him. Braids, Johann. Abe, Winona, Rosa. All the Crawlers fighting for humans and Singers alike.

"Do not return unless you must. You have a connection to this place, but it will lessen the time you have in your current form."

Tashon nodded and looked down. He was right above the Crawlers' main dome. Where he was supposed to be in order to convince the Crawler leaders to end their genocidal plans. That goal was failing miserably.

The muddied ground outside the dome was littered with Crawler corpses and shattered biotech. Others still fought. Crawler slammed into Crawler. Biotech creations decapitated Crawlers, Crawlers destroyed biotech. And in the center of it all, Abe lay unconscious in a puddle. Johann on his knees, wrapped and leashed like an animal. Winona pinned down by a centipede, its long tongue trying to wrap around her throat. Rosa blindly charged at Johann, not aware of the Crawler running at her from behind.

Tashon knew he needed to help. Felt that, perhaps, he was the one to turn the tide of the battle. But he also knew that he did not want to kill.

"All are one. One are all," he whispered.

"You do not have to kill to save them."

"Then how?"

"You will know."

"You speak like I always thought a god would, you know that?"

The being laughed again and told Tashon to leave, reminding him again of the consequences of returning.

Feeling more in control of his body, his mind, his very essence than he ever had, Tashon closed his eyes. Slowed his breathing. Pulled himself down, pushing aside the urge to return to nothing. Searched the scene below, wondering where the most dire need was, where he should come out first. Waited to feel the answer.

The Crawler tethering Johann seemed significant to Tashon. It stood still, making no attack. All the enemy Crawlers and biotech fought and died while that one Crawler did nothing. Tashon realized that must be the leader, the one in charge.

He pulled himself toward it with speed and control. Materialized in the Third between it and Johann, firmly on his feet. Pulled out the clay brick and turned Johann's leash to nothing. Johann laughed, jumped to his feet, and nodded at Tashon.

With conviction, Tashon turned to the startled Crawler leader, pushed the weaponized brick to its head. It shrieked, the piercing sound vibrating the air. The fighting stopped.

Johann nodded to Tashon.

"We don't want to kill more than we have to," Tashon shouted. "But we will if we need to."

As he spoke, an ally Crawler translated for those who had not been given the human language. Tashon waited for it to finish, then continued.

"You fear us. Fear the Singers. We have feared you." Tashon inhaled and then raised his voice. "But none here deserve to die. Not you. Not us. We are offering mercy. End the killing, stop the fighting. Your leader lives. You live. We learn to live together on Aethera."

He waited for the Crawler to finish translating, hoping he would not have to kill the leader, but knowing he would if he needed to.

The Crawler leader clicked three times. Tashon looked to the translator.

"They surrender," it said.

Tashon nodded. The exhaustion of all his travels overwhelmed. His head spun, and he collapsed. Arms lifted him off the ground, and they all set off on the long journey back to the red mountains.

As you foresaw, Mother, they have saved us.
That much is plain, is true.
Yet all that was not seen, not known, caused us doubt.
The new Frames, broken, scarred.
Not as we expected saviors to be. Yet saviors they have been.

Not them alone. We have welcomed Neighbors inside our home.

They have been among us. Read your words, Mother.

Changed by your words.

They silenced their own Family for us.

Saw the wrong among those placed above them, and remedied it.

And now we all Family, Neighbors – old and new,

Go to wake those who sleep.

The End

ACKNOWLEDGEMENTS

Thank you to my Heavenly Father and Jesus Christ. Thank you to my beautiful wife and best friend, Meaghan. Thanks to my parents, and all my wonderful family. Thanks to Luke Dylan Ramsey, this book would not be what it is without his aid and insight. Thank you to Carol Powell and Josh Allen, the two best writing teachers I could have ever asked for. Many thanks to Dave Lane (aka Lane Diamond) of Evolved Publishing for believing in this series as much as I do. Thank you to my editor, Becky Stephens, and to Sam Keiser for providing the phenomenal cover art. And lastly thank you, reader, for taking the time to read this book. I hope you join me again as the journey on Aethera continues.

ABOUT THE AUTHOR

Author J.S. Sherwood has a passion for stories that show the existence of peace and beauty even in the darkest of times. He spent many years teaching English at the junior high, high school, and college levels, and now brings that love of great writing to bear in his own books.

When he isn't reading or writing, he's spending time with his wife, five kids, and two dogs in Arizona. Most likely they're outside, soaking up the fresh air and sunshine.

For more, please visit J.S. Sherwood online at:
Website: www.jssherwood.com
Goodreads: J.S. Sherwood
Facebook: @js.sherwood.7
Twitter: @SciFiSherwood

WHAT'S NEXT?

J.S. Sherwood is hard at work on the rest of the "This Foreign Universe" series, through Book 9. Please stay tuned to developments and plans by subscribing to our newsletter at the link below.

www.EvolvedPub.com/Newsletter

MORE FROM EVOLVED PUBLISHING

We offer great books across multiple genres, featuring high-quality editing (which we believe is second-to-none) and fantastic covers.

As a hybrid small press, your support as loyal readers is so important to us, and we have strived, with tireless dedication and sheer determination, to deliver on the promise of our motto:

QUALITY IS PRIORITY #1!

Please check out all of our great books, which you can find at this link:

www.EvolvedPub.com/Catalog/

Thank you!

www.ingramcontent.com/pod-product-compliance
Lightning Source LLC
Chambersburg PA
CBHW030253270626
47156CB00022B/2569

9781622537457